'I shouldn't be doing this.' The chauffeur held the whip uncertainly.

'I want it,' said Sandra. 'Go on. Do it to me.' She hoped tomorrow she wouldn't have to speak. That she would be plunged into the world of *The Master's Diary* where there was nothing for her to do but obey.

The chauffeur had made up his mind. He raised the whip and brought it down across the meat of her buttocks. They quivered. A thousand needles of pain stabbed into her, followed instantly by a thousand fingers of hot, stinging pleasure.

'One,' she said loudly – just as Clara had done in the book . . .

Also available from Headline Delta

Prisoner of Desire
Secrets
The House on Punishment Corner
Gigolo
Amateur Nights
Amateur Days
Naked Ambition
The Casting Couch
Return to the Casting Couch
Bianca
Compulsion
Two Weeks in May
The Downfall of Danielle
Exposed
Indecent
Hot Pursuit
High Jinks Hall
Kiss of Death
The Phallus of Osiris
Lust on the Loose
Passion in Paradise
Reluctant Lust
The Wife-Watcher Letters
Three Women
Total Abandon
Wild Abandon

The Master's Diary

Becky Bell

Delta

Publisher's Message

This novel creates an imaginary sexual world. In the real world, readers are advised to practise safe sex.

Copyright © 1998 Becky Bell

The right of Becky Bell to be identified as the Author of the Work has been asserted by her in accordance with the Copyright, Designs and Patents Act 1988.

First published in 1998
by HEADLINE BOOK PUBLISHING

A HEADLINE DELTA paperback

10 9 8 7 6 5 4 3 2

All rights reserved. No part of this publication may be reproduced, stored in a retrieval system, or transmitted, in any form or by any means without the prior written permission of the publisher, nor be otherwise circulated in any form of binding or cover other than that in which it is published and without a similar condition being imposed on the subsequent purchaser.

All characters in this publication are fictitious and any resemblance to real persons, living or dead, is purely coincidental.

ISBN 0 7472 5840 6

Typeset by CBS, Felixstowe, Suffolk

Printed and bound in Great Britain by
Mackays of Chatham plc, Chatham, Kent

HEADLINE BOOK PUBLISHING
A division of Hodder Headline PLC
338 Euston Road
London NW1 3BH

The Master's Diary

Chapter One

The first strap was wound around her left wrist. Clara twisted her head to one side to watch as the leather was buckled tightly. The black leather bit into her flesh but there was no pain. The strap was attached to a metal ring set at the corner of the wooden frame. The second strap secured her right wrist and the third and fourth her ankles, so she was spread-eagled across the frame and quite helpless. The position of her arms pulled her pectorals taut and lifted her breasts, which were naked. In fact they had stripped her of everything but a small pair of black satin panties which barely covered the thick growth of her pubic hair.

The woman who had bound her stood back as if to admire her work. She was tall and elegant, her long, red hair cascading over her shoulders. She wore a tight, white blouse and a long, black pencil-skirt that clung to the contours of her buttocks and thighs. She had pinched, neat ankles sheathed in sheer black nylon with a seam rising from her black patent-leather high-heels.

'We have to start somewhere,' she said.

She sat on the side of the frame. Her captive inhaled her musky perfume. The woman's hand ran down Clara's body, over the corded sinews of her neck, down over her breasts, squeezing each one in turn, then on to her flat belly and the black satin of the panties. Her fingers delved between Clara's open legs, then pushed up hard, pressing the material into her labia, screwing it into her.

'After the Master it will be my turn,' she said, the tip of

her tongue licking her top lip. 'Remember that.'

She took a strip of black silk and bound it around the girl's head, blindfolding her with it. She got up, took one final, long look at the bound girl, then turned and walked out of the room, her high-heels clacking on the stone floor. She slammed the heavy door and Clara heard the key turn in the lock.

The book lay on the kitchen table. Sandra Seymour had unpacked all her shopping before taking her shower and had forgotten about it until she came back into the kitchen to pour herself a glass of white wine from the bottle she always kept in the fridge. Then the picture on the cover caught her eye once again, as it had in the shop. The girl it featured was a beautiful and slender brunette, her long, shiny black hair brushed over her shoulders like a mantilla. She was wearing a black lace body through which her heavy breasts and the dark circles of her areolae could be seen quite clearly. The girl was kneeling, her hands clasped behind her back. In front of her, clad in a heavy, dark red velvet full-length robe, a man stood with his back to the camera. He was looking down at her and had his right hand on her head as though he were a priest offering absolution. In his other hand he held a long, coiled whip, though he did not appear to be menacing her with it.

All this, for some reason she did not understand, Sandra had found compelling. It struck a chord in her. There was something about the expression the photographer had managed to capture in the kneeling girl's eyes. There was excitement there, clearly, and a glint of fear, but most of all a look of absolute submission. The man was her master, and she was his slave.

Of course, Sandra knew perfectly well she was probably reading her own reactions into what, for someone else, might well be a blank face. But that was interesting in itself. How did she come to imagine the feelings of a girl in such a situation? It was certainly something she had never thought

The Master's Diary

of before, at least not consciously. Her puzzlement, and the odd, rather sick excitement the photograph had engendered, had made her buy it. She had never bought anything like it before.

She felt the same response again now. She sat at the table, sipped the wine and, opening the book, read on.

His study was dark and dismal, apart from a roaring log fire in the huge, Gothic stone fireplace, its flicking light only occasionally reaching into the shadows.

'Kneel,' he said, his voice betraying no emotion.

Clara did as she was told.

'Good,' he said, smiling a rather odd, thin smile. 'There is only one rule,' he continued, leaning back in the leather wingchair. 'It is simple. You are here to obey. Whatever. Whoever. With no qualifications. Do you understand?'

'Yes, Master.' Her heart was pounding.

'If you obey I will teach you everything there is to know. Things you had not imagined. If you do not, you will be sent away, never to return. Have you ever been whipped?'

'No, Master.' The idea sent a shiver of fear through her. But it was fear laced with an almost unbelievable excitement.

'I shall have you bound and whipped, child. For my amusement. I shall want to see your pretty tears. They will excite me. You do want to excite me don't you, child?'

'Yes, Master.' She wanted that very much. Why else was she here? She would have done anything to give him pleasure because he was her Master.

'Have you been with a woman?'

'A woman, Master?' She did not understand.

'A woman. Have you been caressed by a woman, kissed by a woman, have you come on a woman's mouth?'

'No, Master.' She tried to keep the horror at the thought out of her voice, but then realised that it was not the only emotion she was experiencing. Once again, vivid excitement was interlaced with her fearfulness.

'I shall put you to a woman, child. I shall want to see you being used by a woman. For my amusement.'

'Yes, Master.'

'That is only the beginning. There are no limits, no reservations. You are simply a slave and will be used accordingly.'

Now Clara's emotion was unambiguous. She felt a surge of arousal. 'Oh, Master.'

He had seen the signs. That is why he had brought her here. She was a natural, the perfect submissive. All he had to do was train her, the way he trained all the girls.

'Now I want you to slip your clothes off.'

'My clothes, Master?'

He made a strange little noise of disapproval, clicking his tongue against his palate. 'Don't make me repeat myself. Take your blouse off first,' he said coldly.

Her hands were trembling. She fumbled with the buttons. She wanted to show him her body but was afraid that he would not be pleased by it, that he would reject her.

'Come on, child,' he urged impatiently. He crossed his legs. The scarlet robe he was wearing fell away to reveal his powerfully muscled thighs. She thought she could see the outline of his penis under the silky material.

The blouse slipped off her shoulders. She wasn't wearing a bra and her big heavy breasts, crested by dark, puckered nipples, quivered as they were unveiled. He had instructed her to wear nothing under her outer clothes.

'Very good.' He leant forward and examined her breasts carefully. 'Can you suck your own nipples?'

'Yes, Master.'

'Do it for me.'

She took the weight of her left breast in her hand and fed her nipple into her mouth. Her body shuddered as she let him see her teeth pinching the tender flesh. Without being prompted, she did the same with her right breast. The pangs of sensation this created left her feeling weak. Her nipples seemed to be on

The Master's Diary

fire. They had never felt so sensitive.

'Now your skirt. You may stand, child.' He leant back in the chair again, resting his head against the leather and closing his eyes momentarily, as though the burden he carried was too much for him.

Clara got to her feet, unzipped her skirt and let it fall to the floor. She stepped out of it, unsure whether or not to take off her high-heeled shoes. As he had not ordered her to do so she left them on.

'Come here, in front of me. Kneel again.'

She moved towards him, intensely aware of his eyes roaming her naked body.

As she knelt in front of him his hands unknotted the belt of his robe. He parted the silk to reveal his erection. His cock was circumcised and very smooth, the glans wider than the shaft.

'Clasp your hands behind your back.' His voice had a more serious tone now.

Clara obeyed immediately. The position thrust her breasts forward and her shoulders back.

The Master spent a long time examining her body before he finally said, 'Yes, a very pretty specimen. Very fine. I am pleased.'

Clara felt a wonderful sense of relief. Though she did not properly understand why, pleasing her Master had become the single most important thing in her life, the core of her existence.

At that moment the study door opened. A tall redhead stood in the doorway, her emerald-coloured eyes surveying the scene. She was dressed in tight leather breeches and a black leather blouse. The plunging neckline of the blouse revealed the upper surfaces of her breasts encased in a lacy black bra.

'Is she ready?' she said.

'As always your timing is perfect.'

'A pretty little thing, I must say. Do you want me to take

her downstairs?' The woman walked forward until she was standing by Clara's side.

'Yes. But first . . .' He looked into his lap and the woman laughed. It was a strident noise that did not come easily to her. She put her hand on the back of Clara's head and pushed it forward towards the Master's cock.

'Take it in your mouth, girl, show your Master what you can do.'

The doorbell startled Sandra. She had been so engrossed in the book she had completely forgotten Michael was picking her up at eight. She was still wearing the cotton robe she had put on after her shower. She was supposed to be dressed and ready.

'Hi,' she said, opening the front door to her flat.

'Hi . . . Oh . . . I thought we were . . .'

'Come in. Sorry, I fell asleep,' she lied, not wanting to tell him the truth.

'That's all right.' He looked as if he meant it.

She closed the door. 'Do you want a drink while I get ready? I won't be long.' She was having trouble coming back to the real world. She had identified so strongly with the situation in the book she was surprised the Master and the redhead were not there in the room.

'Thanks . . . wine'll do.'

Sandra walked through into the kitchen. The book still lay on the table. The supplicant girl's eyes seemed to follow her as she walked to the fridge. She poured a glass of wine for Michael, refilled her own and tucked the book away among her shelf of cookbooks. She didn't want him coming across it.

'Here,' she said, back in the living room.

'Cheers.' He sipped the wine. 'Are you all right? You seem a bit distant.'

'I'm fine. You know what it's like when you wake up suddenly.' She wondered what he would think if she said to him: 'Have you ever wondered what it would be like to have a slave, Michael? Have you ever wanted to have a woman bound and whipped, or watch her with another woman? I was just reading about it.'

'I booked the restaurant for eight-thirty,' Michael said, looking at his watch.

'I'll hurry, then.'

Sandra took her wine into the bedroom. She had a small, one-bedroom flat in a purpose-built block off the Fulham Road. Besides the living room and what the estate agents called a kitchen/diner – though it was only just big enough for a table for two – there was a small bedroom and a large, conveniently situated bathroom directly off it. Sandra wandered through into the bathroom and sat down in front of the dressing table she had set up there, because space was so limited in the bedroom. Its surface was littered with a dreadful mess of make-up, nail varnish, tampons, make-up brushes, hair pins, hair brushes and combs. She stared at herself in the mirror. The last thing she wanted to do was go out to dinner.

In a desultory way she applied blusher, eyeshadow and mascara. Immediately her mind drifted away to the image of the kneeling girl on the cover of the book. She put the mascara brush down and clasped her hands tightly behind her back in imitation of the photograph. The pose pushed her large breasts out against the cotton robe.

'Master,' she said aloud. Her nipples, she noticed, were already hard, but the sound of her voice made them throb.

The feeling was too strong to ignore. She got up and walked through into the bedroom. She stripped off the robe and went over to the pine chest of drawers where she kept her lingerie. All her panties were neatly stacked in one drawer. She searched down to the bottom of the pile and found a pair she rarely wore, a thong cut in black satin. Quickly she pulled the panties up her long legs and smoothed the satin against her body. The narrow gusset barely covered her sex and disappeared deep into the cleft of her buttocks, leaving her fleshy bottom exposed.

Sandra looked at herself in the big mirror that hung to one side of the bed. She was an attractive woman. Her slender figure provided a switchback ride for the eye, as it curved out at her full, firm breasts, into her narrow waist then out again at her hips. She had long jet-black hair that hung down almost to her waist. Her face was delicately featured, with a thin, straight nose, small mouth and large brown eyes, the irises flecked with orange and amber.

As the gusset of the panties folded into the slit of her sex she felt a strong surge of sexual pleasure. Pulling at the satin to make it sit more comfortably she discovered, not altogether to her surprise, that her labia were puffy and wet. She thought she could feel her clitoris, hard and swollen.

It was getting dark outside. Sandra pulled the curtains over the window and turned on the lamp on the bedside chest. She stripped the patchwork quilt off the bed with the top sheet and sat on the edge of the mattress. From the bottom drawer of the bedside chest, where she kept all her scarves, she took two: a patterned flowery one whose predominant colour was red, and one of plain black silk. She draped the red scarf over the lampshade, colouring the light in the room a rosy pink.

Picking up the other scarf she wound it into a narrow strip and placed it over her eyes, knotting it tightly at the back of her head. The material pressed against her eyeballs. This sensation thrilled her. She lay back on the white sheet. The bed had an old-fashioned brass bedstead and she reached up over her head to grasp at its corner stanchions. She tried to touch the bottom rungs with her feet, imagining, in the blackness that enveloped her, what it would be like to be spread-eagled and bound to each corner.

'Michael,' she called out.

'Yes.'

'Come in here, will you?'

'Sure.'

She heard his footsteps cross the living room. The bedroom door opened.

'Could we forget about dinner?' she said, arching her body off the bed, her legs wide open, presenting her sex to him on a white-sheeted platter.

'Jesus, Sandra, what's got into you?' They had slept together many times before but she had never done anything as wild as this.

'I need it, Michael,' she said breathily.

'I can see that.'

To give him his due, he did not hesitate. He ripped his jacket and shirt off, kicked away his slip-on shoes and pulled off his socks. As he skimmed his trousers and pants down his legs his cock began to unfurl.

'You look very sexy,' he said. 'Can you see anything?'

'No. Are you naked? I heard you take your clothes off.'

'Yes.'

He knelt up on the bed beside her. Teasingly, he ran his hand above her body, then flicked his finger against her nipple, making her start. He played guess-the-spot again and this time lighted on her thigh.

'Bring it up here,' she said. 'Let me suck it.' There was no need to specify what 'it' was. She felt his weight moving and his knee nudging her shoulder as his hand snaked behind her head to lift it, feeding his erection into her mouth. She gobbled it up hungrily. He was circumcised and, though his cock was not particularly long, it was remarkably thick. She took it as deep as it would go, until her lips were stretched around its base and it was buried in her throat. With equal vigour she sucked hard, dimpling her cheeks and feeling it react with a spasm of movement.

'What's got into you?' he repeated, his hand fastening on her breast.

She didn't answer, concentrating on sawing his phallus in and out of her lips, while still sucking it, so that her hot, wet mouth clung to its length just like her sex would.

'Jesus, Sandra . . .'

His hand slid down over her flat belly and under the black satin panties, his middle finger probing the slit of her labia until he found her clitoris.

'You're so wet,' he said.

His finger pressed down on her clit and she felt her whole body jerk uncontrollably. She couldn't ever remember feeling so sensitive or so needy.

'Use me, Master,' she said in her head, stretching her limbs out across the bed as though bound to some imaginary rack. 'Use me, let me be your slave.' *Slave*. The unspoken word made her feel giddy. She tore her mouth away from his pulsing erection. 'Are you going to fuck me?' she said out loud.

He started to pull her panties down.

'No, leave them on.' She wanted to feel them cutting into her flesh uncomfortably, like a form of bondage.

He caught her mood like a virus. He jumped on top of her and forced his cock up between her legs. The narrow gusset of the panties, already soaked with the sticky syrup of her sex, was easily pushed aside. Thrusting forward he buried his erection in her vagina. It was slick and tight, gripping him as firmly as her mouth had.

'Yes,' she said. In her mind she said, 'Yes, Master.'

In the darkness she could see herself bound to a wooden frame, the black silk over her eyes, her naked body exposed and vulnerable. She could see a woman standing by the frame looking down at her, a woman in a white blouse, a tight pencil skirt and black patent-leather high-heels.

'You're so wet,' he breathed into her ear.

'Thinking about you,' she lied. She was thinking about the Master in his silk robe and the tall redhead. She was thinking about being made to have sex with a woman. She was thinking about being bound and whipped. All the images and ideas from the book were whirling around like a vortex in her head. They provoked an intensity of feeling she had never

The Master's Diary

experienced before. She knew her orgasm was going to be almost instantaneous.

'Fuck me, Master.' She could not help saying it aloud this time.

'Master?' He said, picking up on the word at once. 'You want me to be your Master?'

'Yes, yes,' she gasped, the first throes of orgasm already riffling through her.

'You want to be a little slave, is that it?' His cock hammered into her.

'Yes, yes . . .' Somewhere in the depths of her mind a voice asked her how she could possibly want such a thing. But it was easily disregarded. As she felt his thick hard cock forcing its way into her, her orgasm peaked. Her body, bound to a rack of her own imagining convulsed. In the blackness she saw the redhead leaning forward to kiss her. The Master stood behind her, his eyes watching eagerly. 'Master . . .'

Michael felt her orgasm subside. He rolled off her, the sudden disjunction of his cock causing Sandra's body to convulse again. His hands took her by the hips and pulled her over on to her stomach.

'On your knees,' he commanded, playing the part she had created for him.

'What are you going to do?' Her voice was weak and tremulous.

'Whatever I want,' he said, crawling up behind her and grasping her hips. His cock, drenched with her juices, nudged between her buttocks, brushing the thin strap of black satin buried between them. He pulled the material aside and stared at her vagina. It was open and glistening wet, its lips pursed ready to suck him in. But above it there was another hole, one he had not breached with her before. 'I can have what I want, can't I?'

'Yes, Master, anything.' The little voice told her not to allow herself to be demeaned in this way. 'Anything, Master,' she repeated, ignoring it, knowing perfectly well what he was going to do even before she felt his glans, hot and slippery, butt against the puckered corona of her anus.

'You want it, don't you?'

'Yes.' And it was true. She pushed her buttocks back against him and tried to relax the little ring of muscles that had tensed reflexively at his approach. She had been buggered before and had not enjoyed it but her body was so high now, and so totally absorbed in this new game, she knew this would be different. It was, after all, an assertion of his mastery over her.

He pushed forward but could not penetrate. 'It's too big for you.'

'No, Master. Try again.'

He did. She felt his glans test her sphincter then plunge through it. There was a stab of pain followed by a rush of pleasure so intense it seemed to hit every nerve she possessed simultaneously. His fingers dug into her hips and pulled her back on to his erection, burying it deeper.

'Is that what you want?'

'Oh Master. It's so big, so big, Master.' The words twisted the spiral of her pleasure tighter.

'Take it,' Michael insisted as he began to pump in and out of her, the tight passage lubricated by the juices that had adhered to his cock. Reaching around her body with his right hand, he clutched at the front of her panties. The gusset was already no more than a thick string and he pulled it back into the furrow of her labia, feeling it rubbing against the base of his erection. Then he jerked on the material again, moving it from side to side, rubbing the satin against her clitoris.

'Master, Master!'

Letting go of the panties, he slid his hand underneath them and found her clitoris with his finger. He fondled it quite gently, the little cusp of nerves pulsing conspicuously from his efforts. It had never felt more sensitive or more alive. The blindfold made her feel more acutely, concentrating her attention on her sense of touch.

'So you . . . want . . . to be a little . . . slave . . . do you . . .?'

Each phrase was punctuated by an inward thrust of his phallus. 'Well, I like . . . to play . . . that game . . .'

She could feel another orgasm enveloping her like a crimson cloak. His cock was so hard and powerful it felt like it was splitting her in two. The feelings came in waves, linked precisely to the tempo of his thrusts. She wanted to scream for him to stop, but she wanted to scream for him to push harder too.

His finger left her clit. She felt him stroke the wet channel of her labia, then enter the opening of her vagina. Before she had worked out what he was going to do he had thrust two fingers up inside her, as far up as they would go. Immediately he began stroking them up and down, alongside his cock and separated from it only by the thin membranes of her body. It was as though he was masturbating, using her sex as a means, not an end.

'Oh, God!' she cried. She thought that would be the final straw. Her body was quaking with waves of pleasure, her heart pounding, her mouth wide open to suck in air. But just as she thought she could not possibly feel anything more, the cock buried deep in her anus swelled to new proportions. It spasmed violently and released a chain of spunk with such force that Sandra's body convulsed in an orgasm that seemed to go on forever.

Sandra laid out a plate of cheese and tossed a salad. Neither of them had any desire to go out now. She opened a bottle of red wine and they drank half of it before they started on the food.

'You didn't answer my question,' he said, sitting on the couch in the front room with one of her towelling robes wrapped around him.

'What question?' She sat beside him in the cotton robe.

'What brought that on?'

'You want the truth?'

'Of course I do. Did you see some really gorgeous guy at work?'

'No. I was browsing in a bookshop at lunchtime. And I . . . well, I came across something.'

'A book?'

'Yes.'

'And?'

'I don't know. I started reading it when I got home. It just made me feel strange.'

'Sexy?'

'Yes, if you want the truth, very sexy, but in a way I'd never felt before. It's odd, isn't it?'

'Where is it?'

'In the kitchen.'

'Can I read it?'

She felt herself blushing, then realised it was ridiculous to feel coy after what they had just done.

'If you like.'

'It's a fantasy, right?'

'Yes. I really didn't think I'd be affected by it.'

'Well, you obviously were.'

She laughed. 'Obviously.'

'I'll read it. Then I'll know all your secrets.'

'As long as you act on the information.' She was surprised at herself for saying that, but it was what she wanted. Acting out the fantasy tonight had given her an orgasm she didn't think she would ever be able to forget. She had never thought of herself as submissive. She was the manager of a shop retailing environmentally-friendly cosmetics, and had to deal with a staff of six, including three men. Nevertheless, the little voice that told her that submission fantasies were demeaning her role as an independent woman was easily ignored.

'Oh, I will, don't worry. Variety is the spice of life after all,' Michael said. 'I might even get to like it.'

'Ah, Clara, how pleasant to see you. I hope you don't mind the lateness of the hour?'

She had no idea what time it was. She had been aroused

The Master's Diary

from a deep sleep to be brought up to his bedroom by Angelica.

'No, Master,' she said, only because she felt he wanted her reply.

'Leave us, Angelica, will you?'

The redhead left the room without a word.

The Master lay naked among tousled sheets. Only a small lamp on his bedside table was illuminated and the rest of the room was in shadow.

'Come closer.'

Clara edged near to the bed. The redhead had strapped a leather collar around her neck. Attached to the back of the collar and running down between her shoulderblades was a strap and secured to this, one above the other, were two rigid leather cuffs. Each of Clara's wrists had been buckled into these cuffs, forcing her arms behind her and her elbows out at an unnatural angle.

'Kneel here at the foot of the bed, child.'

As Clara did what she was told the Master got out of bed. His muscular body was covered in hair that, like the hair on his head, was starting to turn white. It was thickest on his chest and around the stem of his cock.

'Put your forehead against the sheets,' he ordered.

Clara leant forward until she touched the white silk sheets.

In this position her rump was forced into the air. The Master stood beside her and caressed it gently with one hand. There were six distinct weals across it, in varying shades of red. As his fingers explored each in turn, Clara gasped.

'Did she hurt you, child?' the Master asked.

'No, Master.' It was not a lie. Angelica was cruel and there had been pain, but the pain had soon turned to a sickly sweet pleasure and the whipping had made Clara orgasm profusely.

'No, I thought not.'

His hand dived between her legs. She felt his fingers toying with her labia and was ashamed that they were already wet.

'You have come a long way, Clara. It has been an interesting journey for you, hasn't it?'

'Yes, Master.' It was true. Clara could not imagine life beyond the castle walls any more. She did not want to have to think of the real world. She cared only for this life and for her Master.

She heard his footsteps crossing the thickly carpeted floor. In a moment he had returned. She caught a glimpse of him. His cock had become hard and was sticking out from his belly. He had an odd-looking instrument in his hand, a braided leather handle into which two long thin strips of whalebone had been bound.

'Open your knees, child.'

Clara obeyed, splaying her thighs apart, knowing he would be able to see every detail of her sex. The thought caused her clitoris to spasm.

The Master stood behind her. His fingers opened her labia, spreading them apart so he could see her vagina.

'You are wet,' he said.

'Yes, Master.'

'What excites you, child? What exactly?'

'Your touch, Master.' The strange instrument in his hand excited her too, but she did not tell him that.

'Do you know what this is?' He held the whalebone in front of her face.

'No, Master.'

'A tawse. Better than a whip. Sharper. More poignant.'

Almost immediately he cut the tawse down on her buttocks, vertically. It produced a deep but very thin weal at right angles to the ones already decorating her arse. He saw her sex convulse but, as her training had taught her, she did not make a sound. He had been thinking about her. She was special. Very special.

'Beg me for it.'

'Please, Master . . . Whip me. please.'

A second stroke landed and a third. He threw the whip

down and dropped to his knees behind her, his phallus pressing against her labia. She could feel its heat. It was throbbing and she knew he was going to come. She wished he would come inside her but he had never done that. As subtly as she could she moved her sex up and down against his shaft, trying to clutch at it with her labia. He raised the tawse again as if to cut it across her back but as he did so his cock pulsed violently. He watched as semen shot out to land in a series of stepping stones all the way along her spine. More spunk dribbled out, running down his phallus and on to her labia.

'Master,' she breathed. Unable to control herself her body took its own pleasure, quivering against him.

Chapter Two

'That's towards the end, right?'

'You remembered.'

'Of course. I've been doing my homework. I've brought you a present.' He held up a small brown paper bag.

'What is it?'

'You'll see.'

'Shall I go and get ready? Or do you want a glass of wine?'

'Getting ready sounds good.' He grinned. He could tell that Sandra was already in a state of considerable sexual excitement. It oozed from every pore.

'Five minutes.' She kissed him on the cheek. 'Are you sure about this?'

'Don't be ridiculous. I enjoy it as much as you do.'

'OK.'

Sandra walked through into her bedroom and closed the door. She stripped off the cotton robe she was wearing and sat on the edge of the bed. Everything was laid out ready. She had tried to be absolutely faithful to the book. For instance, the sheer black stockings she was wearing. They were exactly the same as the ones Clara had worn, a pair with a fully-fashioned heel and a seam. So was the thin, black lace suspender belt. They made her feel wanton. They were a form of bondage, the taut suspenders and tight nylon making her feel constricted. By contrast, her sex was unrestricted, exposed and available, as were the smooth curves of her buttocks.

She dropped the black patent-leather high-heels on the floor and climbed into them. A strap ran from the top of the heel at the back around her ankle and she buckled each one in turn. Clara had been made to wear the same shoes, their heels so high they forced the feet almost vertical. She looked at herself in the mirror, turning this way and that, her naked breasts quivering slightly, the pout of her buttocks and the shape of her legs firmed by the steep angle of the high heels. She had transformed herself into a whore. The harness that lay on the bed would transform her again. She would become Clara. Clara the slave. Waiting for her Master. Clara waiting to obey.

'Ready, Master,' she cried, kneeling down with her hands clasped behind her back, shaking her head so her long, black hair flowed down over her shoulders.

Michael had stripped off his clothes. This was the fourth time they had played this game. Each time had got more elaborate. As he opened the door she saw his cock was already erect. He had strapped it into a black leather cock-strap that made its veins stand out prominently and lifted his balls. He held a brown paper bag in one hand.

'Head down,' he said in a tone that suggested he was relishing his new role.

Sandra bowed her head, staring at the carpet in front of her knees.

'We shall undertake some very special training tonight.' She knew he had read *The Master's Diary*. She wasn't sure whether it excited him because he had a natural penchant for domination, or whether it was merely because *she* found it all so exciting and that rubbed off on him. It didn't really matter which it was. Tonight they were going to re-enact a scene from the book. He'd gone out at lunchtime to buy the equipment he needed.

'Suck on it,' he said, presenting his cock to her.

Eagerly Sandra inhaled his flesh. She drove herself down on him until his penis was buried in her throat and she had to control the reflex to gag. Despite the discomfort she felt a thrill of pleasure.

The Master's Diary

'Good girl.' He clutched her head in his hands and pulled it back. 'Now stand up.'

Sandra got to her feet, watching Michael pick up the harness. She had bought it last week in one of the many specialist shops she had been surprised to discover catered for such tastes. Coming up behind her, he wrapped a thick leather collar around her neck. It was stiff and wide and made her hold her head high. The assistant in the shop had described it as a posture collar. Three buckles held it in place. She felt her body shiver as each buckle was tightened. She could not lower her head to look down at her own body now, and for some reason that thrilled her too. Her eyeline was restricted to the horizontal and above.

A long strap hung down the back of the collar, so long it dangled at her ankles. Two rigid leather cuffs were attached to either end of a short chain approximately half the width of her body, the centre of the chain riveted to the long strap just below her shoulderblades. Another identical arrangement of cuffs was secured to the strap at the base of her spine. Michael pulled her arms back and secured the upper cuffs around them, just above the elbow. The lower set fitted around her wrists, the chains stretched tautly between them. Her arms were held in parallel behind her back, cramping her shoulders and making her thrust her breasts out.

A band of black silk was wrapped around her eyes. It covered half of her face, from her eyebrows to the tip of her nose. Darkness fell. Her whole body began to pulsate.

'Bend over,' he ordered.

Sandra obeyed without question, bending her body at right angles to her legs.

'Legs apart,' he said irritably, as if annoyed that she had not already thought to do it.

Sandra squirmed her feet apart, knowing she was exposing the whole length of her swollen pussy lips. Though the hair on her belly was thick, with wiry black curls, she had carefully shaved away all the hair on her labia, making them perfectly smooth. She thought she could feel them parting, opening themselves for him.

She started at his touch. His fingers were oily. He was massaging some cream into the ring of her anus. Her sex didn't need it. He would be able to see that.

The paper bag rustled. The touch of cold plastic made her start again. He was pushing a hard, smooth plug into her anus. All the way in. She moaned. It was thick. As thick as his cock. The base of the plug was flared to prevent it disappearing entirely. She felt a second, larger object being pressed into her wet pussy. Two cocks. That's what it felt like. Double penetration. Her heart beat faster.

He stooped to catch the bottom of the long leather strap, then brought it up between her legs, so it held the two plugs in place.

'Up,' he ordered.

She straightened. He quickly pulled the strap up over her belly and between her breasts and buckled it into the fastening at the front of the collar, making sure it was tight and held the plugs firmly.

'Legs together,' he said.

She obeyed, feeling the stiff leather biting into the top of her thighs. Why she found that feeling so affecting she did not know, but it made her whole body hum.

He strapped her legs together with three straps, one around the top of her thighs, one around her knees, the last at her ankles. Then he pushed her in the chest and she toppled back on to the bed, unable to stop herself. As she fell, her limbs had reacted reflexively trying to get free. The fact that they couldn't, the sensation of being so powerless that she could not even break her fall, gave her a new thrill. It made her whole body clench, but it was the tight tubes of her sex and her anus that contracted most, hugging the hard plastic and defining every inch of the intruders. Her clit, pressed back against her pubic bone by the impossibly tight leather, was on fire.

The Master's Diary

Catching hold of her ankles he twisted her around until she was lying along the length of the bed.

She knew what he was going to do next, of course. The only difference was that in the book Angelica, the tall redhead, had been watching, her voluptuous body encased in a boned red leather corset. Unfortunately they could not recreate that part of the scenario. She would have loved to see those emerald eyes gazing at her with an expression of cool disdain.

Climbing up on to the bed, Michael knelt above Sandra's head, facing down her near-naked body. His cock hung over her face. Without being told she reached up and licked at his balls. She sucked them both into her mouth. It was his turn to moan.

She had bought the whip in the same shop as the harness. It lay on the bed. He picked it up. She could hear the whistle of air as he flexed it. Just the noise produced new contractions in her body, her front and rear passages squeezing the plugs again. She thought she was going to come then and there, but struggled to hold on.

A line of pain seared across her left breast. Her cry of surprise was gagged on his balls, her mouth loosening around them. She sucked them in again as the pain turned to pleasure and her body clenched even tighter around the plugs as if trying to crush them.

Another stroke. Her right breast this time. Another line of pain, the weight of the stroke perfectly judged, the pain not intense enough to break the spell but quite sharp enough to be converted into aching pleasure by her body's excitement. Then he concentrated on her puckered nipples, snapping the leather loop at the tip of the whip across them. Once, twice on the left. Once, twice on the right. She writhed on the bed, rolling her hips, making the plugs move around inside her, giving up the battle for control, now hopelessly lost in the throes of an orgasm that seemed to go on forever, trying to keep his balls in her mouth but failing finally as the orgasm peaked and her whole body melted, her open mouth the only outlet for all her passion.

He waited for the orgasm to run its course, then rolled her on to her side. He took hold of her head and pushed his cock between her lips. Her mouth was like a furnace. As she began to recover she sucked on him hard. Bound as she was, it was difficult for her to move her head, so he did all the moving for her, fucking her mouth just as if it were her sex, his hips sawing back and forth.

She felt his prick throbbing. The leather cock-strap pushed his balls up under his shaft so they banged against her chin. She licked at the long, thick prick as it pushed forward, then sucked hard as its whole length buried itself in her throat.

His cock jerked. This time he didn't pull back. Instead he pressed forward. His hands grabbed her breasts, digging into the soft flesh. Then his fingers rubbed at her nipples, cunningly torturing the tenderness the whip had created.

He was coming. And, as his hot spunk spattered down her throat, so was she.

The trouble was, it was difficult to think of anything else. Each and every day at work she was plagued by visions, sexual ghosts that refused to be shunted aside however desperately she tried. But the evenings were worse. Especially in bed. Especially after last night. She ached. She couldn't decide whether it was worse with a bra or without. Every time she had moved during the day her nipples had rubbed against the lace of her bra making her moan, but now, lying naked in bed, they seemed even more sensitive. They were slightly bruised too, their colour a ruby red. There were marks on her breasts as well, little pink lines, where the whip had landed.

She could have dealt with the pain. The trouble was the intrusive pain created other feelings that were less easy to cope with. It made her sex tingle and with it her anus, the two plugs leaving an impression inside her quite as distinct as the weals on her breasts.

But it was her mind where the most indelible impression

The Master's Diary

had been left. The sensations in her body provoked her memories and desire. Memories of what Michael had done to her merging with passages from the book. And desire for more.

The character of Angelica had come to obsess her. She could see her. She knew exactly what she looked like. Her flaming red hair, her slender figure, her piercing green eyes, always ready to punish the slightest hint of disobedience with a corrosive stare. The thought of Angelica's long, bony fingers thrusting into her open sex and that fleshy mouth sucking on her nipples excited her more than anything had ever done. She had never considered having sex with a woman until she'd read the book. Now she could think of little else. Even as Michael's cock thrust into her she could not stop herself imagining what it would be like to feel the soft, wet lips of Angelica's pussy pulsing against her mouth.

But not just any woman. She didn't think it was anything to do with a sudden rush of long suppressed lesbian desire. She wanted Angelica because Angelica was part of the story, part of the situation Manville Mason, the author of *The Master's Diary*, had created. She realised that it was simply impossible for her to believe that Angelica did not exist. Equally, she believed the Master was a real person, maybe Manville Mason himself. The setting and the characters in the book were too convincing to be the product of a writer's over-active imagination. She had read and reread the book. She knew every scene. Every paragraph and every line. It had to be real. *The Master's Diary* was exactly what it said it was, a diary of real events that had taken place in a real place. What happened in the book was a description of what actually happened in real life. She knew that as surely as night followed day.

She supposed she should have considered why the contents of the book had affected her so totally. She had never displayed the slightest interest in what she now knew was called sadomasochism. She had masturbated frequently since puberty, but never in the wildest fantasies she dreamt up to stimulate her sexual excitement had she ever imagined herself being bound and whipped, let alone getting pleasure from – yet another new word to be added to her vocabulary – submission. The cover of the book, the kneeling girl, was the symbol for a whole panoply of sexual practices. The fact that Sandra found them so exciting was something her subconscious, for whatever reason, had chosen to keep hidden from her. Until now. Why it had decided to reveal the truth, after all this time, she did not know. But the truth was undeniable. The cover of the book, together with its contents, had inspired her with a sexuality that she could hardly contain. She had never felt this way before.

As she lay in bed, unable to sleep, she reached a decision. She had to find the Master and his castle. Michael's willing acceptance of her sudden interest in submission had been welcome. But it was a game to him. For her it had come to mean much more. It was something she had to explore, a part of her psyche that was no longer prepared to lay dormant.

'Master,' she said aloud.

She pulled the sheet off her body and brushed her palm across her breast. Her nipples throbbed. She crushed the tingling flesh back against her chest and felt her clit flex. Sliding her other hand down, she opened her legs and covered her sex with her hand, her fingers cupped around it. The plugs were in the bedside table. She thought about getting them out, but there was no time.

Arching her buttocks off the bed, she presented herself to Angelica. She could see her standing by the bed. She was wearing thigh-length patent-leather boots in bright red, and a matching leather G-string that clung to the delta of her sex. Her breasts were exposed, large and spherical, her nipples – how had Manville described them? – the size of hazelnuts, and just as hard. She had a look of disdain in her eyes, as if it were beneath her to gaze on such an unworthy specimen.

Why did that idea excite her so much?

The Master's Diary

Sandra thrust her fingers into the channel of her pussy and quickly found her clit. She tapped it with her finger as she imagined Angelica peeling off the G-string. Her pussy would be shaved clean, so her pussy lips were clearly visible. God, how she wanted the woman to press those lips against her mouth.

'Please . . .' she said aloud, the word exciting her so much she trembled.

'You haven't been trained,' the spectre said coldly.

Sandra saw herself bent double and tied to a wooden trestle, its legs splayed apart, and her ankles and wrists tied to them. Naturally she was naked. Angelica was examining her breasts. Something glinted in her hand. Her fingers pinched the nipples, finding a place for the metal clips. There were two of them. And two breathtaking spasms of pain and pleasure lanced through her as the metal bit into the tender flesh. It was the same feeling she had experienced last night as Michael whipped her breasts, the combination of the two feelings producing a third, more vivid sensation. The clips were joined by a chain. In her mind's eyes Angelica was hooking a weight on to it, pulling her breasts down.

'Please, I can't take it,' Sandra gasped.

But she could. Not only could she take it, but she wanted more. The image in her mind was vivid. Clara had been strapped over a trestle in the book, part of her early training. The author had described the bleak cell in which she was imprisoned and the way Angelica's hand had alternated between tenderness and torment.

Sandra forced her clit from one side to the other, her excitement mounting so quickly she could feel an orgasm already unrolling from the neck of her womb, spreading out as rapidly as the flood of juices that ran down her vagina.

Before it overtook her completely she rolled on to her stomach, deliberately rubbing her sensitised breasts against the sheet, that inextricable mixture of pleasure and pain this gave her boosting her feelings until she was quivering helplessly on the bed. In her mind's eye the expression in Angelica's eyes was unchanged, cool and quizzical and implacable.

She had to find her. She had to find Angelica and the Master. It was as simple as that.

'Thinline Publishing. How can I help you?'

'Hello, ah, I wondered if I could talk to someone about Manville Mason.'

'Certainly, hold the line please.'

'Editorial, can I help you?' It was a crisp, efficient female voice.

'Oh . . . yes.' Sandra hadn't really thought about what she was going to say. 'I was trying to get in touch with Manville Mason.'

'Yes . . .'

'I wondered if you had his address.'

'We can't give you that information I'm afraid.'

Sandra felt foolish. Of course they weren't going to give her his address. 'No . . . I mean . . . is there anyway I could get hold of him? An agent perhaps?'

'He doesn't have an agent. He handles all his work himself. But you can write to us. We'll forward the letter to him.'

'Really?'

'Certainly. No problem.'

'Thank you very much. Ah, do you open them?'

'Yes, as a matter of course we do. But if you mark it private we'll forward it unopened.'

'Right. I expect he gets a lot of letters from women.'

'I really couldn't say.'

'Could you just tell me where he lives, I mean what part of the world?'

'In Cornwall, actually.'

'Have you ever met him?'

The woman hesitated. Sandra got the impression she was going to say something but changed her mind. 'No. Now, if that's all . . .'

The Master's Diary

'Thank you for your help.'
'No problem.'
Sandra put the phone down. She saw that her hand was trembling. Even this distant contact with Mason had made her feel slightly giddy.

She tried to calm down. She would write the letter tonight as soon as she got home. Meantime she wondered how many Gothic Victorian castles there were in Cornwall. A lot, she was sure.

Dear Manville Mason,

I'm sure you get many letters from readers of The Master's Diary. *I'm equally sure I know the reason why. The book is so vividly and graphically written it cannot fail to touch a nerve in many women. That is precisely what it has done to me.*

I have never thought of myself as particularly adventurous in sexual matters nor, for that matter, particularly naive. But since reading what you have written about the sensations a woman is capable of, the depth and profundity of feeling that can be achieved, I have come to realise that my sexuality is more complicated than I ever dreamed. Without being aware of any proclivity in that direction the idea of gifting my will to someone else, of being totally and utterly submissive, has started to haunt me.

I wish I could explain why I was so affected by the idea of submission – I didn't even know that was the word for it until I read your book – but the extraordinary thing is that you make it so clear in the character of Clara. I know I would feel what she feels in your book if I were ever to be so fortunate to be in her position, to have a Master as experienced and imaginative as the Master you have created.

You are going to think me very presumptuous, and forgive me if I am wrong, but the psychological reactions you describe are so accurate and so beautifully observed that it is impossible for me to believe that they are fictional. I know the castle exists. I know that Angelica is real and that Clara's trials and training are based on events that actually occurred. I am convinced that everything the Master does in the book has been done by you, not only because it is so accurately described but because I feel it instinctively. I know you are the Master.

If I am wrong, if the book is a product of your imagination, then I can only congratulate you on a wonderful, creative achievement and I hope you will forgive my presumptuousness.

But if I am right, Mr Mason, if you are the Master, I would do anything to meet you and see the castle for myself. That is a euphemism, of course. You are too good with words not to have spotted that. What I am trying to say – and there is no point mincing words – is that I want to be your slave. I want to serve you as Clara does, as willingly and unquestioningly. In fact, without false modesty, I resemble her physically as well as having the same, deeply ingrained, psychological needs. I want to show you that I can be a Clara, as committed and as obedient. I want to give myself to you. I don't think I have ever wanted anything as much in my life.

You may now be smiling broadly, ready to dismiss me as another obsessive fan who has read too much into your writing. If that is the case then it is a compliment to your work. If it is not then it is up to you.

I await your reply eagerly.

She signed the letter with her full name. Going into the bedroom, she found a bottle of her favourite scent and dabbed the stopper against the bottom corner of the paper before sealing it in the envelope. She felt like a naughty schoolgirl writing a Valentine's Day card to a boy in the sixth form. But she didn't care. If Manville Mason didn't reply, that would be the end of it. She would know she had been wrong, that there was no castle and that he had dreamt the whole thing up. She would have to accept that everything in the book was a fantasy, a form of titillation that had no basis in reality. Life would seem duller, less exciting. She would have to content herself with playing games with Michael, in the knowledge that the real thing simply did not exist.

On the other hand . . .

It was Friday evening, six days later when her doorbell rang.

'Ms Seymour?'

'Yes.'

The man standing at her front door was blond and tall. He was wearing a grey uniform and grey cap, the brocade of a chauffeur prominent on its peak. He had bright blue eyes, a rather square face with a firm jaw but high, delicate almost feminine cheekbones. His chest was broad and his stomach flat.

'Ms Sandra Seymour?' he said, as if wanting to make sure he was not making a mistake.

'Yes.'

'This is for you. I am to wait for a reply.' He handed her a cream envelope made from thick vellum.

'You'd better come in.' She was not prepared for visitors. She had just got out of the shower and was wearing a cotton robe, her hair wrapped in a towelling turban while it dried. 'Sorry, I just got out of the shower.'

'That's perfectly all right, miss.'

Sandra was flummoxed. She had no idea who the man was or what on earth this was all about.

He stepped inside the front door and she closed it behind him.

'Would you like a drink of something?'

'No thank you.' He was wearing black leather gloves. He clasped his hands behind his back and stared at the floor.

Sandra ripped open the envelope. It contained a single sheet of thick card with a deckled edge. As she read the signature scrawled across the bottom, her heart almost stopped: Manville. She had not connected the chauffeur with Manville Mason. She felt her pulse drumming in her ear.

She went through into the kitchen, needing to be alone. She sat at the kitchen table and carefully read the note, written in a copperplate italic script. 'Dear Sandra Seymour, I am charmed by your letter. Would you have dinner with me tomorrow night? My chauffeur will pick you up at eight. Please give him your reply.' She read it twice.

The implications were just beginning to sink in. His reply meant that she had been right. She could see the chauffeur standing in her sitting room. There was a chauffeur in *The Master's Diary* and this man was the image of him, living proof that everything in the book was based on reality.

Sandra's excitement was extreme. She could not divorce her emotional shock and pleasure from a purely physical reaction, the thought that this invitation might be the beginning of the catalogue of sexual experience she had conjured up so frequently in the last weeks, making her feel almost lightheaded. Her clit seemed to be squirming against her labia like a little snake.

'Are you sure you won't have a drink?' she said.

'No, thank you. I have to drive.'

'At least come through and sit down. Are you in a hurry?'

'Not really. Mr Mason's not going out this evening. I'm not required again.'

'Well, then.' She wanted him to stay so she could ask him about Manville. She was eager to get any information she could. 'I could make you some tea or coffee?'

'Tea would be nice.'

'Please sit down. Have you worked for Manville long?' The chauffeur in the book had worked for the Master for six years.

'Six years,' he said, sitting on the sofa.

'Really?' More confirmation. She walked into the kitchen and put on the kettle, leaving the door open. 'It must be very interesting.'

'Very,' he said.

'Is Mr Mason married?'

The chauffeur laughed heartily. 'Not so's you'd notice.'

The Master's Diary

She put a teabag in a large mug and took the milk out of the fridge. She wanted to ask about Angelica but didn't want to do it directly.

'Does he have a companion?'

'You mean Marion.'

'Marion?'

'Marion Chandler. She's a sort of companion, I suppose. She's Mr Mason's executive assistant, officially.'

'And unofficially?' The kettle boiled. She poured the water on to the tea bag. 'Milk and sugar?'

'Just milk.'

'Here.' She set the mug down on the occasional table at the side of the sofa, then sat down in the armchair opposite. 'And unofficially?' she repeated, raising an eyebrow.

'Let's change the subject,' he said firmly.

'Why?'

'I think you know why, Ms Seymour.'

'Sandra, please.'

He sipped the tea. 'Nice,' he said.

'Are you not supposed to talk about your boss?'

'Right.'

'What shall we talk about instead, then?'

'Your reply?'

'Oh, yes. Would you tell Mr Mason I'd be delighted to accept his invitation.'

He smiled. It was a knowing smile. 'Certainly.'

'Look, would you excuse me a second. I really ought to get dressed.'

'I must be going.'

'Please, give me a second. I wouldn't like you to report to Mr Mason that I was a complete mess.'

He shrugged as if it were a matter of no importance.

Sandra waltzed into the bedroom and closed the door behind her. She could hardly contain her excitement. Having the chauffeur in her front room was already making the book come alive for her. Tomorrow she would meet the Master, but she could already feel his influence by proxy. Her nipples felt like hard chips of marble and her pussy had turned to jelly. Her mouth felt dry and she was breathless with desire.

Quickly she pulled the towel off her hair and brushed it out. She pulled off the robe and opened the bottom drawer in the chest where she stored all her new collection of exotic garments. She'd ordered the outfit from the specialist catalogue she got by mail order. It had only arrived two days ago. She hadn't even tried it out on Michael yet.

The material was some man-made fibre. It looked like patent-leather, shiny and bright red, but was as stretchy and clingy as rubber. The first garment was a corset with black laces down the front. It fitted snugly around her waist, extending from just underneath her breasts to just above the delta of her pubis. Long red suspenders hung down from it. She pulled the laces tighter, clinching her waist. She sat on the bed and pulled two thigh length 'stockings', in the same material, up her long legs. It took a great deal of tugging and pulling before they were smooth and wrinkle free. She clipped them into place with the suspenders.

The red patent-leather high-heels were exactly the same colour. They tipped her feet up so she was walking on tip-toe.

Boldly, intensely aware of her naked pussy nestling between her creamy thighs, and her big breasts hanging over the top of the bright red corset, she walked back into the front room.

'Do you think Mr Mason would like me in this?' she said. Before she had read the book she would never have dared to be so blatant. One of the things Manville Mason's writings had taught her was to put sex at the very top of her agenda. She could not ignore the sexual excitement the chauffeur's arrival had created.

The chauffeur did not betray the slightest hint of surprise. His eyes examined her carefully, working up from her feet.

'He might,' he said noncommittally.

'And what about you?'

He smiled. 'I'm not supposed to have an opinion.'

The Master's Diary

Sandra weighed her breasts in her hands. 'But surely you must feel something?'

'You're . . . you're a beautiful woman, miss.'

She shook her head. Her long hair brushed her back. 'What's your name?'

'Curtis Canfield.'

'Well, Curtis. I suppose you've read Mr Mason's book?'

'Which one? He's written a lot.'

'*The Master's Diary.*'

'Yes. I've read it.'

'Do you remember the scene where Clara is tied over the chair in front of a cheval mirror?'

'And the Master whips her.'

'Yes. Did that excite you? Do you think I look like Clara?'

'Is that what you want?'

Sandra ran her finger along her bottom lip then sucked it into her mouth. 'Very much.' It was true. She desired Curtis with a passion. He was undeniably an attractive man but that wasn't the reason she wanted him so badly. She wanted him because he was part of the book, part of the reality that had haunted her for weeks.

'I don't have a whip.'

'I do.'

Without another word Sandra turned and walked back into the bedroom leaving the door open. The whip was hidden under the bed. She took it out and laid it on the counterpane then positioned an upright chair in front of the long mirror on her bedroom wall and knelt up on it, staring over her shoulder at her image in the glass. Her buttocks framed by the shiny red material looked creamy and soft.

She saw him standing in the bedroom doorway.

'I shouldn't be doing this,' Curtis said.

'I want it.'

'Yes, but Mr Mason, if he ever found out . . .'

'I'm not going to tell him.'

'I'd lose my job.'

'I promise. No one will ever know.'

He was staring at those creamy buttocks and the deep cleft between them. Then his eyes focused on the whip.

'You like to be whipped.' It was not a question.

'You don't find that unusual,' she said.

'Don't I?'

'Do you want to put me into bondage?' That was the word the Master always used. 'I've got all sorts of equipment.'

'I'm not into that.'

'But you know lots of women who are. You've seen it for yourself, haven't you?'

He smiled. 'Have I?'

'I know the truth, Curtis.'

He picked up the whip. 'Then you'll have to be punished,' he said tentatively, as if trying out for himself the role his boss had written so graphically.

'Do it, then.' She hoped tomorrow she wouldn't have to speak. She hoped she would be plunged into a world beyond her wildest dreams where there was nothing for her to do but obey.

'You little bitch.' Suddenly and decisively he came up behind her, raised the whip and brought it down across the meat of her buttocks. They quivered. A thousand needles of pain stabbed into her, followed instantly by a thousand fingers of hot, stinging pleasure.

'One,' she said loudly as Clara had done in the book, her voice breathless with passion.

He raised his arm again. This time the whip landed high, glancing off her lower back.

'Two,' Sandra intoned.

The third stroke was more accurate. 'Three,' she gasped, hardly able to contain the shock of physical feeling it produced.

She glanced over her shoulder so she could see him in the mirror. He was staring at her rump, his face writhed in indecision. He raised his arm again and she braced herself for the impact but instead he threw the whip aside and began

The Master's Diary

wrestling his trousers down. He unzipped his fly and pulled them down to his knees. She saw his big, circumcised cock poking out from his shirt tails. His glans was wet.

'Master,' she said, wanting to hear the word.

His hand caressed her flanks then took hold of her hips. She felt his cock nose into her labia. She wriggled back against it. Without a second's hesitation he pushed his cock into her pussy. It sank deep. Then he pulled it almost all the way out again, and began plunging it in and out, taking up a rhythm, the copious juices of her body making the penetration frictionless.

Sandra thought she was already coming. The impact of his hard cock reaming into her rear sent a wave of pleasure through her body. He was stretching her cunt in every direction. He was bigger than Michael. Broader and longer.

Curtis pounded into her. He pulled her back on to him as he tried to get deeper.

She could feel every inch of him. His cock was gnarled with veins. Each one provoked her. The pleasure was intense. Boiling, bubbling pleasure. She felt him swell, the knob of his cock growing, filling her, stretching her. He was running one hand over the shiny, red material that clung to her legs while the other gathered up her long black hair, pulling her head back by it like a rider pulls back a horse by the reins. He was coming, his cock pulsing inside her.

'Master,' she said again. Clara had never been allowed the Master's spunk. That was the ultimate privilege. 'Like the book,' she pleaded.

'Like the book?' He didn't realise what she meant. He forced himself deeper. She felt her cunt clench around him as her orgasm pulsed through her body, as she writhed against him using his cock to screw out every last ounce of pleasure.

'Like the book,' she insisted. He had worked it out now. He pulled out of her then jammed his cock and balls into the cleft of her arse with only the glans peaking above it. He let her head fall forward so he could see himself in the mirror, the knob mushrooming to produce a fountain of white spunk arcing into the air and spattering down over the back of the shiny red corset.

'No one must ever know,' he whispered, as he sunk back on to the bed.

'I promise,' she said.

Chapter Three

Cherry Austin was in a hurry. Which was not unusual. She was always in a hurry. Being a tabloid journalist meant life was spent on the run, always looking for the next story to satisfy the paper's, and her editor's, rapacious appetite for news.

But today was even more stressed. She had been working on an idea for a story for some two months now. She'd heard a rumour from a very good source that the daughter of a prominent, knighted actor, who last year had won an Oscar for his role in a Hollywood blockbuster, had broken off her engagement to a chart-topping pop star and disappeared. When she'd managed to interview the girl's best friend – the only journalist to do so – the friend seemed to think that the girl, Angela Blake, had got involved with a writer, Manville Mason, who had exerted a very strong and not necessarily benign influence over her. Angela, or so her friend believed, had become totally obsessed with the man.

The story had all the ingredients Cherry's editor loved, especially when Cherry researched Manville Mason's work and discovered he was the author of several books, including the bestselling *The Master's Diary*, the sexual excess of which could be fairly described, at least in tabloid terms, as 'kinky'. The front page beckoned. ACTOR-KNIGHT'S DAUGHTER SHUNS POP STAR FOR KINKY SLAVE-MASTER. It was too good to be true.

Unfortunately, Cherry couldn't find Manville Mason. His publishers had put up a brick wall and he didn't have a literary agent. She hadn't been able to find anyone who was prepared to talk about him, let alone give her his address.

She only had one hope. Detective Constable Simmons, her man at the Yard. Her hope was that he would be able to use the police computer to find out if Mason owned a car, and thence the address at which it was registered.

That was why she was rushing. She had been supposed to meet Peter Simmons at ten o'clock in the Barley Mow in Kensington, just round the corner from his flat. She had been held up covering a launch party of some new book, the autobiography of a recalcitrant movie star, who had proved true to his nature by turning up an hour late and delaying the proceeds accordingly.

It was ten forty-five when she finally burst through the pub doors, searching frantically for her quarry.

'It's all right, I'm still here,' Simmons said, used to Cherry's habitual lateness.

He was sitting in a corner on the far side of the bar.

'Sorry, Pete, I'm really sorry. Do you want an explanation?'

'Just another large vodka,' he said.

Cherry made her way to the bar. As it was so close to closing time she ordered three double vodkas, and three glasses of red wine for herself, paying with a fifty pound note. She looked back at Peter while she waited for change. He was an attractive man. In his late twenties, he had a wiry figure and a rather long face. He had a mass of thick, curly black hair, very dark brown eyes, and the sort of complexion that might have led some to think he was of middle-Eastern origin.

'Here,' she said, setting the drinks down on the small, marble-topped cast-iron table.

'Cheers,' he said. 'Very generous. You must want something.'

'Right first time.' She raised one of the glasses. 'Cheers.'

He drank the vodka in two swallows. There were already four empty glasses on the table.

'So?'

'So, like you said, I need a bit of help.'

'What sort of help?'
'An address to match a name.'
'It'll cost you.'
'Of course.'
'Who is it?'
'Manville Mason.'

Pete laughed. '*The Master's Diary*. Well, how interesting. I didn't know you were into all that.'

'I'm not.'

'But you've read the book?'

'Only for background research,' she said quickly.

'Pity.'

'Why?'

'Because I read it and thought it was great. I mean really sexy. Come on, be honest, didn't it turn you on?'

Cherry thought about it for a moment. She had read the book in the office one afternoon. It hadn't seemed to affect her at the time but that evening she had behaved fairly disgracefully at a party, propositioning a stranger and taking him back to her flat for a one-night stand, crawling all over him practically the moment they got through the front door. Usually such adventures had proved highly unsatisfactory, but on this occasion she had experienced a profound orgasm despite the fact that her chosen partner had been a less-than-accomplished lover. Later, she suspected it might have been something to do with the book. But she wasn't going to tell Pete that.

'No,' she said, though not very emphatically.

'Why do you want to find him if you're not going to offer yourself as his slave?'

'Can't say. Sorry.'

'Spoilsport. How much are you prepared to pay?' He downed the second vodka and started on the third.

'The usual.'

'How far are you prepared to go for a story?'

'What do you mean?'

'What are you going to do if you meet Mason? Say he asks you to come to his house. Say he wants to get into all sorts of stuff with you.'

'Stuff?'

'Like in the book. Would you do it?'

Cherry felt an odd sensation in her sex. She could swear it was creaming.

'In return for his story, you mean?'

'Yes.'

'I might.'

'And me?'

'What about you?'

'Say I wasn't interested in money this time, say there was stuff I wanted you to do . . . in exchange for his address.'

'You want to fuck me?'

'Something like that.'

She looked him straight in the eyes. 'Done,' she said. 'Your place or mine?' She grinned broadly.

'Just like that?'

'Peter, I've wanted to fuck you for months. You've just talked yourself out of two hundred quid.'

'Worth every penny. And my place, it's closer.'

She kissed him hard on the lips, pushing her tongue into his mouth and enjoying its sticky heat. 'OK, where's the bedroom?' Cherry said as he let her into his flat.

'Why the bedroom?'

'I thought you wanted to fuck me?'

'No. It was you who brought up the subject of fucking. I had something else in mind.' He led the way into the sitting room. It was quite large, with two big sofas, both positioned to face a large television and video recorder. There was a teak bookcase overflowing with books.

'Sounds intriguing.'

Cherry dropped on to the sofa. She was wearing a short black wrap-around skirt over a tight white Lycra body and flesh-coloured tights. She saw Peter examining her. Despite the demands of her job, the long hours and frequent lack of sleep, she had a clear youthful face, bright blue eyes and a small kissable mouth. Her short blonde hair was parted down the middle and her slightly retroussé nose gave her an air of innocence. Her body was slender, with small round breasts and a pert, apple-shaped bottom. Though she was short, her legs were shapely and seemed longer than they really were.

'Do you want a drink?'

'No.'

'Good.' He went to the video recorder and sorted through a pile of tapes that lay on the garishly patterned carpet. 'Vice squad had a clear-out the other day. I managed to save some classics from the incinerator.'

'Porn?'

'Yes. Very high-quality porn, actually. Dutch, I think.'

He slid one of the tapes into the video recorder and turned on the television, then came back and sat down beside her. He picked up two remote controls.

'I really don't need to see a whole load of dicks to get me in the mood, Pete. I'm in the mood already.' She dug her hand down between his thighs and groped for his cock.

'This is special.' He pressed the remote controls one after the other. The television screen crackled and the video whirred.

An oddly anonymous bedroom appeared on the screen. It had pine-panelled walls, a pine-framed bed and very garish orange and yellow patterned curtains across the single window. Sitting on the edge of the bed, looking ill at ease, was a young girl with short, chestnut-coloured hair. She was wearing a pair of tight denim shorts and a white T-shirt. She kept looking towards the camera as if unsure what she should do next.

A man walked into the shot. He was young too, with curly brown hair and a thin face. He was stripped to the waist, wearing only black leather trousers. His body was lean but not muscular. He was carrying several items of black leather which he dropped on the bed beside the girl.

Taking her face in his hands he tilted it so she was looking up at him. He said something in an odd guttural language Cherry did not understand. The girl appeared to nod her agreement. She stripped off her T-shirt. She wasn't wearing a bra and her heavy, pear-shaped breasts quivered like jelly as she threw the white cotton to one side. She unzipped the denim shorts but did not attempt to take them off.

The man picked up a black leather garment from the bed. Cherry saw it was some sort of hood with eyelets and laces at the back. The man opened the laces out and pulled the hood over the girl's head and hair, wriggling it down until it encased them completely. There was a large, oval hole at the front for the girl's mouth, and a small opening that fitted the base of her nose, but there was no provision for her eyes or ears. Resting the girl's face against his belly, the man drew the laces tight, pulling the leather against her face until it fitted like a second skin.

The man picked up a second item of black leather, a two-foot long rectangle with a series of buckles and straps attached to each side. He laid it flat on the bed then again said something to the girl. Without any hesitation she lay back, then rolled over on to her stomach on the top of the black leather.

The camera moved into a tight close-up. Attached to the inside of the rectangle and positioned so they could be used to bind the girl's arms to her sides Cherry could see six thin straps, three on each side. The man carefully fastened these in place, one just under the armpit, one above the elbow and the other at her wrist, then wrapped the leather over her back and used the buckles to fasten it around her. He tugged on the buckles to get them as tight as they would go. The girl's flesh bulged out over the top and bottom of the garment.

Satisfied that it was secured properly, the man rolled the girl on to her back. The girl's breasts flopped over the top of the black leather which encased her so tightly. Her hands poked out of the bottom of the garment though she could not move them at all.

The man took hold of the denim shorts and wriggled them down the girl's hips. Under the shorts she was wearing a pair of white satin panties. As soon as he had wriggled the shorts off her legs he returned and pulled the panties down too. The girl's mons was almost bare. The chestnut-coloured hair had been trimmed away to form a tiny inverted triangle which pointed down to the fleshy slit of her sex.

'Well?'

Peter's voice startled Cherry. She had become completely engrossed in the video.

'Well what?' she said.

'What's your reaction?'

'I'll tell you in a minute.'

The man on the screen had picked up another item of leather. It was a rigid leather cuff. Quickly he wrapped it around the girl's left ankle. A second cuff followed on the right. He stooped, rummaging under the bed, and came up with a long metal rod. A shiny metal chain was attached to the centre of the rod and snap hooks dangled from each end. The man spread the girl's legs wide apart and clipped the snap hooks into small D-rings on the leather cuffs. Then he took hold of the chain, pulling it up until the girl's legs were bent double and attaching it to the underside of the leather garment effectively preventing her straightening her legs again, forcing them back until her heels were hard against her thighs.

The camera closed in. In this position the girl's sex was completely exposed. The camera roamed the area in tight close-up, moving from the little puckered corona of her anus to the thin lips of her sex. The quality of the picture was high and Cherry thought she could see where the girl's pubic hair had been shaved away. Her labia were pursed and glistening. It was clear that this extreme bondage excited her.

When the camera panned out again, the man in the leather trousers had gone. The girl lay helplessly on the bed, writhing around and straining her arms, trying to twist her left hand around on to her belly and down between her legs, desperate, it appeared, to touch her sex, as if to get some relief from an overwhelming frustration. But it was impossible. There was no slack in the bondage. In fact, there was no way she could bring any pressure to bear on her clitoris, the position of her legs, bent and spread apart, even making it impossible for her to roll on to her stomach where she might have been able to rub herself against the sheet. She was making little mewing noises, repeating a single word over and over again, its meaning, if not the word itself, recognisably corresponding to 'please'.

Cherry realised that she was squirming her buttocks against the sofa, her thighs pressed together, trapping her clit. She looked over at Peter. A large bulge tented the front of his trousers.

The camera began to close in on the girl's face. The black leather that covered it so tightly made her mouth, by contrast, seem almost obscene, a gash of scarlet and pink, quite as wet as her pussy. Her tongue flashed out, wiggling up and down as though trying to draw attention to itself.

A man's voice said something in the foreign language, but it was clearly a different voice, with a deeper tone. The whole picture was tight on the girl's face so Cherry could not see who was speaking, but suddenly a large circumcised, fully erect penis appeared on the screen, its under surface sliding against the girl's lips. It had been oiled and was very wet, the oil dripping over the black leather.

The girl sucked on it eagerly. She made an attempt to reach up and take the whole shaft into her mouth but this brought what sounded like an angry rebuke. Instead she concentrated on moving her lips up and down underneath it, her tongue occasionally darting out to lick around the top of the glans.

The camera pulled back. Cherry saw the man who was kneeling at the top of the bed. He was strong and athletic, with muscles that had obviously been used to pump iron, each rib clearly delineated. As the girl attended to his cock, his hand caressed her thigh, down the inner surface until it

The Master's Diary

was resting against her labia. Very delicately, his middle finger probed her slit. Cherry saw him winkle out her clitoris and press his finger against it. This obviously produced a huge wave of sensation in the girl. Her body rocked on the bed. Immediately the man took his finger away, and said something to her that sounded like a teasing admonishment. Clearly she was not intended to have her pleasure yet.

From behind his back the man produced a large, black dildo. It was a crude representation of the real thing, with a smooth glans at the top, a ridge underneath it and a curved shaft that had been distressed to resemble veins. As the girl continued to ply her mouth up and down his cock, the man brought the dildo down to the mouth of her sex. Very carefully, making sure it did not touch her clitoris, he nosed the tip of the glans between her labia. The camera followed the movement, filling the screen with a view of the girl's sex as her nether lips parted to admit the black rubber. Cherry heard the girl moan loudly but with the dildo no more than an inch into her vagina, the man merely held it there, her labia pursed tightly around it.

The camera went back to a shot of the whole bed, the girl still sawing her head from side to side so her lips caressed the man's erection. Then it closed up on her mouth again, and Cherry saw the way the man's cock was pulsing, its wetness increased by the girl's saliva. She was sure he was going to come. She saw him hold the base of his cock with his free hand and squeeze it tightly. This made the flesh balloon, swelling against her lips. The girl redoubled her efforts, sliding her lips up and down the length much faster. As her tongue moved to caress the tip of his glans, Cherry saw the slit flare open and a big gob of white spunk spattered out over the girl's leather-bound face. More followed. He pulled back so most of it spattered into the girl's mouth, which she held open eagerly, spunk running all over her lips and tongue.

The camera went back to her sex. She was struggling against her bonds to push herself down on to the dildo, but Cherry could see that the man was holding it back, parrying her every attempt. The girl began a rapid stream of words, at first appearing to beg him to give her what she so badly wanted, then cursing him for not doing so. Neither approach worked. The dildo held her sex open but did not penetrate enough to relieve her frustration.

Cherry found herself wriggling in sympathy. Her own sex was pulsing wildly. She had never seen anything like this. Though she could not explain to herself why, the idea of being so helplessly bound and totally vulnerable was incredibly exciting. She could imagine exactly how the girl felt, her frustration at not being able to do anything to bring herself off increasing her very desire to do so. It was torture. Delicious torture.

The long stream of invective stopped. This time the girl used her body to plead with the man. The picture cut to a shot of the whole bed again, the girl's leather-swathed flesh arched up towards the man. He took hold of one of her breasts in his hand and squeezed the full flesh. Then he took the nipple between his finger and thumb and pinched it. At exactly that moment he plunged the dildo into her. It disappeared completely in one smooth movement, the juices of her body so copious the penetration was frictionless. Instantly, the girl began to quiver, as though she were being given an electric shock. Her head snapped over to one side, then to the other, her whole body lifted clear of the bed, supported only on her shoulders and heels. The man took his hand away. Cherry saw the dildo slowly begin to slip out of the girl's sex. When it was finally expelled and fell to the bed, the girl gasped and collapsed back on to the bed with it. The picture froze.

Credits rolled up against the background of the naked girl. Then the screen flickered and turned a uniform blue.

Cherry looked over at Peter. He was watching her, a strange expression in his eyes. He raised an eyebrow.

'Don't tell me you're not turned on. I can see that you are.'

'I wasn't going to. Are you into this? Have you got a bedroom full of equipment or something?' She definitely hadn't put Peter down as a man who would be interested in anything like this.

'No. I happened to be going through some of the latest confiscated videos. This one just appealed to me.'

'What do you want me to do?'

'Co-operate.'

The way that he said the word, coldly and calmly, sent a chill through Cherry's body. At that moment she wished he had just pushed her back on the sofa and fucked her. On the other hand, her empathy with the girl had aroused a whole new set of emotions. The thought of being tied and teased in the way that she had, of going through what she had experienced, was an enticing prospect.

'I thought you said you didn't have any equipment?'

'I can improvise,' he said, the tone of his voice still icy.

Cherry sprung to her feet. 'Wouldn't you rather just fuck me?'

'No,' he said emphatically.

'All right, if that's what you want.'

He smiled, a thin almost imperceptible smile. 'It's what you want too, isn't it?'

'I think so,' she said quietly.

He stood up and took her hand, leading the way out into the hall and through to the bedroom. The bedroom was neat with a small double bed, covered with a blue and green check counterpane, and a wallpaper patterned with tiny cornflowers. There was a bathroom to one side, its walls and floor tiled in white ceramic tiles.

'Like in the video,' he said, nodding towards the bed. 'I'll wait in the bathroom.'

Cherry could feel the tension in his body. She wondered how long he had been watching the video, waiting for the opportunity to get a girl to act out the part.

'You want me to strip, right?' she said.

He nodded and disappeared into the bathroom, closing the door behind him.

Cherry looked around the bedroom. She had had her fair share of sexual encounters with men, but nothing like this. Normally she would have expected Peter to throw her on the bed, fumbling to undo her clothes, their bodies creating a flame of passion that would eventually consume them both. This was completely different. They hadn't even kissed. The odd thing was that the coldness of it, the element of calculation, was exciting in itself.

Cherry unbuttoned her skirt and laid it over the top of a mahogany chest of drawers. She stooped to unclasp the three poppers that held the crotch of the body in place. As she struggled to free them, she felt the heat and distinct dampness of her pussy underneath. She pulled the body over her head then shook her hair out and combed it back into place with her fingers. As the Lycra of the body had been tight, she had not bothered with a bra. Her breasts were small and round with disproportionately large nipples that had already puckered, the deep brown buds of flesh wrinkled and hard. She pulled the tights down her legs and sat on the bed, kicking off her shoes, then extracted her feet from the nylon. She thought about the girl in the film. There must have been a camera crew in the room with her. How did that feel? She shuddered as though someone had just run over her grave.

'Ready,' she said quickly, before she changed her mind.

The bathroom door opened. Peter was wearing a dark blue cotton robe. He stared at her body for a moment. She had downy blonde hair that was shaped like a fat cigar. He closed the bathroom door then opened the top drawer of the mahogany chest. He took out a white silk evening scarf and brought it over to the bed. Without a word he fitted it over Cherry's eyes and wrapped it around her head, knotting it tightly.

'Can you see anything?' he asked.

'No.'

The blindfold was effective. Cherry was suddenly plunged into darkness. Her body responded with a sharp pang of arousal. The darkness made her anonymous and the anonymity was welcome. She didn't have to be herself, hemmed in by conventions and long-held taboos. She could respond on a purely instinctive level.

She felt Peter's hand on her shoulder, pushing her back on to the counterpane. She lay on her back. His hand pulled her ankles around so she was lying along the length of the bed. His hands moved to her arm, rolling her over on to her stomach, just like the girl in the video had done.

The loss of one sense seemed to dramatically increase the sensitivity of all the others. The rather harsh material of the counterpane rubbed against her nipples provoking a marked response. She seemed to be able to hear more acutely too, the noise of Peter's breathing suddenly pronounced.

She heard him walking back to the chest of drawers. A drawer slid open and there was a rustling sound. Then another drawer and more rooting around. Footsteps came back to the bed, and things were dropped on the counterpane beside her. She started as his fingers touched her upper arm. Something cold and hard wrapped around it and over her back. It was threaded through her other arm and she felt them being cinched tightly together and heard the metallic click of a belt buckle. A second belt followed just above her elbows, drawing her arms even closer together. He crossed her wrists one over the other, then wound a third belt around them and buckled that tightly too.

Cherry experienced a surge of sensation. The constriction of her arms was exciting. It produced all sorts of feelings in her she had never had before. She had tried to imagine how the girl in the video had felt. Now she knew for herself.

Peter was rolling her over on to her back again. She sensed that he had paused, standing over her, looking down at her naked body. The position of her arms, bound so tightly behind her, made her thrust her small breasts forward, and arched her torso off the bed. She started again as she felt the tips of his fingers stroking her flat belly. Briefly, they toyed with her pubic hair. She opened her legs, by way of invitation, but the fingers moved away.

A weight depressed the mattress at her side. She felt a hand gripping her ankle. Something soft and silky was being wound around it. The ankle was pulled back, until her heel was hard against the back of her thigh, then the same material was wrapped around the top of her thigh and tied tightly, making it impossible for her for to straighten her leg again. Peter repeated the process with the other leg.

Cherry saw a picture of herself in her mind's eye, lying on the bed, with her legs bent double. The girl in the video had been bound more expertly but the result was virtually the same.

There was a clicking noise, the noise of belt buckles, she thought. But they were not being buckled around her. She heard Peter's breathing and felt the brush of something against her side but she could not imagine what he was doing.

A hand touched her knee. The tongue of what felt like a leather belt was threaded underneath it. The belt was pulled through then slotted under her other knee. She felt Peter shift his position on the bed, then her knees were being pulled back by the leather belt up towards her chest. Cold, hard leather wrapped around the back of her neck and a buckle clicked as it was fastened. She tried to stretch her legs back down but they were effectively doubled up against her torso, her neat, pert buttocks tilted upward, and the whole slit of her sex exposed. Not only that but the bondage completed her helplessness. Apart from squirming around on her back she could not move.

Almost immediately Peter's weight shifted again. She felt something hot and wet nudge against her cheek and realised it was his cock. Eagerly she tried to gobble it into her mouth.

'No,' he said. 'Like in the video.' His voice sounded strained and hoarse.

The Master's Diary

Cherry pursed her lips and ran them along the underside of his cock. She could feel it pulsing and could taste the sticky wetness his excitement had produced. She knew her own response had been no less liquid. With her sex tipped up like this she was sure she could feel her own juices running down between the cleft of her buttocks.

Licking the hot, hard cock produced a flood of hot, hard arousal. But it was not like anything she had felt before. The impulse was the same, of course, but it was twisted by the constriction of her body into something quite different, a feeling that seemed to be trapped by her bonds just as her body was trapped. She had been tied into a tight little ball, her limbs rendered useless, but the more helpless and constrained she was the more her sex, so rudely exposed, seemed to feel unrestricted and curiously free. Her clitoris was throbbing violently and she was sure she could actually feel her vagina gaping open, like a mouth desperate for air. The vision of the girl in the video haunted her too. In her mind she saw the girl's body quivering as the dildo had nosed between her labia. Now she was in virtually the same position as the girl she realised why she had been able to empathise with her so completely. Her body was responding to the same treatment with just as much passion.

She tried to concentrate on his cock, licking his glans with her tongue, just as the girl had done, and sliding her mouth under the whole length of it.

Suddenly he pulled away. His weight moved down the bed. Cherry felt his hands on her ankles. They moved up to her knees, caressing her flesh gently. She was sure she could feel the heat of his cock an inch or two from her upturned labia. She tried to wriggle herself down on to it, but he held her legs firmly. His hands squeezed between her legs and her chest until he could grasp her nipples. He pinched them both at the same time and she moaned loudly, the sharp pang of sensation making her sex clench fiercely.

'Please . . .' she gasped.

She felt his cock butt against the little corona of her anus, then move up into the slit of her labia. Just as a minute before her lips had sucked on the underside of his erection, now her soaking wet labia were doing the same. She was sure that she had never in her entire life wanted to feel a cock riding up into her cunt as much as she had wanted it at that moment.

Peter pushed himself to and fro, sawing his cock between her labia, without making any attempt to penetrate her.

'Please,' Cherry said.

He stopped. She felt his hands on her buttocks, then the heat of his glans nosed into the mouth of her vagina. She remembered the way the girl's labia had pursed to greet the head of the dildo and was sure hers were doing the same. A huge wave of sensation coursed through her. He had hardly penetrated her at all but the nerves in her pussy were responding wildly. She felt a flood of her juices running over him. She was coming, her whole body geared up for orgasm.

'Please,' she begged him.

'Not yet,' he said quietly.

Her sex clenched around him. Though it grasped the top of his glans, the feeling of emptiness it encountered in the rest of its length only increased her desperation.

Without thinking she tried to straighten her legs. The sudden bite of whatever bound her legs so tightly, the sudden reminder that she was completely helpless, gave her a whole new set of sensations to cope with. She couldn't understand why she should find this so exciting, but it was. Just as the blindfold had increased the sensitivity of her other senses, so the fact that she couldn't move seemed to amplify the feelings from her wildly throbbing sex. As if to test this proposition she tensed the muscles in all her limbs, struggling to get them free. The resistance she encountered pitched her into a frenzy of sensation, her sex contracting like a fist, desperate to grasp something more substantial than the teasing penetration it encountered.

Peter must have felt it. He must have seen it. She was sure

he was staring down at her sex. But he did not move. She could feel the pulse of blood in his glans, and his fingers pressing into her buttocks, but that was all.

'I need it,' she said. The sound of her voice surprised her. It was calm and detached, not two emotions she felt.

Later she would remember it as one of the most extraordinary sensations she had ever experienced. Without a sound, and without the slightest movement, his glans swelled, stretching the mouth of her vagina around it, and a jet of red-hot spunk spattered out into her open pussy. The glans recoiled, then swelled again, even larger this time, and produced a second jet. Others followed. Cherry felt every one, the spunk shooting up inside her, seeming to travel for inches before it spattered against the wet, silky walls of her vagina.

She was coming. Instantly. The bondage concentrated everything on the explosion inside her. She screamed because she had never felt anything so intense, but just as her orgasm exploded, Peter plunged into her, driving his cock all the way up into her cunt, riding on a flood of her juices and his own spunk. He filled her completely, turning her orgasm into something new, the impact doubled, her mind wallowing in a pit of scarlet pleasure. Her body tried to express its pleasure by stretching outward, the fact that the bondage prevented that so effectively adding another dimension to her already overwrought feelings.

Eventually he untied her. She squeezed her eyes tight shut against the light as he pulled off the blindfold. When she opened them she saw the jumble of scarfs and belts he had used to bind her.

'What did you do to me?' she said, unable to believe her own response.

He grinned. 'Guess I must have touched a nerve.'

Chapter Four

Sandra Seymour looked at herself in the mirror. The deep, wired cups of the black silk and lace bra lifted her breasts into a billowing cleavage. She could see the shadow of her dark nipples under the lace. A wide suspender belt in the same material banded her waist, its long, thin suspenders snaking down over her thighs to pull the jet-black welts of the very sheer stockings into peaks on her creamy thighs. A triangle of black silk cupped her mons, the thick pubic hair underneath it making it look as if it had been inflated. Satisfied with what she saw, she picked up the black silk and lace slip. She raised it above her head and allowed it to float down over her body. The silk was so soft it seemed to caress her flesh.

She had spent her whole lunch hour selecting the lingerie and the new dress. She'd even bought a new pair of shoes. She had dashed home, had a bath and spent nearly an hour on her make-up, carefully lining and shading her large brown eyes, and emphasising her long eyelashes with mascara.

Her excitement was extreme. All day she had tried not to think about what was going to happen tonight, but it had proved impossible, and every spare moment had turned into a daydream, the scene from the book in which Clara is taken to the Master for the first time playing over and over in her head.

Sandra had laid out the dress on the bed. She had chosen everything carefully. She had thought of wearing one of the more outrageous outfits that she had bought for use in her games with Michael. But she had decided that approach lacked subtlety. She wanted the Master to desire her and thought him more likely to do so if her appearance suggested that she was a novice when it came to *his* area of expertise. A novice, but not naive. She didn't want him to think her prudish. That is why she'd chosen the sheer stockings and the black lingerie.

She climbed into the dress and wriggled it up over her body. It clung to the rich curves of her body, the shiny black material woven with a strand of silver thread that caught the light. Its box-neck was low and revealed more than a hint of her luxuriant cleavage.

The new black, spiky high-heels completed the outfit. She looked in the mirror again. She brushed her long hair out then tied it into a single silver band at the nape of her neck, letting the rest of its length flow over her back.

She looked at her watch. It was seven-fifty. Thankfully, the time had passed quickly. She'd hoped she wouldn't have time to sit with nothing to do but think about what was going to happen. That would only make her even more on edge and she was nervous enough already. She glanced out of the window just as the black, long wheelbase Rolls Royce pulled up outside. The windows of the car were opaque and she could not see if Curtis was driving.

Quickly, she drew a line of dark red lipstick over her lips, and adjusted her hair. Then she turned the bedroom light off and drew the curtain aside again to watch. At exactly one minute to eight, Curtis got out of the double-parked car and headed for the entrance of her block.

The entryphone rang. She picked the receiver off the wall. 'I'm coming down,' she said.

Her pulse was racing as she locked her front door. She walked down the two flights of stairs instead of waiting for the lift, but tried to remain calm. That was, she thought, asking the impossible.

'Hi,' she said brightly. Curtis was waiting outside the front door as she opened it.

'Good evening, Ms Seymour,' he said stiffly.

The Master's Diary

That should have signalled something to her but it didn't. 'Very formal,' she said. 'What's got into you?'

He frowned and nodded towards the car surreptitiously, side-stepping her attempt to take his arm.

'Give me your house keys,' he said.

She handed him the keys as Manville had told her to do.

Curtis trotted back to the car and opened the rear passenger door. She gave him an old-fashioned look as she caught up with him. Then she realised the reason for his demeanour.

'Good evening, Ms Seymour.' The voice was deep, rich and cultured.

Sitting in the back of the car was a tall, dark-haired man. He was dressed entirely in black, a black silk shirt, jacket and trousers and black shoes. He had deep-set eyes that were so dark a brown they looked almost black too. His face was smooth and square, his large features and high cheekbones not conventionally handsome but unmistakably attractive. Though he did not match the description of the Master given in the book, nor the mental picture Sandra had formed from it, there was absolutely no question in her mind that this man was Manville Mason, and that the force of his personality was the inspiration for the character he had created.

'Good evening,' she said, climbing into the car and sitting beside him on the long leather bench seat. Now she realised why Curtis had been so off-hand. He didn't want his master to get any hint of what had happened between them last night.

'Manville Mason, and you are Sandra Seymour,' Manville said, extending his hand. He had long, thin fingers and wore a gold signet ring embossed with a black stone on his left hand.

'Pleased to meet you,' Sandra said, shaking his hand. His fingers were cold to the touch.

Curtis had got back behind the wheel. The engine started, though it was barely audible, and the car glided away. The soft suspension added to a sudden sense of unreality.

'Would you care for a glass of champagne?'

She had barely taken her eyes off Manville. Now she glanced round the vast interior of the car. She had never been in a Rolls Royce before let alone this specially constructed, stretched version. It was large and luxurious. There was a walnut cocktail cabinet on top of which was a silver ice bucket containing a bottle of champagne. Two flutes, one of them half full of wine, sat in custom-built wooden holders.

'Thank you,' she said. She realised she was breathless and tried to breathe more naturally.

Manville leaned forward and poured the wine. He handed her a glass and picked up his own. 'What shall we drink to? New beginnings?'

'Yes,' she said. She looked into his eyes. They were staring into hers. She had the impression that they could see into her soul, that he now knew everything that really mattered about her. She also knew, without the slightest doubt, that everything he had written about was, as she'd suspected, a reflection of a reality he lived every day of his life. Manville Mason was physically dissimilar, not as old or craggy, but there was no doubt that he was the Master.

He touched his glass delicately against hers. The wine was cold and delicious.

'I was very touched by your letter,' he said.

'I'm sure you get a lot.' She tried to sound breezy and non-committal but she knew he only had to look at her to see that she was not.

'I do. But not all as charming and revealing as yours. It appears my work has provoked something in you.'

'Yes.' She felt herself blushing and struggled to stop it.

'You think you are what I like to call a submissive. Isn't that what you said in your letter?'

There was going to be no small-talk, no asking her about the weather, or what she did for a living. 'Yes,' she said, because she couldn't think of anything else to say.

'You mentioned Clara. Is that how you see yourself?'

'Yes.' She seemed to be stuck on that monosyllable.

The Master's Diary

'Have you thought about what it means? It amounts to a sort of operation, an amputation of the will. Free will that is. Your ability to do anything for yourself, to think for yourself. All that is removed. What you are left with is a single, solitary motivation, day and night. The need to obey your Master. And his surrogates. Whatever is asked of you. Have you thought about that?'

Sandra had not. In fact, she realised, all she had done was play games, toying with fantasy. She knew that was different from living it from day to day. But the prospect did not frighten her. If anything it served only to excite her further.

'I want to obey,' she said, trying to keep her voice steady.

'Good. You are right, of course. I do get many letters. For some women my books are an amusing fiction. For others, like you, they stir something deeper. They realise, as you did, that they are based on a fundamental reality. I am a rich man. I have used my wealth to develop certain themes in life that I think are redolent in human nature. What I write about is based on that reality. Occasionally I read a letter, like yours, that makes me think that its author might be suitable material to spend time with me at the castle.'

'There is a castle, then?'

'Oh yes. You were absolutely right, my dear. The point is that some of the women who write letters may believe that they are submissive, but the truth is very different. They have only experienced what they have read at a very superficial level. They are only interested in being whipped, or being put into bondage, as a way of enhancing their sexual pleasure on a short-term basis. They are not true submissives. It is a great mistake to take such a woman to the castle. To avoid that mistake I have, over the years, devised a number of tests.'

'Tests?'

'In order, shall we say, to separate the wheat from the chaff. Which means that you have a choice. We can have a perfectly pleasant dinner, and talk inconsequentially about all manner of things, and then I will send you home, or . . .' he paused, turning to look right into her eyes again, '. . . you can be tested.'

'You know which I will choose, don't you?' she said. He knew everything she was likely to do.

'Yes. Nevertheless you must let me hear you say it.'

'I want you to give me the tests.'

He smiled. His teeth were very white and regular. 'Good,' he said quietly, sipping his champagne. 'So, where shall we start?' He made a small chattering sound that might have been a muffled giggle. 'Extraordinary isn't it? Sitting here in a car with a man you've never met before, talking about sexual slavery.'

'I have met you before. I know you very well,' Sandra said decisively.

He made that odd giggling sound again. 'A good retort,' he said. 'So, where are we to begin? I want you to answer a few questions. There is no point lying. Lies will be found out. Have you always thought of yourself as submissive?'

'No. Never. Never before I read your book.'

He smiled. He pressed his hands together as though in an attitude of prayer and touched the tip of his fingers against his lips.

'And you hadn't the slightest idea that you possessed such a . . . a proclivity?'

'None.'

'How interesting. How would you characterise your sex life?'

Sandra crossed her legs. The nylon stockings rasped. She was intensely aware of her nipples rubbing against the lace of the bra. It seemed to have turned into sandpaper, creating a fiendish itch that she dared not scratch. 'In what way?' she asked, trying to relax. She sipped the champagne but it did not help.

'Sensational, average, dull . . . ?'

'I don't have any trouble achieving an orgasm, if that's what you mean,' she said boldly. 'I never have. I like sex. I enjoy it.'

'With men?'
'Yes.'
'Have you had sex with a woman?'
'No.'
'Never?'
'Never.'
'There is a great deal of lesbian sex in my book.'
'I know.'
'Did that excite you?'
'Yes.'
'But it hasn't made you want to go out and try it for yourself?'
'It excited me in the context of the book.'
'But in real life?'
'If the context was the same, I'm sure my reaction would be the same also.'
'Well put,' he said, patting his hands together as though giving her a round of applause. 'Are you wearing panties?'
'Yes.'
'I want you to take them off.'
'Now?'
'Yes.' His eyes stared at her intently again, waiting to see the slightest hesitation. She gave none. Lifting her bottom from the leather seat, she wriggled her skirt and slip up until she could reach the waistband of the black panties. She saw his eyes examining the black stocking tops and the suspenders.

She was about to draw the panties down when he stopped her. 'No,' he said. 'Not like that. Get on to your knees. Pull your dress right up over your hips, then take them down.'

Sandra knew she must obey immediately. There was plenty of room in the Rolls. She replaced the glass in the receptacle on the cocktail cabinet and dropped on to all fours on the thick black rug that carpeted the floor. 'Like this?' she said.

'Yes.'

She reached behind her and pulled the hem of the dress up over her thighs and buttocks until it and the black silk slip was bunched around her waist. He would have a clear view of her buttocks, the back of the panties stretched tightly over them, the flesh smooth and curvaceous. She reached up to the waistband and pulled them down to her knees, angling the pursed lips of her sex up towards him. She knew the windows of the car were opaque but she wondered if the glass division between the passenger compartment and the driver was too. Could Curtis see what she was doing? Had he seen it all before with a dozen beautiful and supplicant women?

'Do you always wear stockings?'

'No.'

'Why did you wear them tonight, then?'

'To please you.'

'How sweet.'

He reached forward and ran his hand over her buttocks. The touch was like an electric shock. Sandra could not suppress a gasp.

'Have you ever been buggered?' He asked it as casually as if he was asking if she could swim.

'Yes.'

'It was not to your taste?'

'I . . .' She wasn't sure what to say. It was another experience that Manville's book had transformed.

'It will be required of you.'

'I know.'

'Open your legs a little bit more, would you, my dear?'

Sandra wriggled her knees apart but the panties prevented her from spreading them fully.

'Shall I take the panties off?' she asked.

'No, no, that's quite satisfactory.'

She wasn't sure how much he would be able to see. The interior was lit by the streetlights outside, the intensity changing from minute to minute. She hoped he would be able to see that this bizarre experience had excited her so much her labia were wet. All day her imagination had run wild speculating on what he was likely to do with her. She had not imagined this.

'Good,' Manville said quietly. 'I want you to touch yourself now. Touch your clitoris.'

Sandra's clitoris throbbed. She slid her right hand over her belly and down to her pussy. She was astonished by how wet her labia were. Not only that, they were radiating heat like the bars of an electric fire. She pushed her finger between them. Her clitoris was swollen and hard.

'Good,' Manville said. 'Press on it.'

She did as she was told, trapping her clit between her finger and the underlying bone. It reacted with a huge wave of feeling. She gasped.

'Is that the best you can do?' he said, his voice suddenly cold and critical.

'I don't understand?'

'I want to hear you, hear you moan.'

'Oh . . .' she said at once. It did not require any acting. 'Oh, oh . . .' She had tried to suppress her exclamations of pleasure. It was wonderful to feel she didn't have to.

'Don't move your finger,' he remonstrated, seeing her finger move her clitoris from side to side. 'Just press it back.'

She did as she was told. 'Oh God . . . oh . . .' She repeated the word over and over again.

'Louder,' he ordered.

'Oh . . . oh . . . oh . . .' Each time was louder, and longer. The extraordinary thing was that the crescendo of sound was making her come. Or that's what it felt like. The sound seemed to vibrate through her body. She was moaning continuously now, her orgasm peaking. Somewhere in the back of her mind she wondered if Curtis could hear her. Would it remind him of how she had wailed when they had been together? 'Oh, God . . .' She screamed the words out, as her whole body shuddered, her clitoris pulsing against her finger, her vagina contracting as if searching for something to grip.

She collapsed forward on to the floor of the car. It was

only as her orgasm drained away that she realised that the car had stopped.

'Are you ready for the next stage?' Manville said.

Sandra rolled on to her side, then sat up, the dress still around her hips, the panties falling to her ankles. She looked out of the window. The car had pulled up outside a large Victorian house, with a semi-circular carriage driveway. The front door was painted white, its brass locks and knocker polished brightly.

Manville reached forward and plucked the panties from her ankles. He held them up to his face and stroked the material against his cheek. She saw him inhale, then exhale again, his body shuddering. His lap was veiled in shadow and she could not see whether he had an erection.

'All right, Curtis,' he said loudly.

Sandra heard the driver's door opening and Curtis's footsteps moving around the car. The passenger door was opened. Curtis stared in, looking at her long legs sheathed in the sheer black stockings.

'Out,' Manville said, his voice cold and commanding, with no hint of the warmth it had possessed moments before.

Sandra began to pull down her dress.

'Did I tell you to do that?' Manville snapped, leaning forward, the smiling face replaced by a look of fierce disapproval. 'Learn to do nothing unless you are told,' he said.

Sandra scrambled out of the car with the help of Curtis's arm. Manville followed. The front door opened and an exterior light was switched on. Standing in the doorway was a tall, statuesque redhead. Sandra stared at her. It was Angelica. From the toes of her black high-heeled shoes, to the rich curves of her breasts, to the haughty arrogance of her manner, the woman was an exact incarnation of Angelica.

'Is this her?' she said, her eyes roaming Sandra's body very much as if she were appraising a horse.

She was, Sandra decided, one of the most beautiful women she had ever seen. Her face was rather long and thin, but she had high, sharp cheekbones and a narrow, straight nose, her curly red hair falling in soft waves all around it. Her eyes were large and very green and her complexion was flawless. The neck that held her head so high was slender and elongated. She wore a grey suit with a black silk blouse. The blouse was unbuttoned enough to allow a glimpse of her extensive cleavage, haltered in a black bra, her breasts high and firm. The skirt of the suit was short and showed off her long legs, encased in shiny, gunmetal-grey tights. Her thighs were contoured with muscles, her calves taut and neat, and her ankles pinched and slim.

'Take her upstairs, will you?' Manville said.

The redhead took two steps forward. She grasped Sandra by the arm, her fingers pinching the flesh, and led her into the house. There was a large hall and a wide staircase facing the door, its newel-posts elaborately carved with a coat of arms in which an eagle appeared to be tearing the heart out of some small mammal.

'This is Marion Chandler. You understand you must do everything that she tells you to do, without question?' Manville said once they were inside.

'Yes,' Sandra said. Marion, not Angelica. The sight of the woman had excited her so much her heart was beating like a drum. She tried not to think what the woman might ask her to do. She realised that what had happened in the car had only strengthened her desire to be part of the world Manville had created. The way he had treated her, made her display and touch herself, had had a profound effect on her. It was the reason she'd come so quickly. In his book the scenes with Clara and Angelica had aroused her. But this was no longer fiction. Faced with the reality of a woman, of doing the things Clara had been made to do with Angelica, Sandra hoped desperately that she would not lose her resolve. She wanted to obey. She just hoped she would be able to.

Manville nodded to Marion, then turned and disappeared through a door at the far end of the hall. Marion's grip on her arm tightened again and she guided Sandra upstairs. At the top of the staircase there was a wide, but windowless corridor at the end of which Marion opened a door on the right and pushed Sandra inside.

Sandra found herself in a small, windowless room, the walls, ceiling and floor all covered in dark grey carpeting. The light came from a bar of spotlights set in the ceiling, all of them dimmed so the room was barely lit. Two heavy wooden beams ran across the ceiling, set into which were a series of metal hooks and rings. Dangling from these were a leather harness and thick metal chains. In the centre of the room were two columns, rising from floor to ceiling, and positioned between them was an upright steel frame about the size of a small double bed. The frame was slatted with steel. There were four leather cuffs attached to its corners and leather straps at various points all over.

Sandra felt her body go cold. *The Master's Diary* had descriptions of several rooms like this, but she had never seen one before.

Marion closed the door. It closed with a clunk. The redhead smiled. She had a wide, fleshy mouth and large very regular teeth that filled it in two perfect semi-circles. 'So,' she said. 'Another recruit.' The smile disappeared. 'You know who I am, don't you?' The woman had a very slight American accent Sandra thought.

'Angelica.'

Precisely.' The smile reappeared. This time one corner of her mouth was slightly higher than the other. 'I was Manville's inspiration. Do you think he described me well?'

'Yes. You're very beautiful.'

'Don't try to flatter me. It won't make any difference. Angelica is a dedicated lesbian. So am I. Angelica is heartless and cruel. So am I. Angelica demands to be obeyed. So do I. Do you understand?'

'Yes.' She looked straight into Marion's eyes. They were as cold as sharply cut diamonds.

The Master's Diary

'Get your dress off,' Marion snapped.

Sandra unzipped the dress and wriggled out of it, intensely aware that Marion was watching her every move. As she stepped out of it the redhead snatched it from her hands and hung it on a hook on the back of the door.

Marion stepped forward, took hold of the hem of the black lace slip and pulled it over Sandra's head, hanging that on the door too.

'Very pretty,' she said. 'Did he take your panties, or weren't you wearing any?'

'Manville took them.'

'Yes, he usually does. Take your bra off now.'

Sandra reached behind her back to the clip of her bra. She unfastened it and let the shoulder straps fall over her arms. Leaning forward she allowed her breasts to slip out of the black silk and lace cups. Marion took hold of one of the straps and pulled the garment away roughly.

'Now, over here.' Marion said, indicating the metal frame. Sandra walked over to the frame. She would have liked to hold her breasts to stop them jiggling up and down as she walked but was sure that would bring a rebuke, especially as Marion's eyes were glued to them. She had been briefly semi-naked in changing rooms with other women, but apart from that couldn't remember ever having exposed herself to another woman's gaze, certainly never as blatantly as this. She tried to pretend to herself that she found it exciting, but in fact the truth was she was breathless with another emotion: fear.

Marion took her arm and turned her round so her back was pressed against the metal slats. She stared into her eyes and had no difficulty reading what they contained.

'Everything is by consent,' she said with that odd, twisted smile. 'You only have to say no and you will be released.'

Sandra knew that was the case. She had read it in *The Master's Diary*. In fact it was that principle that was making her frightened. At that moment she could not say she was in the slightest bit aroused at the thought of Marion touching her, or of being ordered to touch Marion. She was afraid she would have to say no, which would bring a premature end to her adventure.

'Do you understand that?'

'Yes,' she said.

'And you do want me to go on? I don't like to think I'm wasting my time.'

Sandra could not look her in the eyes as she said, 'Yes.'

'Reach up to the top of the frame,' Marion said with barely a pause.

Sandra did as she was told. She tried to remember how Clara had felt as Angelica had stripped her for the first time. It was a tribute to Manville's skill that she thought the fictional Clara had felt fear of exactly the same thing. But at what point had fear turned to excitement? She couldn't remember that.

Marion wrapped one of the leather cuffs around Sandra's left wrist and buckled it tightly. The cuff was attached to a chain which in turn hung from a metal ring in the top corner of the frame. She moved to the right wrist and cuffed that to the opposite corner, spreading Sandra's arms wide apart. With practised ease she knelt at Sandra's feet and strapped her left ankle into a third cuff.

'Feet apart,' she ordered, as she tried to force Sandra's right ankle over to the opposite corner of the frame. Sandra stumbled as she tried to obey, the cuffs on her wrists jerking against her flesh. Marion wrapped the last cuff around her nylon sheathed ankle, then stood up to admire her work. 'Much better . . .'

She turned to the door and took off her jacket, hanging it over Sandra's dress and slip. She unbuttoned her blouse, pulled it out from the short skirt and stripped it off, hanging that on the same hook. The wired cups of her plunge-fronted bra were voluminous but barely managed to contain her ballooning breasts. The cups were so low cut that Sandra could see the upper surface of the very wide areolae that surrounded her nipples. It was a dark reddish brown.

She walked back to her captive. Reaching around Sandra's back she picked up a wide leather strap that was also fastened to the frame, and buckled it around her waist. Another equally wide strap was tightened around both Sandra's arms just above the elbow, and around her legs, just above the knee. Each bound her tighter, reducing the possibility of movement, her helplessness complete.

'I want you to struggle,' Marion said calmly. 'As if you wanted to escape.' She was looking straight into eyes. 'Come on,' she prompted when Sandra did nothing. 'Or shall I give you an incentive?'

Sandra tried to move her arms. She tensed her muscles and tried desperately to free them. The leather held. She wriggled her legs against their straps and twisted her whole body but achieved little, the leather biting into her flesh. And that's when it happened. As she felt the bonds holding her so tightly, their grip unyielding, she experienced a surge of arousal. Her clitoris throbbed as strongly as it had in the car, her face turned red and her misgivings simply evaporated.

'Again,' Marion said with a knowing smile. She had seen what had happened and knew what it meant.

This time Sandra used all her strength, struggling wildly to free herself not because she wanted to escape but because the harder she struggled the more she felt how completely powerless she was, a feeling which created a second wave of sharp, palpable pleasure. Her breasts slapped against each other and sweat broke out on her forehead with the effort.

'All right,' Marion said. 'That's enough.'

Sandra relaxed, slumping against the leather. But that was exciting too. She did not need to support herself. The bonds held her of their own accord.

'Do you want to go on?' Marion asked, though it was perfectly obvious what the answer was.

'Yes,' Sandra said.

Marion extended her hand. She had slender fingers with

long fingernails varnished in dark scarlet colour. She traced one of the fingers down Sandra's cheek, then over her lips. 'From my point of view, I must say, I hope he accepts you. You're a very attractive woman. There would be many occasions when I would have you at my mercy like this.' That twisted smile appeared again. She brought her face to within a couple of inches of Sandra's. 'Have you ever kissed a woman?'

'No,' Sandra said breathily.

'Really? How very interesting.' The redhead's eyes were blazing with excitement. 'Reach forward and kiss me now,' she said.

There was just enough play in the leather to allow Sandra to push her head forward and brush her lips against Marion's, but not enough to allow her to bring any real pressure to bear. She brushed her lips from side to side and strained to press them closer. Her breasts were crushed against Marion's black bra.

With what seemed like infinite slowness, she saw Marion lift her hand. It snaked around the back of her neck, under the hair band, then held her head firmly as she pressed her mouth forward, their lips crushing together, the redhead's tongue plunging into her mouth.

Sandra's heart lurched. She sucked in air and the woman's tongue at the same time. Another wave of pleasure coursed through her. She had never been kissed by a woman before and she was astonished at how different it felt. Though Marion was kissing her hungrily and as hard as any man, her mouth felt soft and pliable. Struggling against the limitations of the bondage Sandra kissed her back as best she could, trying to stretch forward.

It wasn't only her mouth that felt different. Her breasts were crushed by Marion's. Even through the black bra she was sure she could feel the redhead's nipples, like her own, as hard as stone.

Marion stepped back. The clasp of her bra was in the front between the two cups. She unhooked it and allowed her big

The Master's Diary

breasts to spill out. Her breasts were round and high though, unlike Angelica's, her nipples were surprisingly small. Without stripping the bra from her shoulders she kissed Sandra again, this time their breasts squashed together and ballooning out to the side. The heat and fleshiness of them made Sandra swoon, her nipples pushed back into her own orbs until they were grinding against her ribs. She could feel Marion's nipples just as distinctly, two pebbles in a sea of sponginess.

As if reluctant to stop, nibbling at Sandra's bottom lip then sucking at it, Marion slowly pulled away. She stepped back and surveyed her captive appreciatively. She put out her hand and touched Sandra's left breast, then let her fingers drop to her nipple, flicking her fingernail against it and making Sandra shudder.

'You could not begin to imagine the things I could do to your breasts,' the redhead said, her voice cool and calm.

Giving her a little smile Marion walked behind the frame. Sandra turned her head but could not see what she was doing. She thought she heard a cupboard door being opened but could not remember seeing any conventional furniture in the room. Her body ached. Marion's finger seemed to have left an indelible trail over the skin of her breast and nipple. The flesh there seemed to be alive.

She sensed the redhead coming back behind her. A hand reached through the metal slats and she glimpsed a black silk sleeping mask, its interior softly padded, before it was pulled up over her eyes and darkness descended. 'No,' she said, before she realised she had said it.

'No?' Marion's voice repeated harshly. 'You mean you want to stop?'

'I didn't mean it,' Sandra said hastily. That was the last thing she wanted to do. The short grey skirt that was pulled tautly against the redhead's stomach and the lush curves of her buttocks and the shiny grey tights seemed, by contrast, to point up the nakedness of her big breasts. Though the sight of a woman's body had never provoked her before, she realised it was exciting her enormously now, and she had only exclaimed in distress at the prospect of being deprived of it.

'Never say anything you don't mean,' Marion warned with venom. She adjusted the blindfold, making sure it fitted snugly over the bridge of Sandra's nose.

The enforced darkness had the effect of concentrating Sandra's thoughts. Her fear had melted away to be replaced by sensations she had never felt before. Even as she had been bound and used by Michael she had never felt like this. What Michael had done was a game and a game orchestrated, in the end, by her. Not only was this not a game, it was not of her making. And, more essentially, it depended absolutely on one thing: her submission. She only had to say the word, to withdraw her consent, and it would stop, instantly and forever. That was what created this unique sensibility. Whatever current Manville's book had tapped deep in her psyche, she was now plugged into it directly. Her fevered arousal as Marion had kissed her had been part of this phenomenon.

She heard a loud clicking noise followed by a whirring sound. Very slowly she felt her weight shifting. Disorientated by her loss of sight it took her a moment to realise what was happening. Her feet were being lifted and her head falling back. The metal frame must be pivoted at its centre between the two columns. In a matter of seconds it was horizontal. The whirring stopped.

Again Sandra listened, trying to hear what Marion was doing. She heard the unmistakable rustle of clothing, then the rasp of nylon against flesh. She imagined her stripping off the rest of her clothes. Then the noise of the secret cupboard again.

She started as Marion's hand touched her thigh. The fingers moved across the top of her stocking to the suspender, then over it and down between her legs. Her reticence had gone completely. She found herself trying to strain her sex up towards Marion's hand, anxious to be touched by a woman for the first time.

The Master's Diary

But it was not a finger that she felt probing between her labia. It was something hard and cold. She caught her breath as she felt her labia being prised apart, exposing her clitoris but not touching it, the fourchette above it spread open. Another part of the same device curved down over the rest of her labia and slipped into the mouth of her vagina. It did not penetrate far, but stretched the little mouth tightly around its obviously considerable breadth.

She felt Marion's naked breasts rest briefly against her thigh as if she were reaching down under the metal frame. Then the fingers that held the odd device in place moved away and Sandra felt a leather strap digging into the cleft of her buttocks and up between her legs. It was pulled over her belly then buckled tight into the wide belt around her waist, which she guessed it was also attached to at the back. The belt held whatever was sitting on her sex more tightly than Marion's hand had done, squeezing it against her tender flesh and making Sandra moan.

Sandra felt Marion's body move away. Then she could hear nothing. She turned her head from side to side as if to try and sense where Marion was but it didn't work. Suddenly the device began to vibrate, a strong, rhythmical oscillation. At the same time, a finger of plastic had extended down from the centre of the contraption to settle, lightly, against her clit. This was vibrating at the same frequency and produced waves of sensation that were impossible to ignore. The blindfold made them worse, each perceived in the blackness as a flash of colour, each concentrated by the fact she was not distracted by what she could see.

She knew she was coming. It felt as if her whole sex was vibrating, the mouth of her vagina stretched around the stubbly plug and her clitoris both responding with equal vigour. She moved her buttocks up and down, as though fucking some imaginary lover. It was delicious. She didn't care that Marion was watching and could see she was bringing herself off. Each surge of pleasure from her clit made her vagina contract around the dildo, gripping it tightly, testing its hardness. That produced a second wave that rebounded back to her clit, creating a vicious circle of pleasure.

Sandra pulled against her bonds, wanting to feel the restraint. As her orgasm mounted she struggled wildly, each bite of the leather that held her so tightly adding fuel to the flames that consumed her. She wanted to show herself to Marion. She wanted the woman to see what she was capable of. As she tried to arch herself off the frame, every strap straining to contain her, she came, a thousand needles of pleasure lancing through her, every nerve in her body alive. At the centre of it all, in the middle of the storm, she saw Manville's black eyes looking at her and through her as they had in the car. In the end she had come for him.

Her body melted. She sunk back on to the frame. At that moment she felt Marion's leg against her side. The vibrations stopped. In a second she had straddled her chest, Sandra's breasts pressed into the side of her thighs. She felt the heat of her buttocks descending towards her face. She could smell the musky aroma of sex.

Despite her orgasm, despite all the reservations she had felt earlier, Sandra was overcome with a new wave of excitement.

'Don't let me down,' Marion said coolly.

For the first time in her life, Sandra felt a woman's sex pressed against her mouth. Unlike Angelica, in the book, Marion's sex was not shaved and Sandra could feel pubic hair lining her rubbery labia. She had no idea what to do, but pushed her tongue out and up, searching for the redhead's clit. It was not difficult to find. The little nub of flesh had already escaped its protective hood and was throbbing as blood coursed though it.

Sandra nudged her tongue against it. She tried to remember what she liked men doing to her and used the tip of her tongue to push it from side to side, as rhythmically as she could. The rest of Marion's sex was wet and her juices dripped over Sandra's chin.

Thwack. It seemed Sandra heard the noise at the same time as she felt the pain, a burning jolt of it across her left nipple. A second followed immediately across the right and then another on the lower camber of her breast. She gasped, her tongue losing its place on Marion's clit. Apparently the redhead didn't care. Another jolt of pain exploded on her inner thigh, and another just above her knee. At the same time Marion squirmed her buttocks down on Sandra's face, forcing her nose deep into the furrow of her labia.

'Come on,' Marion said, increasing the speed of the whipping. The flicks of the whip were not hard but they were well-aimed, each exploding on virgin territory. The extraordinary thing was that each stab of pain turned in seconds to squirming hot pleasure, each site where the whip fell transformed into a new erogenous zone, throbbing as strongly as her clit.

Sandra could do nothing but react. She wriggled her mouth against Marion's wet, squashy sex, each gasp of pain as a new stroke fell producing a hot exhalation of air against Marion's sex but that was enough. Even with everything else that was happening, Sandra knew Marion was coming.

The girl reared up on her haunches, then sank down again. Her sex opened, melting over Sandra's mouth at exactly the moment that Sandra experienced the same release, one intense flood of pleasure, her body clenching around the plug that held the lips of her vagina so wide apart.

The voice seemed a long way away. It was a man's voice. It was speaking very quietly. She couldn't make out what it was saying at first. Then she felt Marion's body lifting over her own and the blindfold being removed.

She crunched her eyes against the light. She raised her head to look down her body. A fat, pink butterfly was curled around her sex, held in place by a white leather strap. She saw Marion standing at the side of the frame, pulling on a towelling robe over her voluptuous body. Standing next to her was Manville Mason. He was also wearing a robe.

'Did you hear me?' he said.

'No.' How long had he been standing there? Had he seen everything?

'From now on, my dear, you must call me Master.'

'Master?' She was having trouble grasping what that meant.

'Yes. You will have to arrange to take some time off work. Is that a problem?'

'No, Master.' That phrase sounded so right.

'Five days to be precise,' he said. Sandra could see a distinct bulge distending the front of the robe. She hoped he would use her to ameliorate that condition. 'Curtis will come and pick you up as soon as you are ready. He will bring you to me.'

'Does that mean I've—'

'It means it is the beginning. The end is a very different matter.'

The fact that he turned and walked away, without any further intimacy, was her only disappointment.

Chapter Five

'Cherry?'

'Hi, Peter.' She recognised his voice immediately.

She was sitting at her desk in the newsroom, the bustle of activity all around her creating a cacophony of noise.

'I've got the information you wanted,' he said.

'Great. Shoot.' She didn't have to pick up a pen. It was already in her hand, poised over an empty page in her spiral notebook.

'Mason's got a Rolls. Quite a car. Longwheel base stretch. Registration number MST One. Not very original. It's registered at an address in Hampstead.' He gave her the address.

'You're a doll,' she said.

'I'm was hoping you might like to come round again.'

Cherry felt a sharp pang of desire. 'More videos?'

'Yes, as a matter of fact. There's one I think might interest you a lot. Judging from the last time.'

'You were very inventive.'

'And you were very . . . compliant.'

She lowered her voice, though she doubted anyone else could hear her in all the din. 'I've never done anything like that before.'

'Neither have I. It was fun.'

'It was better than fun.'

'So how about you come around next week?'

'As soon as I've tracked down Mason, I'm yours. On a plate.'

'Trussed up like a chicken?'
'Sounds interesting.'
'I won't have to improvise this time.'
'Why not?'
'Another vice squad raid. They got some very unusual items in a raid the other night.'
'Really? That and new videos. Can't wait.'
'Give me a call, then. Make it soon.'
'It will be.'

As she put down the phone, Cherry wasn't sure which she was most excited about: the prospect of at last tracking down Manville Mason, or the thought of going to Peter Simmons' flat again and trying out whatever equipment the vice squad had confiscated.

Sandra had phoned the area manager first thing in the morning. It was not difficult to arrange the days off. In fact, Sandra had three weeks owing to her from last year, as well as her whole entitlement for the current year. The area manager of the chain had often told her that she should take more holidays and was only too pleased when she phoned him to announce she wanted to have a five-day break. There was a replacement manager available to take over in three days.

And that was that. Sandra called the number Manville had given her and told him that her holiday would begin on Wednesday morning. He appeared delighted with the news and told her that he would have her collected on Tuesday evening at six. She would be driven straight to the castle in Cornwall.

Then she had to deal with Michael. It was not as though they had made any commitment, but she liked him and she certainly had to find a way of explaining why she was about to disappear. She decided to tell him her company were sending her on a management training course. As Michael was a social science lecturer at a College she hoped he would not realise that such courses rarely took five days.

The Master's Diary

And he didn't. Though he was suitably disappointed that he was not going to see her, he wished her well and hoped he would see her as soon as she got back. He had bought his own copy of *The Master's Diary*, he told her, and had been studying it carefully, gleaning ideas for their next encounter.

She could arrange for a neighbour to water her plants and pick up her post from the box downstairs. There was nothing else to plan. She didn't have milk delivered. All she had to do was wait. For three days. Three days that would seem like a lifetime.

The stretch, black Rolls Royce pulled out of the driveway and into the road. That was unusual. For three days the Rolls had remained in the large garage at the back of the house. Cherry Hughes had camped outside in her Ford Escort watching the house through the telephoto lens of her camera. There was no sign of life. She had seen the blond chauffeur washing the car, and watched the cleaners arrive first thing in the morning. But there was no Manville Mason, and definitely no Angela Blake.

Presumably, Cherry had reasoned, Manville had a country house and was resident there. But it didn't matter. Sooner or later he was bound to come back to London, and Cherry would be waiting for him. The enticing prospect of a front-page exclusive, with a large by-line, made the wait worthwhile.

Cherry started her car. As the blond chauffeur drove the Rolls out into traffic she tucked her Ford Escort in behind it. She hoped it was on the way to pick up Manville and bring him back to town, in which case she would get his country address as well. Angela Blake was bound to be at one or other house.

Sandra got home at five-thirty on Tuesday evening. Everything was ready. Manville's instructions were precise. She was to bring nothing with her. Marion had given her a plain cream, cotton dress, a white cotton bra and panties and a pair of flat-heeled, brown shoes. She was to bring nothing else but the keys to her house. She was not to wear any make-up and her hair was to be brushed out with no bands or pins of any sort. She was even to clean off her nail varnish and make sure she wore no perfume.

She had laid out the clothes on her bed. As soon as she had showered, removed all her make-up and brushed out her hair, she picked up the cotton panties and pulled them on. They were an old-fashioned cut, the legs low, the sides high. The bra too was unflattering, its straps thick and its cups full and cone-shaped. But oddly, as Sandra looked at herself in the bedroom mirror, the white cotton banding her body, the sight excited her. She would never have dreamt of choosing this underwear for herself, and the fact that she was wearing it was the first example of what Manville had called the amputation of her will. She was no longer free to decide what she should wear.

Sandra pulled the dress over her head. The material was rough and stiff and the dress shapeless. It hung from her body like a sack. But again her reflection in the mirror provoked a pulse of excitement. With no make-up and these odd clothes, she already looked like a different woman, which was, she suspected, exactly why Manville had insisted on her wearing them. She was not Sandra Seymour any more. She had given up that persona, for the time being at least. What replaced it did not depend on her. She had gifted that right to her Master.

She glanced out of the window hoping to see the Rolls double-parked outside, but it was only fifteen minutes to six and the car wasn't there. She sat on the edge of the bed, uneasily, trying not to think of what was awaiting her. But that was asking the impossible.

Her experience at Manville's house was everything she'd imagined it would be and much more. She'd conjured up all sorts of scenarios, based on scenes from the book, but what Manville had done to her in the car, and Marion in the strange windowless room, had far exceeded anything she had read.

The Master's Diary

Her impulse to write to Manville, to find out the truth about the book, had been justified not for the simple reason that she needed to satisfy her curiosity as to whether it was based on reality, but because it had become a way of finding out about herself.

Games with Michael were one thing, what had happened at the house quite another. The leather bonds that had strapped her so tightly to the frame had left physical impressions on her flesh, on her wrists and ankles and her upper arms especially, as had the cuts of the whip. Both had faded quickly. The psychological impressions the experience had left were much deeper and had not faded at all. She could relive every second of that evening, recite every word that had been said to her, and re-visit everything she had felt. She could feel Marion's pussy pressed down against her mouth, taste the redhead's juices, smell the musky aroma of her sex mixed with some exotic scent, and see her eyes as they'd watch her undress. Three times in the last three days, despite having masturbated herself to sleep with dildoes pushed into both passages of her body, she had woken in a hot sweat, needing more. Her body had become insatiable.

She glanced at her watch and realised she had forgotten to take it off. Manville had expressly forbidden her to wear that too. She had also forgotten to take off the ring she always wore on her left hand. As she got up to put both away in the drawer of her bedside table, she saw the huge black Rolls gliding to a halt outside the block. She watched as Curtis got out and marched up to the front door.

The entryphone buzzed.

'I'll be right down,' she said. She picked up her keys and went out into the hall. It felt extraordinary to be going out with nothing, not even a handbag, but that too reminded her of where she was going and why and she felt almost light-hearted as she ran to the lift. Curtis stood by the front door.

'Good evening,' he said as she walked out.

'What happened to, "Good evening, Ms Seymour"?' she

asked jauntily. 'Does that mean you're alone?'

'I am.'

He went to the passenger door of the car and opened it for her. She climbed inside, remembering the first time she had got into the spacious interior. The black leather felt cold against her bare legs.

Curtis got behind the wheel without a word and drove off, the glass partition between driver and passenger wound up. Sandra found the switch that controlled it on a panel of other switches set in the side of the door. She pressed the button and it slid down slowly with a whir of electric motors.

'Aren't you speaking to me?' she asked.

'I didn't think you'd want to talk,' he said.

'Why's that?'

'You've got enough on your plate.'

'I kept my promise, didn't I?'

'What promise?'

'To say nothing about what had happened between us.'

'That was a mistake.'

'Not for me.'

'I should never have agreed.'

'Oh, come on, Curtis, you know what goes on. You don't expect me to believe you just close your eyes to it. I'm not the first and I'm sure I won't be the last. You get lots of opportunities. And you take them. Isn't that true?'

'If you say so.'

'I do. Tell me something, did you watch?'

'Watch what?'

'Watch last week when you came to collect me with Manville. Can you see through that glass?'

'Yes.'

'So what did you see?'

'I saw what you did.'

'Did it turn you on?'

'What do you think?'

'And is that what he always does, your Master, I mean? With all the others?'

'I'm not supposed to tell you anything.'

'You're not supposed to have fucked me either, but you did.'

'He does all sorts of things. It's never the same.'

'Like what?' For the first time, Sandra felt a pang of jealously. It came as a shock. In the book it was perfectly clear that there was more than one slave at the castle, and Clara had been forced to watch her Master with other women on many occasions. The emotion Clara felt, however, the envy and jealously and feeling of rejection, had been hard for Sandra to associate with. Until now. She hadn't thought she would be affected in that way. But now she knew Manville and was involved with him, the thought of seeing him with another woman, of him preferring another slave over her, filled her with exactly the same emotions Clara had presaged in the book. 'How long will it take to get there?' she said, changing the subject.

'Three hours if the traffic's not too bad. Four if it is.'

He pressed a button on the dashboard and wound the partition up, clearly anxious to end the conversation.

Sandra sat back in the luxurious seat. The rolling ride of the soft suspension was soporific and she found her eyes drooping. It had been a hard day, getting all the paperwork prepared for the relief manager, and she found she was tired, three interrupted nights' sleep not helping.

The car stopped. Curtis came round to open the door. Marion was waiting outside the Hampstead house. Sandra couldn't work out why until Marion got in beside her. Had she got to go to the castle too? Marion was dressed in a tight black leather skirt and a white silk blouse. There was still something wrong about all this. Curtis had got into the back of the car too. Instead of sitting on the seat beside her, Marion was kneeling on all fours pulling her skirt up over her hips. Sandra could see the gusset of the panties that covered her pussy and long black suspenders clipped on to sheer black stockings. She was pulling them down to her knees. Sandra wanted to touch her but as she leant forward Curtis pushed her back. He had unzipped his flies.

'My turn,' he said. He crawled up behind the redhead. Sandra could see his big cock pushing between Marion's buttocks. He raised his hand and slapped her bottom as hard as he could.

The thwack of flesh on flesh started Sandra awake.

The car had stopped. She looked around, still dazed by the vividness of the dream. The car was parked among a rank of huge articulated trucks in the car park of a transport cafe. Curtis wound the partition down. He turned around.

'Got to pee,' he said. 'How about you?'

She shook her head as he got out and headed into the cafe.

The dream had caused a distinct feeling of arousal, and a sticky dampness between her legs.

She watched as Curtis came back out of the cafe. He had his chauffeur's cap in his hand and his long blond hair caught the rays of the sun, now sinking in the west. She remembered his strong, muscular body, and how he had used it to please her.

'Curtis,' she said, as he got back into the car.

'Yes.'

'Are we making good time?'

He started the engine and drove out on to the road.

'Yes, as a matter of fact, we are.'

'Good. Can you find somewhere nice and secluded?'

'I told you to pee back there.'

It was like an act of defiance, she supposed. On the brink of giving up her ability to do anything but obey she wanted to assert her own needs.

'That's not what I want,' she said. 'You know what I have in mind. Don't tell me you haven't thought about it too.'

'I could get fired.'

'You said that last time. It didn't stop you.'

The Master's Diary

'Last time was different.'

'Not for me.'

'You hadn't seen Manville then.'

'What difference does that make?'

'Don't you know?'

'If you don't find somewhere to stop you know the first thing I'm going to say to him when we arrive . . .'

'That's blackmail.'

'Exactly.'

The subconscious impulse presented in the dream was growing rapidly now it had come to the surface. The thought of having Curtis thrusting inside her created a wave of desire that was impossible to ignore. She needed him. Her sex spasmed involuntarily. With what Marion had done to her and her own masturbation, she had been penetrated comprehensively by large dildoes, but that was not and could never be a substitute for the real thing.

'What do you want me to do?'

'What you did last week.'

He lapsed into silence. They were travelling along a motorway and it was another ten minutes before the next exit, but as they approached it she realised he was signalling to turn left. She could see his eyes looking at her in the rearview mirror.

The countryside was hilly, the fields on either side of the road surrounded by tall hedgerows of hawthorn. The big car rolled as it rode the narrow, bumpy lanes. At the crest of a hill there was a gap in the hedge. Curtis slowed, then pulled the car through into a small copse of trees in one corner of a field of wheat, the longevity of two of the oaks no doubt the reason they had not been cut down to make more room for cultivation. One of their branches had rotted and crashed to the ground forming a low bridge between them.

'Is this what you want?' he said.

'Ideal.'

The sun was setting now and from their vantage point they

could see it was just about to touch the horizon in the valley below. Sandra opened the car door and got out. The air was balmy and fresh. She took a deep breath. The ground under the trees was carpeted with grass.

'Aren't you going to get out?'

Curtis opened his car door. 'If he finds out about this . . .' he said.

'Your secret is safe with me,' she said. She leant back against the car and caught his hand, pulling him to her and kissing him full on the mouth, her tongue plunging between his lips. He responded by wrapping his arms around her and lifting her clear off her feet, his erection growing against her belly.

He dropped her back to the ground. 'This is a bad idea,' he said.

'Oh, come on, Curtis . . .' She pushed against him, grinding her belly against his erection. Then she pulled away and lifted the hem of her skirt. 'Or would you rather I did it myself?' She ripped the leg of the cotton panties aside and pressed her finger into the slit of her sex.

Curtis caught her by the arm, tearing her hand away from her pussy. She could see anger in his face. 'All right, if that's what you want, I'll bloody well give it to you.'

He dragged her to the back of the car, roughly, then opened the boot. A light came on. Sandra saw him pick up a coil of rope, then slam the boot closed again.

'This is what you want, isn't it, you little bitch?' he said. His fingers still dug into her arm. He marched her over to the two oak trees and the fallen branch between them. The branch was as thick as the trunk of most trees and curved upwards in the middle like an enormous bow. 'Here,' he said. Curtis caught hold of her other arm. He had large, powerful hands and had no trouble forcing Sandra's wrists together, holding them in one hand while the other wound coils of rope around them. He tied the rope off tightly then pulled her toward the branch of the tree by it. Throwing the rope over the highest point he pushed Sandra across the fallen branch, picked up the rope again and wrapped it around her ankles, making it impossible for her to straighten up.

The bark of the tree was coarse against her belly, her head was a few inches from the ground, her long black hair draping on the grass. The rope chafed her flesh, but her arousal turned the discomfort into cause for further excitement, especially as she felt his hand raising the hem of her dress and pushing the plain cotton up over her buttocks.

'This is what you want, isn't it?' he said crossly. He was angry at himself for allowing her to provoke him.

'You know it is.' She struggled against the rope, trying to stand up straight, but he had bound it tight. That was one lesson Marion had already taught her. The unyielding bondage, and the feeling of helplessness it produced, made Sandra shiver. The more tightly bound she was the more her sex seemed to turn to a molten liquid core and seethed with sensation. Curtis was right. This is exactly what she wanted.

His hand was pulling down the cotton panties. They fell to her ankles, trapped there by the coils of rope. With her bottom unveiled he raised his hand and slapped it down on her left buttock, making her pliant flesh vibrate. The noise echoed around the little copse. He raised his hand again and aimed it at her right side this time. This blow was harder, the noise louder. Sandra gasped.

Curtis stepped back. He tore off his jacket and unbuttoned his trousers, pulling them down to his knees. Hanging upside down as she was Sandra could see him behind her, his erection sticking out as he pulled his white briefs down. It glistened in the shafts of orange light from the spectacular sunset, the sticky juice it had produced smeared across his glans.

He grasped her hips. Sandra tried to angle her sex up towards him. She felt the underside of his shaft pressing against her labia before he pulled back. His glans nudged into her anus and she thought he was going to bugger her, but then it slipped lower. He bucked his hips and his cock buried itself in her, right up to the hilt. He wriggled his erection around inside her, grinding his pubic bone from side to side.

Instantly Sandra felt her whole body tense around the sword of flesh. She tried to pull her arms up but the rope wouldn't budge. The fact that it wouldn't created another surge of arousal. Her sex clenched around the invader, gripping it tight. She was coming. With her legs bound together she could not open herself for him, but in this position his penetration seemed just as deep and she was sure his glans was touching the neck of her womb.

He began battering into her, his fingers digging into her hips, pulling her back on to him as he plunged forward, the slap of his belly against her buttocks quite pronounced. Sandra's orgasm was arriving rapidly. The dildoes she'd used to masturbate had filled her just as completely, but they had never felt like this, hot and hard and pulsating. She could feel every inch of him. The ridge of his glans seemed to be catching on a part of her inner surfaces that had developed an incredible sensitivity, each strike making her moan with pleasure.

He hammered into her, increasing his pace, using all his strength to project his cock into her as far as it would go, his balls banging against her labia. In contrast to the cramped, uncomfortable position of her body, her sex, at the very core of her, was free to respond without limit. She felt it clench and she came, her body rigid, her limbs pulling against the rope reflexively, the feeling of restraint inevitably adding to her pleasure.

She recovered her senses only to feel Curtis pulling out of her. 'No,' she cried in alarm. 'Don't stop, not now.'

'I have to, you idiot,' he said. He vaulted over the branch and knelt in front of her. 'What if Manville wants you when we get to the castle? Don't you think he'd notice?' He knelt in front of her. He combed her hair with his fingers, pulling it up around the back of her neck. Sandra raised her head. She saw his cock sticking up from the top of his thighs. He was right, of course. She had acted without thinking of the consequences, but she didn't want her foolhardiness to result in Manville's wrath. If he found out what they had done he might even change his mind about letting her stay at the castle.

'Like this then,' Sandra said, edging forward and managing to brush her mouth against the front of his cock. That was clearly what Curtis had in mind too. He raised himself on his haunches, allowing Sandra's mouth to close over his erection.

She sucked it hard and he moaned. It was impossible for her to move very much in this position, the muscles in her neck cramped as her head was forced back, but that didn't seem to matter. Curtis held her head in his hands and began sliding in and out of her, using her mouth as her substitute for her pussy.

Sandra tasted her own juices. He was forcing his cock down her throat. She could feel it swelling and she knew he was very close to coming. She used her tongue to lick at the underside of his erection, the thick tube that formed the urethra pulsing as his spunk pumped up into it. She wanted to hold his balls, to force her finger into his arse, but the ropes prevented her. That was going to have to be something she got used to. What she wanted and what she was able to do were going to become two very different things. She felt her sex throb at the thought. Her clitoris, still trapped in the folds of her labia, flexed too, the feelings linking together to create a sharp pang of lust. This thrilled her more totally than anything else had. Bent over the tree, bound with rope, with her dress around her hips and her panties around her ankles, she was completely helpless.

She felt his cock recoil. Then his glans inflated and a thick jet of spunk spattered into her throat, followed by another, and another, his whole body shuddering. Then he withdrew slightly, and more sticky wetness oozed from the slit as Sandra used her tongue to lick it clean.

'We're going to be late,' he said gruffly. He reached forward and unknotted the rope, then got to his feet and pulled his trousers and briefs back around his waist. His wilting cock disappeared.

Sandra straightened up with an effort, her muscles protesting at their sudden freedom. She pulled the cotton panties up and adjusted the dress. 'Come on, then,' she said. 'I'm ready.'

As she got back into the car she realised that was true. She had had her fling. Now she was ready to face her master and obey.

Neither of them had noticed, Cherry was sure of that. As soon as she'd seen the Rolls pull into the copse, she'd looked for a place to park further down the road. She had grabbed her camera and headed back to the little copse on foot.

Cherry had followed the Rolls from Hampstead. She had watched as the handsome blond chauffeur rang the doorbell of a modern block of flats and collected the stunning, though oddly dressed, brunette. She'd followed it on to the motorway and into the transport cafe.

In the copse she hid behind the hedgerow. With the telephoto lenses she didn't need to risk getting too close. Almost before she had settled herself down the brunette was out of the car and quite obviously throwing herself at the chauffeur. Cherry had photographed the first kiss. She watched as he'd got the rope and dragged the brunette over to the fallen branch. She'd photographed the girl being bound over the fallen branch. There was just enough light from the spectacular sunset to get a close-up as he pulled down her panties. In the viewfinder of the single lens reflex camera she could see the girl's sex, pressed tightly between the curves of her buttocks. She'd photographed the blond chauffeur pounding into the girl. She had moved around slightly to get a particularly well-framed shot as he held back the girl's hair while he knelt in front of her, his erection causing Cherry's own sex to spasm involuntarily. She couldn't use the photographs in the newspaper, of course. But she had a feeling they would be useful. Manville Mason might be well aware of the fact that his chauffeur was taking liberties with females

The Master's Diary

under his charge, but on the other hand he might not. And if that were the case the photographs could prove very useful indeed.

As the brunette was released and got to her feet, Cherry took one final shot as the girl pulled up the odd, old-fashioned panties, then ran back to her car. She needed to get her car turned around and ready to follow the Rolls as soon as it reversed out of the copse.

She just made it in time. She pulled the car into the verge on the other side of the road and hoped they wouldn't notice the parked car. As the Rolls backed out into the road she ducked down below the windscreen. It sped off.

Ten minutes later they were back on the motorway heading south-west, with darkness descending rapidly.

Cherry shifted uncomfortably in her seat. The crotch of her panties seemed to have worked itself into a tight string that cut into the crease of her sex. She tried to concentrate on her driving, but what she had seen through the camera lens was difficult to forget. She thought about Peter and what he had done to her. Perhaps she should suggest to him that they went for a drive in the country and found some remote and secluded spot. As she'd watched the girl shudder under the chauffeur's assault it had been impossible for her not to remember exactly what she had felt as Peter had given her similar treatment.

Cherry had always thought of her sex-drive as perfectly normal. She had never had fantasies about anything other than what she liked to think of as straight sex. That is why she'd found it difficult to admit to herself that what Peter had done to her had aroused her in a way that nothing else had. But the truth was that the thought of a repeat performance, the promise of watching another video and trying out the mysterious items he had mentioned on the phone, had kept her sexual temperature well above normal for the last three days.

What she had seen in the copse had only served to increase it to fever pitch.

Chapter Six

The big car rolled along the country road. They had left the motorway and were driving through an area of thick forest, the long beams of the headlights glaring out into the darkness to reveal a canopy of overhanging leaves, the branches of the trees reaching out to touch each other above the road.

Sandra stared out of the side window but could see nothing, the forest on either side dark and deep.

After three or four miles the car slowed and turned down a much smaller single lane leading right into the forest. After no more than a thousand yards the trees gave way to a clearing. Sandra saw a tall brick wall, stretching away into the night, and two huge wrought-iron gates, mounted on brick pillars, barring the road.

Curtis drove the car to a small post sticking out from the verge on the right side of the road. There was a small pad mounted on the side of it like a calculator. Curtis punched in four numbers and immediately the gates began to creak open. Sandra watched them, close behind them as they drove through.

The driveway beyond was so long there was no sign of the castle at first. Ancient cedars and oaks on rolling lawns appeared in the headlights as the car twisted this way and that, following the winding drive. Then, lit by powerful floodlights, Sandra saw the imposing, castellated battlements and spiral turrets of the castle itself, a grand Victorian folly. She knew what to expect. It was exactly as described in *The Master's Diary*, right down to the monstrous gargoyles that decorated the downspouts of the guttering and the huge lion rampart that had been carved into the columns on either side of the massive oak front door. She knew many features of the house by the same means: its large Gothic fireplaces, the minstrel-galleried ballroom, the Master's book-lined study and, of course, the medieval dungeon that the original owner had insisted had been added for the purposes of true 'authenticity'. There was a modern extension at the back too, with a swimming pool and a large conservatory, and of course, at the very top of the house, the small 'cells' where the four slaves were accommodated. According to the book, there were never more than four slaves in residence at any one time. Sandra wondered if this too would turn out to be based on fact.

The big car glided to a halt in front of the oak door. Without a word, Curtis got out and came round to open the passenger door. Sandra knew exactly what to expect. If the castle ran true to form the front door would be opened by a small, incredibly muscular Frenchman who, Manville had written, had once been a circus acrobat. According to the book the man had suffered a terrible accident in the ring which had left him, effectively, a eunuch, a quality that had proved useful in a household where naked and semi-naked female slaves were regularly paraded.

She was not disappointed. The front door swung back and a short, ball of a man bowled out on to the gravel drive. He was completely bald, the pate of his head polished and shiny. He was wearing a stiff black suit, its pockets bulging, a white, winged collar and a black bow-tie. He moved with a rolling gait, dipping his left shoulder and favouring his left leg.

'*Bon soir*,' he said looking at Curtis. '*Vous etes en retard.*'

'Traffic,' Curtis said.

The short man smiled. He had very irregular teeth, some of which were pointed as if they had been sharpened. There was a gold tooth in the upper set, which caught the light. Sandra thought it was a knowing smile. '*Bien sur*. Traffic.' He pronounced the last word with two distinct syllables.

He looked at Sandra for the first time. He had small piggy eyes but they sparkled with life. He moved to her side, pushed his face against the dress, barely above waist level and sniffed her. 'Traffic,' he repeated, grinning broadly.

He took her arm and led her through the front door as Curtis got back into the car and drove off. His fingers bit into her arm. The vestibule had a tall, vaulted ceiling and a stone-flagged floor, with medieval armour, swords and lances hanging from the walls. A large stone staircase led up to a gallery on the first floor, but he guided her behind it. Again, Sandra knew what to expect. There, set against the back wall was a lift, its cage gilded like some Arabian fantasy, with an ogee-shaped cupola for its roof. It had been installed by the previous owner, according to the book, who had only one leg. Fiction and fact were inextricably linked.

The man opened the grille of the cage and thrust Sandra inside. Closing the grille with a bang he pressed a button on the control panel and the lift groaned and clanked as it rose up through the centre of the castle.

On the top floor it stopped with a jolt. The man led her out into a short, stone-walled corridor. There were two doors on each side and a large one at the end which he opened and pushed her through.

'Sit,' he said.

The room was large. It had a polished, wooden floor and a long oak table pushed against one of the stone walls. There was a huge walnut cupboard and a matching chest of drawers and a single Windsor chair.

Sandra sat on one of the chair.

'*Je m'appelle Henri*,' he said studying her critically. '*Vous me connaissez, déjà?*'

Manville had changed Marion into Angelica, and Curtis into Brian, but for some reason not bothered to change the eunuch's name.

'Yes,' she said.

'That is good. Then you know what I am for?'
'Yes.'
'And that if you do not obey me, it is the same, *le même*, as disobeying *Le Mâitre*. *D'accord?*'
'Yes.'
'*C'est bon.*' He turned on his heel, walked out of the door and closed it behind him. Sandra heard the unmistakable grind of the key in the large box mortice lock she could see on the back of the door.

And that was that. She was here in the castle that for the last weeks, from the time she had sat in her kitchen and picked up *The Master's Diary*, had haunted her every waking moment; every sleeping moment too, for that matter, bearing in mind how much her dreams had been dominated by what went on here.

She got to her feet. There were thin, narrow windows cut in what were obviously thick stone walls, built to replicate the shooting slots used by medieval archers. They had been glazed, but provided no view. The windows looked out on to the back of the house, which was not floodlit, and though Sandra thought she could make out a conservatory she could see little else.

The experience with Curtis had left her feeling anxious. She didn't want Manville to guess what had happened and hoped Henri wouldn't tell him what he obviously suspected. She had been worried that the rope might have left tell-tale marks on her wrists and ankles but as she examined them carefully now she was glad to see that they had not. There was a slight indentation on her right wrist but vigorous rubbing soon made it disappear entirely.

She wondered what the walnut cupboard and chest of drawers contained. She dared not look. Instead she went back to the chair and tried to relax. That proved impossible. She shifted from side to side, not able to get comfortable, knowing that this wait was all part of the routine. It was intended to make the point that from now on her life was entirely

The Master's Diary

dependent on the whim of another. If Manville did not care to see her tonight, or tomorrow, or at all, she would remain locked in this room, waiting. It was not up to her. The true submissive would find that exciting, Angelica had told Clara, in the book, and it must be that Sandra was exactly that, because she found that she was profoundly excited at being locked in the anonymous room.

With no watch, time seemed to stretch out ahead of her without end. She had no idea how long it was before the key ground into the lock again and the door swung open.

'Stand up,' Henri said as he walked in and closed the door behind him. He went over to the walnut cupboard and swung its doors open. Sandra glanced inside as she got to her feet. Hanging from a series of hooks screwed into the top of the cupboard was a whole collection of straps and harnesses, some leather, some bright chrome or a combination of the two. There was a rack of clothing, mostly leather in red and white and black. At the bottom of the cupboard was a shoe rack, very high-heels in the same colours as the clothes neatly arranged in pairs.

Henri struggled to unhook one of the harnesses, standing in the cupboard itself so he could reach. He brought the harness over to Sandra and smiled, revealing his uneven teeth. It was made from bright red leather.

'Kneel, *ma petite*,' he said.

Sandra thought she recognised part of the harness, a thick, wide collar that fitted around her neck. It was the same sort of posture collar she had bought for her games with Michael. But there the resemblance ended. There were thin straps hanging down from the collar and another much wider circle of leather suspended from these.

Henri wrapped the leather around her neck. There were three buckles to hold it in place. The thick leather butted into the underside of her chin making it impossible to lower her head.

'Stand,' he ordered.

Sandra got to her feet. Henri was arranging the rest of the harness. Two straps descended from the collar at the back, to the wide belt that was made to fit around her waist. A more complex arrangement was attached to D-rings set into the front of the collar. Two straps hung down as far as the top of her breasts where they were looped into a metal ring. At the bottom of each metal ring two further straps formed an inverted V, around the sides of the breast. These straps were looped into a metal ring between the breasts and on each side of them, hanging from which were further straps so the breast was enclosed completely. The lower straps were then looped into yet another ring immediately under the breast, and from this a further strap descended on each side to the thick leather at her waist.

Henri arranged the straps carefully around Sandra's chest, without taking off her dress. The straps were all buckled and could be adjusted and he spent a great deal of time getting them positioned correctly, the leather pinching her flesh so her breasts were pushed out more prominently. He then wrapped the waist-belt around her body. It was stiff and unyielding, boned in some way so it was cinched in at its centre like an old-fashioned Victorian waist-nipper. The belt was secured with four buckles at the back.

'Breathe in,' he commanded as he fed the tongues of leather into the buckles. He pulled them tight, straining to get them as tight as they would go. Sandra felt the leather biting into her, so inflexible it was difficult to breathe.

Attached to the sides of the waist-belt were two leather cuffs. Quickly Henri fed her wrists into the cuffs and buckled them tight too. In this position, with her wrists at her waist, her elbows were bent and stuck out behind her.

'*C'est bon,*' he said. '*Maintenant, kneel.*'

Sandra found it difficult to kneel without the help of her hands to balance, and dropped to her knees to the wooden floor with a thump. She saw Henri going back to the cupboard, but dared not turn to see what he was doing.

His footsteps came back to her. She felt him combing his fingers through her hair, gathering it together at the back of her neck. Something was wrapped around it holding it together, then she saw the front of a leather hood being drawn over her head. He pulled it over her eyes and mouth and down over her chin. It was loosely laced at the back and he fed the hank of hair through the laces, so it created a sort of ponytail, high on her head, her long black hair cascading down from it like the mane of a horse.

To Sandra's relief, unlike some of the hoods Clara had been made to wear in the book, this had holes for her eyes as well as for her mouth. Henri began pulling the laces tight, stretching the leather against her face.

'*Ca va*,' he said when he was finished. 'Up.'

Sandra got to her feet, the inability to use her arms again causing her problems. She staggered and Henri caught her by the elbow to stop her falling.

She saw he still held a single, very thin strap in his hand. He wound it around her left elbow, extended it across her back, under the two straps that joined the collar to the waist belt, then looped it around her right elbow. As he buckled it Sandra felt her elbows being drawn together, forcing her to thrust her chest out and hold her shoulders back.

Henri went to the cupboard for the third time. He took out a long metal chain, with a snap hook on one end and a looped leather handle on the other. It was a leash. He clipped the snap hook into a D-ring on the posture collar and pulled Sandra forward by it.

They marched out into the corridor. Next to the lift shaft was a narrow stone staircase. Henri led her down it to the first floor. The grilles clunked as Henri closed them and the lift descended a single floor.

The corridor on the lower floor was wide and the stone walls had been plastered to give a more normal appearance. A thick, dark blue carpet deadened the sound as Henri led her forward.

'Do you need to pee?' he asked.

'Yes.'

'*Ca va.*' He opened one of the doors on the left-hand side and led her inside. The bathroom was vast, with every modern amenity, its walls and floor lined in grey marble. A big mirror over the two wash hand basins gave Sandra the first glimpse of herself in the bizarre harness. The cotton dress was bunched and creased by the leather straps.

Henri guided her over to the toilet. He pulled the skirt of the dress up over her hips and quite casually took hold of the front of the cotton panties and pulled them down to her knees.

'Come on, come on,' he said when she failed to sit down immediately.

It was another small test of her resolve. Though Henri seemed totally uninterested, standing with the leash in one hand, tapping his foot impatiently, she had never peed in front of a stranger before. Fortunately her need overcame her modesty.

When he heard the torrent stop he tugged her to her feet, quickly pulling up her panties and re-adjusting the skirt of the dress. Out in the corridor again they turned to the right and she saw, at the far end, a pair of doors, panelled and elaborately carved. He led her up to them. To the left of the doors was a solid brass hook set in the wall at eye level. Henri strained on tip-toe and wrapped the leash around the hook.

Without a word he walked away. Sandra could see him getting into the lift and heard it clanking loudly as it descended. Then there was silence. She listened intently, trying to hear any sound from what was obviously Manville's bedroom, but the leather hood had no provision for her ears and she could hear nothing but the pounding rhythm of her own blood.

The effect the constricting leather harness had on her was extreme. The tighter and more uncomfortable her restraint, the more – or so it seemed – her body responded with waves of arousal. The cotton dress and bra offered little protection against the leather which bit into the soft flesh of her breasts,

The Master's Diary

but the discomfort had puckered her nipples so strongly they felt like stone. They were throbbing too, creating an overwhelming desire to be touched, a desire she could not meet. And perhaps that was the most exciting thing of all. She strained her hand up towards her breasts, pulling against the leather cuff, trying to twist her body down towards it, but her fingers were still inches away from their target, achieving nothing but an ache of protest from her straining muscles as the leather harness dug into them. She could not reach her panties either. Henri had pulled them up carelessly, and the elastic of one leg was stretched tightly across her sex, sawing into it. She would have given anything to be able to pull it out and settle it into a more normal position. She could not do even that simple thing. It was the same feeling of helplessness that had excited her in the copse with Curtis. Now, standing in the corridor of the castle, it was total. She could do nothing. And there was no escape.

She tried to calm herself. She wanted to take a deep breath but the tight belt prevented that. She wanted to be able to lower her head, to relieve the cramp that was building up in the back of her neck, but the posture collar thwarted that ambition too. As little as four hours ago she had been free to come and go as she pleased, to do anything she wanted to do. All that had changed dramatically. She had been plunged into a world where the bizarre was commonplace, where totally different rules of behaviour held sway. She have never dreamt such a world existed, even as a fantasy, before she had read Manville's book. Now, faced with the fact it was a reality, she could hardly believe how quickly she had responded to it, and how readily she had come to accept its dictates as normal.

She thought she heard a sound and tensed, standing up straight, as if to attention, staring at the brass handles on the doors. But nothing happened. She found by pulling her elbows inward she could relieve the pressure from the small thin strap wound around them. But this made her shoulder muscles spasm. If she pushed out against the thin strap, the pain in her shoulders was afforded temporary relief but only at the price of a stinging pain in her elbows and wrists. Relieving the cramp in her neck meant forcing her chin down against the thick leather collar, its upper edge made, she suspected, deliberately rough. These little diversions, however, helped to pass the time.

She wondered where Marion was. And the other slaves. The castle was quiet enough to be deserted. No one appeared to move.

'Good evening, my dear.'

In the end she had not heard the door open, or seen it. She had been leaning against the wall with her eyes closed. As she started to attention she saw Manville standing in front of her, the handle of one of the doors in his hand. He unwound the leash from the brass hook and let it drop. 'Follow me.'

The bedroom was large and luxurious. There was a huge double bed and two vast white sofas facing each other, with a large coffee table between them. A door to one side of the bed was open and Sandra could see a marble-lined bathroom beyond. Next to it another partly opened door revealed a large dressing room, its walls lined with racks of clothes. The floor of the bedroom was carpeted in a thick, deep red carpet, a colour that was picked up in the curtains and the counterpane. The cream coloured walls were dotted with spectacularly bright oil paintings. Apart from a small Max Ernst and a large Kokoschka the rest seemed to be by the same artist. All featured nude or semi-nude women, their attitude suggesting an extreme voluptuousness as vivid as anything Sandra had seen on canvas. The largest of them all was of a redhead, kneeling on a white double bed. Though the technique of the painter was more impressionistic than photographic it was obvious that the woman was pressing her sex down on to a face, a tongue lapping at her labia. It was not possible to tell whether the face belonged to a man or a woman, though Sandra was quite sure the redhead had to be Marion, in which case the figure between her legs would undoubtedly be a woman.

The Master's Diary

'Stand just there, by the sofa, would you?' he said.

Manville was dressed in a dark blue silk robe, its sash knotted around his waist. His legs and feet were bare. He sat on the sofa opposite Sandra and looked at her.

'You know what I am going to say to you, because you have read it. I will say it nevertheless. Your only purpose, your only function here is to obey. It is as simple as that. If you refuse to obey you will be punished . . .' Sandra could have completed the sentence for him. He was right, she'd read it many times before. '. . . and if you refuse to be punished you will be sent away. Do you understand?'

'Yes.'

'Haven't you forgotten something?' He raised an eyebrow.

'Yes, Master.' How could she have forgotten something as fundamental as that? The word seemed to reverberate around the room.

'Good.' His eyes looked at her steadily. She had the feeling they were looking into her soul. At that moment there was nothing about her he did not know. 'I want you to kneel, there on the coffee table in front of me.'

Sandra started forward. The coffee table was made from ash, its surface covered with a sheet of plate glass. There were some art books piled to one side and a large wooden bowl, formed by scooping out the interior of a solid piece of wood. Awkwardly, Sandra edged herself towards the table. She could not lower her head to see what she was doing, so had to rely on her sense of touch. She pushed her knees against the edge of the table, then inched forward on the glass top until she was right in front of Manville.

'Open your legs,' he said quietly.

Her knees slid easily across the glass.

He leant forward until his face was no more than a foot away from hers. His deep brown eyes were hypnotic. 'I want you to touch me,' he said.

'I can't, Master,' she said.

'Don't argue, just do it,' he snapped angrily.

Sandra leant forward, hoping she would be able to butt her head against his body or get close enough to touch him with her out-stretched fingers, but as she approached he backed away.

'I gave you an order,' he said.

She crawled closer. She tried to look down to see the edge of the table but the collar prevented it. She strained her fingers forward, fighting against the leather cuff and the waist-belt that held it. 'I can't, Master. I can't.'

'Not a very good start,' he said. He got to his feet. As he brushed past her she lunged forward and managed to touch his thigh with her fingers, but the gesture did not improve his temper. 'Follow me,' he said gruffly.

He walked towards the bathroom. Sandra found it hard to get off the table. She pushed her legs out to the side and sat on it, then got her feet on the floor and stood up. By the time she had accomplished all this Manville had disappeared through the bathroom door. She hurried to follow.

'Not very good,' he tutted. 'I had hoped for a better start.'

Though she knew it was ludicrous, that he knew as well as she did that what he has asked was impossible, Sandra felt dejected. She knew she hadn't failed him, but on another level felt as if that was precisely what she had done. Perhaps he'd expected her to lunge forward and use her mouth to touch him, but if she'd have done that, she'd have overbalanced and fallen on top of him. She supposed she should have taken that chance.

Manville picked up the chain leash. The large bathroom had a big circular bathtub and a separate shower cubicle. Manville led her over to the shower cubicle.

'Inside,' he said, and all the earlier warmth in his voice had gone.

Sandra stepped into the shower. Manville leaned in after her and tied the leash to the top of the shower head, winding it around and around until Sandra was forced up on tip-toe. Then he turned the mixer taps on full and a gush of warm

The Master's Diary

water cascaded over her, hitting her full in the face and soaking her immediately. The cotton dress and lingerie were drenched, the material clinging to her body and becoming semi-transparent. She spluttered and gasped as the water splashed over her, the position of her head, raised up towards the shower jets, allowing the water to splash into her nose and eyes and mouth. She closed her eyes and turned her head to one side but it didn't help much. She just had to stand there, allowing the needles of water to play over her face and body, pounding against her forcefully.

The flow stopped. Manville pulled her out of the cubicle then unhooked the leash from the collar. Water dripped on the marble floor. She hadn't even taken off the flat-heeled shoes and they were full of water and squelched as he manoeuvred her to the middle of the room. She saw herself in the huge bathroom mirror that lined half of one wall. She looked like a drowned rat, the red leather darkened by the drenching. The cotton dress and bra were almost transparent and she could see the shadows of her nipples under the material. The water had worked its way between the leather helmet and her face and was ringing in her ears. It also pooled on the floor at her feet.

'Now I think it's time you did something right, isn't it?'

'Anything, Master.'

He came up behind her, running his hands around her body and cupping her breasts, his cheek pressed against the side of the leather helmet. It was the first time he'd touched her so intimately. She felt as though she had been connected to a source of electrical energy. Her whole body trembled.

'You have to learn to be good,' he whispered. The palms of his hands made circles against her rock-hard nipples, pressing them back into her squashy flesh. 'Tell me what you feel?' he said.

Even soaked to the skin and humiliated like this, Sandra felt a sense of absolute arousal that she had never experienced before. None of this had been in the book. If anything she had been expecting him to dress her in silk and satin and lace, as Clara had been dressed. Not this. But the more bizarre the experience the more, apparently, she was moved to a profound exhilaration. 'Turned-on,' she said. 'Unbelievably turned-on, Master.'

'I'm really too busy for this,' he said, as if to himself. He went to the bathroom cabinet above the wash basins and opened it. He took out a large pair of scissors. He returned to face her, then plucked at the material trapped by the leather harness over her left breast. He pulled it out, then snipped it away. He grabbed the front of the bra and pulled that out too, then cut at it. Her puckered nipple was exposed.

He snipped away until her breast was completely uncovered, then did the same with the other one. Poking out from the leather harness and still surrounded by sodden cotton, they looked obscene.

Manville walked around behind her and began cutting up from the hem of the dress. He cut all the way up to the waist-belt, then inserted the scissors in the back of the neck and cut downwards to it. He cut through the bra strap, then started methodically cutting the rest of the dress into strips.

Sandra watched him in the mirror. To her relief she saw a large bulge tenting the front of his robe.

He could not pull the shredded remains of the dress out from under the waist-belt because it was so tight, but instead he cut around the top of it, until all the rest of the dress had gone and only the leather harness and the panties remained. He inserted the scissors in each side of the panties and cut them in two. The weight of the water made them flop down against her thigh.

'Open your legs,' he said.

As Sandra obeyed, the panties dropped to the floor.

'Take your shoes off and come with me,' he said. His tone of voice had changed again. He was no longer cross.

By the time Sandra had managed to extract her feet from the clinging, wet leather and walk back into the bedroom

Manville was lying in the middle of the bed, with his head propped up against two pillows.

'Kneel up, here,' he said, patting the mattress at his side.

She crawled on to the bed as best she could, the thought that this might lead to some intimacy between them immediately making her pulse race.

'The harness makes it difficult for you, doesn't it?'

'Yes, Master.'

'Poor thing,' he said softly. 'Open my robe,' he said in the same tone.

Sandra felt alarm. It would prove to be another reason to get cross with her. 'I can't, Master.'

'Sh . . .' he said, putting his finger to his lips. 'Use your mouth, girl,' he said with the tiredness of one who had had to explain an infinitely simple problem to an imbecile time and time again.

Sandra crawled forward though she felt no relief. She wasn't sure she could do what he asked and if she failed he would be angry again. But she had to try. With the posture collar making it impossible for her to lower her chin, she couldn't just lean forward and gather the knot of the sash in her mouth. She had to lie out flat. Rolling on to her stomach she wriggled herself round until her face was alongside his hip and her body was stretched out at right angles to it. She pushed herself forward up on to his belly, until her mouth could reach the knot. She caught the end of the sash between her teeth and squirmed back, pulling it with her. The silk knot parted. But she still had to get the robe open. She wriggled back up and sucked at the upper edge of the robe, then tried to rear up and pull it back to the other side of his body. She was only partially successful.

These antics were clearly exciting Manville. As the first part of the robe was pulled away she saw his erection forcing its way out of the silk.

Sandra caught the second fold of the robe between her lips, backed away with it, pulling it over on to her side of the bed. For the first time she gazed at his naked body. It was lean and muscular, and covered with a thick matt of hair, some of which was turning grey. His circumcised cock was almost fully erect. It was an odd shape, the smooth pink glans slightly larger in diameter than the shaft that supported it, giving it a resemblance to a mushroom. He had reproduced this element of his physical appearance faithfully in the book.

'Very good,' he said. He reached up and touched the wet red leather that covered her cheek. 'I want you to straddle my hips now,' he said.

Eagerly, Sandra rolled on to her side and managed to force her way up on to her knees. Trying to balance herself, she threw one leg over his thighs so her knees were resting either side of his body.

'You see what you can do when you try,' he said in a soft, mocking tone.

'Yes, Master.' She could feel the heat of his cock. It was radiating out from him. Her clitoris began to throb. She couldn't see him at all now, her head held high by the collar, making it impossible to view anything below the horizontal. But she knew she could find him with little difficulty by squirming forward and down.

She had dreamt of this moment. In the last four days she had developed a thousand scenarios as to how he would take her for the first time. She knew, inevitably, she would be bound, but how and where had been a matter of endless speculation. She had never imagined this, the wet red leather and her soaking wet hair still dripping on to the bed, her discomfort extreme. But that only served to make the feelings more intense. She would have to get used to the fact that everything in the castle was likely to be beyond her experience. The way he had treated her tonight was just the beginning.

'Oh, Master,' she gasped as her sex clenched involuntarily, wanting him so badly.

'I don't enjoy getting cross with you,' he said indulgently.

'No, Master. I just . . .' She didn't know what to say.

The Master's Diary

'Sh . . .' he said. 'However good you are, Sandra . . .' Her name sounded completely different on his lips. '. . . there will come a point of no return, a point when you will rebel. That is inevitable. It is how you cope with that moment which will determine your future. Do you understand?'

'Yes, Master.' But she wasn't sure she did. She couldn't imagine not wanting to obey him.

'A little closer,' he said.

Immediately, Sandra edged forward. She felt the silky smoothness of his glans brush against her labia and could not suppress a gasp of pleasure.

'Stop,' he said.

She remained still. She wished she could have looked at him. She wished she could have seen that large cock pointing directly at her sex. The urge to sink herself down on to it, to feel it plunging into her, riding up on a tide of her juices, was almost irresistible.

She heard him move. A second later she felt his fingers closing on her nipples. They pinched them lightly, then used them to hold up her big, round breasts, the leather harness on each side biting deeper.

'So much to do, and so little time,' he said. 'All right, that's enough.'

'Master?' She didn't know what he meant.

'I said, that's enough.' He was sitting up, pulling himself away from her. She desperately tried to 'walk' forward on her knees to maintain the same position.

'Master, please, please don't leave me . . .' She stopped herself. What was she saying? She was a slave. This was a test. She realised that in a sudden flash of revelation. He had given her a graphic demonstration of how easy it would be to disobey. If she said another word, moved another inch, it would all be over. But she was still in control. As hard as it was, she managed to swing her leg off him and tumbled on to her side, the leather harness digging into her flesh. She welcomed the pain. It took her mind off the expectation of pleasure. She stretched her elbows against the thin leather strap, sending sharp needles of pain all the way up her arms and into her cramped shoulders. She found she was literally biting her lip to stop herself from begging.

Manville left his robe open. There was a low armchair with a matching stool to the right of the bed and he sat on it, putting up his feet and crossing his ankles. There was a circular occasional table alongside the chair and on it a small, brass bell. Manville picked it up. It rang sweetly.

They must have been waiting outside the bedroom door, listening for the signal.

One of the doors opened. Sandra caught a brief glimpse of Henri as he pushed the girl inside.

'Come over here, my dear,' the Master said in the gentlest of voices.

The girl was blonde, very, very blonde, her hair golden and shimmering. It was cut into a neat bob an equal length all the way around, the hair not quite touching her shoulders. She was wearing a black silk slip, with thin spaghetti straps, and high-heeled satin slippers. Her hands were gloved in black leather and bound together by a pair of metal handcuffs that were, in turn, attached to a ring on the thin leather collar around her neck. It made her look as though she were praying. She had bright blue eyes and a rather round, but very pretty, face. The slip was short and did not veil her shapely legs. Oddly, Sandra had the feeling she had seen her face somewhere before.

'Undo her collar, Angela,' the Master said.

The girl came up to the bed. Kneeling behind Sandra she managed, with some difficulty as a result of her own bondage, to unbuckle the posture collar. She unclipped the two straps at the back, allowing it to fall forward, dragging the harness that had encased Sandra's breasts with it. The waist-belt remained in place however, still tethering Sandra's wrists to it.

'I want you to watch,' he said, obviously addressing Sandra but not looking at her.

The Master's Diary

He beckoned the blonde to come over to him. She knelt by the armchair and leant forward, pushing her head towards his belly so it was possible for her to gather his erection into both her gloved hands.

Sandra struggled against her bonds. Now she could lower her head she could see everything. The hem of the black slip had ridden up as the blonde reached forward and Sandra could see her small, neat buttocks and her slender thighs.

'That's lovely, my dear,' the Master said. He raised his hand and stroked the girl's head with such tenderness Sandra felt a fierce attack of jealously. Why hadn't he treated her like that? She would have loved to be touched with such gentleness. 'Doesn't she look pretty?' The question was addressed to Sandra. He turned his dark brown eyes on her too and she knew he could tell exactly what she was thinking.

'Yes, Master.'

'Angela is a natural, you see. Like you, she hadn't the faintest idea what she really needed. She has come a long way. Now you must learn, like her. This is your first lesson.' He took the girl's hands and pulled them away, then pushed the footstool to one side, and lowered his feet. She wriggled around so she was kneeling between his legs. Sandra watched as he held her head in his hands and guided his cock between her lips. It sunk deep. The girl's cheeks bulged. She began to bob up and down on the mushroom-shaped staff.

Sandra felt her clitoris spasm. As she saw the long, hard shaft of flesh sinking between the girl's rather thin lips it was as if it had been plunging into her. She could not suppress a moan. He was right, of course. This was her first lesson. She had taken too much for granted and this was the result. He was teaching her that his reality was not a game.

The girl's head moved faster. Sandra saw Manville's muscular body begin to arch over the chair. It was a privilege to be chosen by the Master and the girl was enjoying every moment of it. She sawed her mouth up and down, licking and sucking at his flesh with unbounded enthusiasm. Suddenly his body went rigid, every muscle locked. Immediately the girl pulled her mouth from his cock and dropped it to his balls, sucking them in while her gloved hands grasped his phallus. A jet of pearly white spunk shot up in an arc and landed on her shoulder. Another hit the black silk slip. Sandra watched as her gloved fingers massaged the rest of the spunk out of him, sucking his balls to ensure that she had milked him of every last drop.

And that was the end of the lesson.

Chapter Seven

The room was small and windowless, with stone walls and floor. Its only furniture was a single bed and a wooden chair. There was a narrow doorway with a stone alancet arch leading to a separate shower room, toilet and wash hand basin, though the door had been removed. A single opaque light fitting screwed into the ceiling was the only source of light.

On the wall opposite the bed, a metal spike had been driven into the wall at well above head height. Set into the spike was a metal ring.

The ring became the focus of the room for Sandra. She stared at it hour after hour. The 'cell' was exactly as it had been described in *The Master's Diary*, even down to the sandy colour of the single sheet that covered the thin, striped mattress. The metal of the ring was bright, not rusty like the spike that supported it. Sandra knew why. Clara, and all the slaves like her, had been tied to it, their wrists hoisted high above their heads, their naked bodies turned to face the stone wall, while Angelica administered punishment. The fate of the non-fictional slaves was sure to be the same.

Last night, having taken his pleasure with the petite blonde, Manville had summoned Henri, the diminutive Frenchman, who had led both girls up to the top floor of the castle. Having locked Angela into her cell on one side of the corridor, he had marched Sandra into identical accommodation on the other side. Removing the leather harness, half of which hung awkwardly from the thick belt around her waist, and the remnants of the dress that still clung to her body underneath it, he'd left her without a word. Naturally, the door had been locked. It was exactly as the slaves had been treated in the book.

Breakfast had been pushed through the door without Sandra seeing who had delivered it, and lunch, at least she assumed that's what it was, arrived by the same means. She estimated she had been alone in the room all day, though she had no way of knowing precisely, with no watch or sunlight to give her clues. She had slept, dreamlessly, and woken feeling refreshed.

There was nothing to do but sit and think. And she had a lot to think about. What had happened last night had affected her deeply. She had prepared herself for all sorts of physical hardships, but though she had read about it, she was not prepared for the psychological ordeal. Manville had shown her graphically that not only could her sexual satisfaction be denied at his whim, but that her dependence on him was on a much more profound level. The conflicting emotions she had experienced as she had watched the blonde enjoying the privilege that she so desired for herself – a desire as strong as anything she'd ever felt – resolved into a single sentiment. She had felt anger and jealousy and almost overwhelming lust, but at the same time, and perhaps most fundamentally of all, she had felt the constraint of obedience holding her more tightly than any bondage could do. Manville had teased and tormented her, let her see him with another slave, to show her exactly what was required of her. The fact that she had not protested, and had remained passive, gave her a sense of satisfaction far greater than any sexual thrill. And that, in the end, was how she knew that the extraordinary feelings that the book had aroused in her had roots deeper than her libido. She did not understand why or how, but there was no denying that, to her, the idea of being a slave had a profound resonance.

Which didn't mean that her libido had been by-passed. Far from it. Even sitting alone in this dreary, stone-walled cell

The Master's Diary

aroused her. She was naked, of course, which made it difficult to forget the sexual agenda, and her whole body seemed to be tingling with life and expectation. She knew at any moment the door could open and a new adventure would begin. On the other hand of course, they might leave her for another day, letting her frustrations increase, reinforcing the point that what *she* wanted was no longer relevant.

She thought about Marion. Since what she had come to think of as her initiation, she had not seen the redhead, but she had thought about her a lot. The thought of what she had done to her turned her sex liquid instantly. She could feel the softness of her body, and her musky scent, and remembered exactly how it had felt to part her labia and nose her tongue against her swollen clitoris. She wondered what it would be like if she were able to hug her superb body, and press herself into it, feeling those big, heavy breasts squashed against her own, while she dug her fingers down into the cleft of her buttocks. The thought made her shudder.

So far everything that had happened had been presaged by Manville's book. If it continued to run true to form, Sandra knew that Marion would not be the only woman she had to face. It was common for the slaves to be made to perform all sorts of intimate acts in front of the Master and his guests. But though that prospect was daunting, she hoped that what she had felt with Marion could be transferred in equal measure to other women. She could certainly imagine kissing and caressing the soft silky skin and neat curves of the blonde she had seen last night. The point was, of course, that whatever her feelings, she simply had no choice.

With her body in a state of permanent arousal, and the frustrations of last night, the temptation to masturbate was extreme. But she resisted it. Though neither Manville or Henri had forbidden it, she knew it was wrong. To touch herself was an act of her own volition and that, in itself, had no place in her world now.

When she heard the key being inserted in the lock for the

third time that day she assumed it was probably time for her evening meal. It was not.

'Good evening.'

Marion Chandler's high-heels clanked on the stone floor as she walked in. She was wearing a short, strapless cocktail dress that clung to her voluptuous figure, its pink silk voile overladen with red sequins, her flaming red hair falling to her shoulders in soft, shiny waves. Her long legs were encased in glossy, sheer, flesh-coloured nylon and her high-heeled shoes were a bright red. There was a long valley delineated by muscle on her inner thigh. It disappeared under the hem of the skirt. The perfume that had lingered in Sandra's memory soon filled the small room.

She was carrying a small make-up case and some black lingerie, which she dropped on to the bed. Her eyes examined Sandra minutely.

Sandra felt her sex churn. Her nipples had not softened all day but now they puckered even more tightly, knotting themselves like the end of a balloon.

'I'm not sure whether I don't prefer you like this,' Marion said. She took Sandra's chin in her hand and tilted her face up towards her. 'You don't really need make-up. Stand up.'

Sandra obeyed, her heart beating rapidly. She had never in her whole life felt sexual desire for another woman but now, as she got to her feet, she looked at Marion's magnificent body with new eyes. She stared at the billowing cleavage that escaped the tight bodice of the dress, her breasts pressed together to form a dark, deep tunnel. She imagined herself pulling the dress down and sinking her mouth on to Marion's pulpy flesh.

Marion read the look in her eyes perfectly. 'It would be nice, wouldn't it?' she said. She raised her hand and trailed her fingers across Sandra's breasts, the edge of her long fingernails touching both nipples.

'Yes,' Sandra said.

'Yes, Mistress,' Marion corrected.

The Master's Diary

'Yes, Mistress.'

'There're lots of things I want to do to you. I can be very cruel.' As if to confirm it, Sandra saw a glint of steel in her eyes. 'But there's no time for that now.'

Marion opened the make-up case. It had a tray which levered itself upward as the lid was pulled back. Sandra saw an assortment of cosmetics and brushes to apply them. Marion took two small objects from the upper tray. They were made from silver and were cone shaped. Marion took one between her thumb and forefinger and pressed its outer rim. The cone was hinged on some sort of spring so that it could open out, splitting down the middle. The redhead seized Sandra's left breast with one hand and fitted the open cone over her nipple with the other. As she let it go, the metal trapped Sandra's nipple so that the puckered bud of flesh stuck out, the apex of the cone unable to close. Taking the other breast Marion repeated the process with the second silver cone.

'Pretty,' Marion said admiring her work.

The clips bit into Sandra's tender flesh, causing a flush of pain. But the pain was infused with a strong streak of sexual pleasure. Sandra felt her sex turn molten.

'Put those things on.' She nodded at the garments on the bed. 'Someone will come to do your make-up.' She took Sandra's left breast in her hand and squeezed it. The swelling flesh put extra pressure on the clip and Sandra felt a stab of pain. It turned so instantly to pleasure that she moaned.

'So sensitive,' the redhead said. She marched out of the door without giving Sandra another glance. The key ground in the lock.

Sandra went to pick up the clothes. Raising her arm caused her pectoral muscle to flex and lifted her breast. This made its flesh stretch and that, in turn, pulled against the clip, producing another mild shock of pain. Learning her lesson, Sandra moved more carefully, doing everything slowly and trying to avoid brushing her arms against her chest.

She picked up a black silk garment. It looked like a basque, except it was not boned. It had a half-cup bra and long suspenders extending down from its hem, and the centre of the garment was criss-crossed with black laces. Sandra pulled it over her head, the movement causing another tremor of feeling from her imprisoned nipples. The silk fitted tightly, barely covering her breasts, the silver cones peaking over the top of its bra.

There was a pair of black stockings on the bed too. Sandra sat on the mattress to pull them on. It seemed that no matter how she tried, it was impossible to move without provoking little pangs of feeling from her nipples. The initial shock of pain had subsided into a dull, and not unpleasant, ache, but as she leaned forward to fit the nylon stocking over her foot, her thigh pressed against her breast and a much sharper sensation coursed through her.

The stockings were a very dark black, though they had the same glossy finish that Marion's tights had had. Sandra tugged them into place, smoothing the material out over her long legs and making sure it was not wrinkled.

There was a pair of panties on the bed too. She eased these over her hips and smoothed them against her sex. They were high-cut, no more than a broad chevron of material that cut across the long black fingers of the suspenders at the front. At the back, another chevron banded her bottom, its apex rising from deep within the cleft of her buttocks.

As she adjusted the crotch of the garment, settling it over her sex, she could feel the heat of her labia underneath.

She sat on the bed, waiting. It was impossible to ignore the silver clips. Even without any movement at all they produced a whole range of sensations, the dull ache suddenly becoming a sharp, stinging pain, or a throbbing spasm that sent thrills of pleasure directly to her sex. If she looked down, she could see the tortured flesh poking out of the top of the silver cones, just above the black silk. The constriction had turned them ruby red.

For most of her time in the cell, there had been silence.

When the meals had been delivered she had heard the noise of the other doors being opened too but between times the thick stone walls and oak door had prevented any less obvious sounds. But now, after what she estimated to be no more than half an hour, she could hear a bustle of activity in the corridor outside.

Then the key was inserted in the lock of her door. The door swung open and Henri marched in, his appearance unchanged from yesterday. A small, nondescript woman followed him. She was in her forties and wore a black nylon overall, her face stern and uncommunicative. She carried a pair of black patent leather high-heels which she dropped on the floor by the bed.

'*Mais oui,*' Henri said, examining Sandra.

The woman pulled over the wooden chair and sat in front of the bed. Without a word she took out cosmetics from the case and began making-up Sandra's face under Henri's critical gaze.

It was yet another new sensation. She had had her face made-up by another woman before, but never without being able to see what she was doing. With no mirror in the room she had no idea what she was being made to look like. Apart from the fact that she could see the mascara was thicker than she normally used she had no clue as to what the woman was doing. Eye-liner and shadow were applied with a brush. Blusher emphasised her cheekbones. Her dark eyebrows were plucked of stray hairs. Last of all the woman painted on a lipstick.

Taking a brush from the case the woman brushed out Sandra's long hair, even this freedom denied to her. She arranged it carefully, pinning it into a tight chignon, leaving her neck bare.

Henri pronounced himself satisfied. The woman left.

'Stand,' Henri ordered. 'Hands together,' he said, demonstrating by holding his hands out in front of him, his palms almost touching.

As Sandra obeyed she saw him take a long chain from his

ever bulging pocket. Its metal links were shiny. Attached to one end was what looked like a miniature pair of handcuffs, their circular shackles already open. Henri placed the shackles over Sandra's upturned thumbs and swung them closed, the ratchet that locked the shackles in place clicking loudly.

'Shoes,' he said, standing with the chain from the cuffs in his hand.

Sandra climbed into the high-heels. They were much higher than anything she'd ever worn before, making her feel as though she were walking on tip-toe and cramping her toes in the process.

'Follow,' Henri said.

Sandra found she could only take diminutive steps. She tottered out into the corridor. The doors of the other cells were all open. She glanced inside. Each one was identical to hers in every respect and each was empty.

They got to the lift. The grille was open and Henri pushed her inside. Without getting in himself he pressed the button for the ground floor, dropped the chain and closed the grille. The lift began to descend.

Sandra looked down. As the cage approached the ground floor she could see through the latticed metal lift shaft that Marion was waiting in the hall below.

'Very pretty,' the redhead said, opening the grille and pulling Sandra forward by the chain. They headed down the corridor and turned right. At the far end Sandra saw three other girls waiting by a pair of panelled doors. They were all dressed in lingerie and all wore the same black patent-leather, precipitously high-heeled shoes. As Marion led her forward, Sandra recognised Angela, the petite blonde who she had seen with the Master last night. She was wearing a wide red lace and satin suspender belt, with a matching, underwired half-cup bra and tiny G-string panties. Even with the high-heels she was the shortest of the three. The girl to her right had a mass of wavy chestnut-coloured hair. She had been dressed in white hold-up stockings with a wide lace welt, a pair of white French knickers, their high-cut legs inset with lace, but no bra. She was much heavier than her companions, with pear-shaped breasts that hung down to her belly, a thick waist and huge, oval buttocks. Her thighs too were meaty and rippled with cellulite.

The third girl was also blonde and her long hair was pinned, like Sandra's, to her head. She, however, was slender, her slim figure cinched into a tight, dark blue boned basque. Dark blue stockings and silky, dark blue thong-cut panties completed her outfit.

All the girls had their hands bound together by the tiny cuffs, their thumbs turned up, a long chain hanging from them just as it did from Sandra's. All three had the same silver cones clipped around their nipples.

'In a line,' Marion said.

In what had obviously become a well-practised routine, the three girls formed up behind each other leaving about a yard between them. Marion pulled Sandra to the end of the line. Taking the free end of the chain, which Sandra saw had a small snap hook attached to it, she pulled it through the legs of the girl immediately in front of Sandra, who happened to be the blonde in the dark blue basque, and clicked the hook into the links of the chain that held the thumb-cuffs together. She then picked up the trailing edge of the loose chain that hung from that girl's cuffs and swung this up between the thighs of the girl in front of her, the chestnut-haired woman, following the same procedure to link her to Angela, who was at the head of the line.

She then caught hold of the loose chain from Angela's cuffs and rapped twice on one of the panelled doors.

'Come.' The voice belonged to Manville Mason.

Marion opened the door and yanked on the chain, pulling the blonde forward, the other girls having to follow.

'Ah, we were wondering what had happened to you.'

They were walking into a large dining room. There was a huge Gothic fireplace at one end, its grate, set between two cast-iron fire dogs with heads of dragons, ablaze with a log fire. Candles flickered from silver candelabra set on a seventeenth-century oak dining table in the centre of the room. It had been laid for three. Two of the places were still occupied by Manville Mason and a large, corpulent but young man with a round, moon-like face and staring, wide-apart eyes. The third, Sandra guessed, had recently been occupied by Marion.

As if to confirm this theory, Marion dropped the chain when the girls had tottered right up to the table and sat in the vacant chair. There were *demitasse* cups of coffee on the table and crystal balloon glasses of brandy. Marion picked up her glass and sipped at the amber liquid.

'Well, I must say, Manville, you certainly have the very best *petits fours*,' the man said. He turned his chair outward from the table so he could view the girls without twisting round.

'Thank you, Malcolm. And, as usual, the choice is yours.'

The man took a slug of his brandy, then got to his feet. He came up to Angela and stared down into her red satin bra. He prodded the silver cone on one of her nipples with his fingers. The blonde moaned but did not move.

'What are these?' Malcolm asked.

'An invention of my own. I'm trying them out for the next book.'

'The next book?'

'*The Master's Castle*. It's a sequel to *The Diary*.'

'Do you try out everything before you write about it?'

'Oh yes. I like to make sure everything I write has been tested out first. Especially all the bondage harnesses and the various punishments.'

'Test them for what?'

'The line between pleasure and real pain can sometimes be a very thin one. As far as I am concerned, pain is only a prelude to pleasure. It is never an end in itself.'

'And everything is based on what happens here?'

The Master's Diary

'Oh course I can't write about the other establishments. That would be breaking a confidence.'

'We must have some secrets, mustn't we?' Malcolm said, tapping his finger against his nose.

'Precisely,' the Master agreed.

The man moved on to the fatter woman. With her breasts unfettered, he was able to examine the silver cone more closely but did not touch it this time.

'She needs to go on a diet,' he said, forgetting the same could be said of him.

'Some of my friends prefer a fuller figure. I do myself some times.'

'Not me,' Malcolm said. He moved to the third girl in the line, running his hand down the silky, dark blue basque. He caught hold of the chain that ran between her legs, yanking it up so it creased the crotch of her panties and dug into her sex. He sawed it from side to side while he stared into the girl's eyes, looking for a reaction, but she gave none.

'She's gorgeous,' he said.

He dropped the chain and moved to look at Sandra, who stared back at him steadily. His hand cupped her breast under the black silk and squeezed it. The silver cone bit more deeply but Sandra managed to suppress a moan.

None of this was exactly a surprise to her. There had been scenes like this in the book and she had expected something similar. But there was a big difference between reading about it and imagining she was one of the slaves being examined by the Master's guests, and actually experiencing it for herself. Her excitement was tempered by her reaction to Malcolm. He was not an attractive man. He had a chubby face and greasy, lank hair. She could see his belly straining to escape his shirt, the buttons looking as though they might tear at any moment. She was afraid of her reaction if he chose her.

'It's terribly difficult,' he said.

'Take your time,' Marion told him.

'I never understand why they are so obedient,' he said.

Manville knitted his fingers together on the table. 'Because they want to be,' he said simply.

'But you train them, don't you?'

'I train them in what to do, not why to do it.'

'Now you come to mention it, I'm tempted by her,' he said, going back to the chestnut-haired woman. He weighed her breast in his hand. 'Something different.'

'Exactly,' Manville agreed.

He was wavering. He danced up to the front of the line and stared at Angela again. Then he came back to Sandra. He looked her in the eyes and she returned his gaze, trying to suggest an indifference that might make him think she was not the right choice. It didn't work.

'Her,' he said.

No, Sandra screamed inside, only just managing not to say the word. She felt her face blush and her heart begin to race. She looked at the Master, trying to concentrate on him, trying to remember how much she had wanted to be his slave. She had to find a way to convince herself that serving this man was part of that.

Marion got to her feet. She unhooked the chain from the long-haired blonde's cuffs and let it fall between her legs. Stooping to pick it up she handed it to Malcolm.

'She's new. She hasn't been trained,' the Master said. 'Perhaps you should take one of the others too.'

The man grinned. 'What a good idea.'

'Her, then,' he said without any hesitation. He was pointing at Angela.

Marion unclipped the chain that ran between Angela's legs, then picked up the loose chain hanging down from the girl's thumb-cuffs. She handed it to Malcolm.

Sandra's pulse raced. It looked as though she was going to be put to yet another test. She knew, whatever happened, she could not refuse. She did not want her adventure to end before it had really begun.

'You know where to go?' Marion asked. 'There's a special room on the ground floor.'

'My room will be fine,' he said, without looking at her, unable to tear his eyes off the two women he had been gifted.

Marion took a small key from the table next to her coffee cup. 'You might need this,' she said, handing it to him.

'Good night, then,' Manville said. 'See you at breakfast.'

Sandra saw him staring at her, the message in his eyes as clear as if he'd spoken it. 'Don't let me down,' they said.

She saw him turn to the other two girls and beckon them forward with his finger. The chestnut-haired woman reached him first and knelt by his side, her big thighs spreading out like tree trunks. He indicated that the blonde should sit up on the table in front of her, the chain still linking them making the movement awkward. He then pushed her back so she was lying across the uncluttered part of the table with her legs dangling over the edge. The Master's hand slid along her leg over the stocking top to the tightly stretched silk of her panties. As his fingers caressed it, his other hand dipped down to the kneeling woman's face. Sandra watched as the woman opened her mouth and he slipped his fingers inside it. She saw her suck them hard and thought Manville's body shuddered as a result.

'Come on, then,' Malcolm said. He jerked on the chains, forcing Sandra to turn away.

Out in the corridor, he pulled them along to the lift. It was a tight fit for all three of them and Sandra felt herself pressed into Angela's back, the silver cones protesting as her breasts were squashed.

Malcolm's bedroom was on the first floor. It was large and luxurious, just like the Master's room, with a double bed and a separate *en-suite* bathroom.

There was also a large mirror hanging from one wall. For the first time since she had been dressed in her cell, Sandra caught a glimpse of herself. At least, she saw two women, standing side by side, one in red lingerie and the other in black. It took her a long moment to realise the brunette in the black was her. Her face looked completely different, her makeup darker and more dramatic than the way she would have done it for herself, and her hair pinned to her head in a style she would never have used. Her long legs appeared to have been elongated even further by the height of the heels, their muscles stretched and firmed. Her breasts spilt provocatively from the top of the black silk, the silver cones catching the light.

Malcolm dropped the chains. There was a tray of drinks on a burr yew chest of drawers. He poured himself a brandy.

'Got to pee,' he said, heading for the bathroom. He closed the door after him.

'I'm Angela,' the girl whispered. Her eyes were flaring with excitement.

'Sandra,' Sandra said. 'You've done this before?'

'Of course. You know you have to do everything he asks? If you don't we'll both be punished.' She had seen the fear in Sandra's eyes.

'I'll try.'

'It's what Manville wants,' the girl said. 'Just remember that. How long have you been here?'

'I arrived yesterday.'

'I thought so. That's why Manville was so good to me last night. He always does that in front of newcomers.'

'You're very beautiful,' Sandra said, though she was not sure why.

'That makes it easier, then,' Angela said.

The door opened. Malcolm came out wearing a white towelling robe. He had the little key in one hand and his brandy glass in the other. He put them both on the five-drawer bedside chest and sat on the bed.

'Over here,' he said.

The two women tottered over to him.

'Is there any equipment?' he said.

'It should be in the bottom drawer, Master,' Angela said

nodding towards the bedside chest.

Malcolm opened it and peered inside. He pulled out a large, cream plastic vibrator. 'Could be useful,' he said. He looked again and found a smaller dildo in the same material. 'Get down here then,' he said, a little irritably, as if they should have known what to do. 'Let me see a bit of action.'

Angela knelt on the bed. Sandra followed her, unsure what she was meant to do. The blonde raised her still shackled hands to Sandra's shoulder and rolled her back on the bed. Kneeling beside her she pulled Sandra's hands up over her head, producing a pang of pain from the nipple clips in the process, then leant forward and kissed her gently on the mouth. Sandra felt an instant surge of passion. The blonde's mouth felt deliciously soft. Her tongue licked Sandra's lower lip as her hands glided down her body. With her hands cuffed together she could not get to her objective without breaking the kiss, so when her hands reached Sandra's midriff she sat up, allowing them to travel further down over Sandra's belly to the black panties, the lower hand of the bound pair resting against them and stroking the silk.

Sandra's feelings were terribly confused. There was no doubt about the sharp sexual pulse the girl had provoked. If she had entertained any doubts that the lust she felt for Marion would not be easily transferred to another woman they were instantly quelled. If they had been alone she would have been unequivocally excited by the girl's touch and eager to experiment further. If they were with Manville the same would have been true. But they were not. She was only too aware of Malcolm's eyes roaming her body.

There was another factor too. She couldn't seem to rid herself of the image of the Master's hand travelling slowly up the blonde's thigh, or the way he had shuddered as the fat woman had sucked on his fingers. He had done it deliberately, she was sure, another way of reminding her that she was not in a position to express her own desires. That didn't make the desire any less strong, however, and she couldn't help wishing she had been left behind to serve her master for the first time.

Angela's fingers were delving under the leg of the black panties. She felt her finger slotting into the channel of her labia. It rubbed against her clitoris. With her thumbs cuffed she had to flatten the palm of the upper hand over Sandra's mons in order to get the lower one down between Sandra's legs, and the material of the panties was caught up between the two so it was far from easy, but she managed to drag the little nut of flesh up and down, producing a wave of pleasure.

Sandra felt another hand on her thigh. She looked up and saw that Malcolm was stroking the black silk suspender and the welt of the dark stocking, his eyes staring intensely at what he was doing. At the same time she saw Angela's head dip down towards her belly. The girl's tongue lapped around the flesh immediately above the panties as her hands co-operated to pull the crotch of the material to one side. Malcolm, meanwhile, was pulling her thighs apart.

Sandra rested her head back on the bed, the effort of holding it up between her raised arms cramping her muscles. Angela's mouth was hot. Sandra felt her tongue darting down between her labia. She moaned as it came into contact with her clit. Instinctively she arched herself up towards the girl, opening her legs wider. The tongue circled her clit with artful delicacy. Lower down something hard and cold probed between her pussy lips. It found the mouth of her vagina and pushed inward tentatively. She recognised the familiar feel of a dildo. Malcolm pushed it right up into her body, causing a surge of pleasure.

Sandra wriggled herself down on the hard phallus. She was eager to reciprocate, confident now that she would be just as aroused by giving as she was by receiving. Besides she hoped she could try and overcome her distaste for the man by submerging herself in the sea of desire she felt for Angela. 'Let me,' she said, hoping the girl would understand.

She did. Immediately she swung her left leg over Sandra's body and straddled her shoulders, all without breaking the rhythm that her tongue had established on Sandra's clit. Sandra found herself staring up into her sex. The gusset of the panties was no more than a narrow string and it had buried itself between her rather thin labia. An oval of pubic hair surrounded them. It was already wet.

Angela held herself above Sandra's face for a moment then slowly lowered her sex until it came to rest against Sandra's chin.

With her arms raised over her head, and Angela's knees firmly planted on either side of her shoulders, there was no way Sandra could lower her hands to pull the panties aside. She had to use her tongue. She managed to hook it under the red silk but it was too tight for her to manoeuvre to one side.

'Please,' she said loudly.

Malcolm's fingers left the dildo. She saw his face appear alongside hers. He saw the problem. His fingers grabbed the thong of silk and pulled it over to one side.

'Don't say I never do anything for you,' he grinned.

Sandra saw he was watching as she nudged her tongue into Angela's labia. It was only the second woman she had ever touched so intimately, and despite the leering face to her right she could not suppress a tremor of passion. But this was totally different from what had happened with Marion and created a whole new set of resonances. As the first thrill flooded over her she was aware of a harder, more insistent pleasure than she'd felt before. As she found Angela's clit and began to circle it, just as Angela was doing to hers, she realised she was feeling a double hit of sensation. She could feel the effect she was having on Angela almost as acutely as she could feel the effect Angela was having on her. She tried to imitate what the girl was doing, circling her tongue at the same speed, using the same pressure. The girl's body tensed, the muscles in her thighs and buttocks hardening. She was not surprised. Her own had done the same thing, and for the same reason. They were both coming.

Perhaps with all the frustrations she had experienced over

the last twenty-four hours, on top of all the excitements, it was not surprising her body was responding so quickly. Angela's tongue was perfect. It had found the spot on her clit that must have been the most sensitive place on her body, and swept past it on its tiny circuit with monotonous regularity, every sweep producing a new surge of feeling. The dildo was still buried inside her too, though it was difficult to keep it there. She tried to hold it inside but the natural lubrication of her body, and the force of gravity, were making it slip down.

She tried to concentrate on Angela, tried to roll her tongue around in the same way, but then the dam burst and all her pent-up feelings escaped, flooding over her, inundating her with pleasure. At exactly that moment she lost the battle to keep the dildo inside her. It fell out with a plop, the sudden shock winding her orgasm to new heights. She found herself writhing up against the softness of the girl's body, wanting to feel every inch of it. The cones that pinched her nipples and the cramping cuffs added another dimension too and she found she was trying to pull her hands apart to increase the sensation of helplessness that she had come to love so much.

She knew Angela had come too. She could feel it through every nerve in her body as if by some sort of osmosis. They clung to each other, shivering and shaking, their bodies as one.

'Quite a performance,' Malcolm said. 'And now it's my turn.'

Angela rolled off Sandra and sat up. 'What do you want us to do, Master?' she said.

'Take her panties off,' he said, indicating Sandra's hips.

As Angela used her shackled hands to skim the black panties down her long, stocking-sheathed legs, Sandra co-operated by raising her bottom. The silk snared on the high-heeled shoes and had to be plucked free.

Malcolm raised himself to his knees on the bed. He started to take off the towelling robe, then stopped. 'Hey, you should do this for me, shouldn't you?'

The Master's Diary

'Yes, Master,' Angela said.

She got off the bed and walked around behind him. She looped her arms over his head then ran her hands down to his waist and pulled the belt of the robe apart. Her hands continued down, opening the robe up, then encircling his erection.

'May I do this too, Master?' she said.

The excitement Sandra had seen in her eyes had not diminished. Malcolm was not prepossessing. Now, with his robe open, she could see his flabby chest, round belly and white skin. But Angela seemed not to have noticed. She was rubbing her body against his back and wanking his cock in both hands with obvious delight, while her mouth planted little kisses on his shoulders and neck. It was quite clear that her enthusiasm was genuine.

'Come on,' he said to Sandra, nodding down towards his cock.

'What, Master?' The word sounded wrong. He was not her master.

'Suck on it, girl,' he said irritably.

Angela grasped the base of his cock in both hands. He was not circumcised and she pulled his foreskin back, revealing his pink, slightly wrinkled glans. She held the base of his shaft in one hand and his balls in the other. 'Come on,' he encouraged.

Sandra had read *The Master's Diary* over and over again. She knew what happened at the castle. She knew it was the fictional master's habit to give his slaves to his guests. But though the guests in the book had not been romanticised and had often been described as fat, or balding, or otherwise unattractive, when they had taken one of the slaves back to their rooms, or into one of the punishment chambers that dotted the castle, they had always been transformed by Sandra's imagination into carbon copies of the Master himself, their described characteristics discarded.

That was not going to happen in reality. Sandra had been

able to concentrate on the delights of Angela's body up until now, but the crunch had finally come. The distaste she had felt in the dining room was welling up in her again.

Angela must have been able to read it in her face. She scowled at her over Malcolm's shoulder and mouthed the words, 'do it' without pronouncing them.

Sandra pulled herself up to her knees. She was within a breath of getting to her feet. She would walk downstairs and tell the Master that it had all been a mistake, that she could not be his slave because she could not bring herself do what Malcolm asked of her. But as she straightened up, the silver cone that enclosed her left nipple so tightly caught on the upper edge of the black silk bra. Sandra gasped as the cone bit into the sensitive flesh. The wave of pain turned into hot, throbbing pleasure, her whole body responding, the orgasm she had had only minutes before revived in miniature. She looked at the hard cock Angela held in her fist. A tear of fluid had escape the single eye-like slit at its tip.

Without thinking she leant forward and used her tongue to wipe the fluid away. It tasted sweet. She ran her tongue around the head of the glans then down over the ridge. Under the same impetus she slipped the cock between her lips and sucked on it gently. It pulsed in her mouth. She sucked again, then drove herself down on it, feeling it riding up into her throat.

Her reticence disappeared. She bobbed her mouth back and forth on it eagerly. Her sex responded as if it, too, was being used. Her clitoris spasmed against her labia. Her mental state rapidly caught up with her physical arousal. She realised that the more difficult the tasks she was given by her master, the more she should embrace them. Having to obey a man like Malcolm, a man who was not attractive and handsome, was a test of her obedience and submissiveness, and the realisation that she was capable of submitting herself to him gave her the same thrill as she had experienced last night in the Master's bedroom, watching him taking his pleasure with

Angela. That was her role, after all. It was not for her to choose. The more unpleasant the duty the more it reinforced her feeling for her position. And wasn't that exactly what she wanted? Wasn't that what all the slaves in *The Master's Diary* had craved? Wasn't that why the castle existed in reality as well as in fiction?

She was sure this was the reason Angela had appeared so clearly aroused right from the beginning. She had been used in this way before, probably many times before. She welcomed the opportunity to submit because it was a way to tap into that fundamental impulse that Manville had written about so accurately.

The paradox was, that as the truth dawned, the task was no longer odious. Sandra's physical excitement coursed through her body. She sucked and licked and drove her mouth down on Malcolm with renewed vigour, trying everything she knew to give him pleasure. She wanted to make him come in her mouth, to make him lose control. She wanted to ravish him.

But he had other ideas. He took her head in his hand and pulled her up so he was staring into her eyes.

'You're very good at that, but it's not what I want.'

'What then, Master?' Her tone of voice had changed completely. It was breathy now and hoarse.

'Lie on your back.'

'Oh yes, Master.' A few minutes ago the thought of having him inside her had horrified her. Now just the words had produced a huge surge of feeling. She threw herself back on the bed, raised her arms above her head and spread her legs wide open, wanting him to see her sex. She knew it was perfectly framed by the black silk, the suspenders and the jet-black welts of the stockings. She thought she felt her labia wink open and hoped he would be able to see the mouth of her vagina, scarlet and wet. Malcolm stared at it. She saw Angela staring too.

For a second Malcolm did nothing. Then he allowed Angela

to pull her arms away and strip the robe from his body. He crawled forward until he was kneeling between Sandra's legs. He picked up the discarded black panties and wound them tightly around the base of his cock, lifting his balls.

'Looks pretty,' he said.

'Very pretty, Master,' Angela said. She knelt on the bed beside him and plucked at his nipple, pinching it with her fingernails. His cock twitched upward as a result.

He leant forward. Sandra felt his belly pressing into hers. She raised her buttocks off the bed and thrust her sex up towards him. He nosed into her labia.

'Very hot,' he said.

'Yes, Master,' Sandra said.

He pushed down to the mouth of her vagina as he lay out on top of her, his weight crushing her breasts and putting renewed pressure on the silver clips. It was a measure of Sandra's excitement that this produced no pain. Her body was so aroused it converted the sharp, stinging feeling into instant, intense pleasure. She moaned.

She moaned again as he plunged his phallus into her. She felt the velvety, wet walls of her sex parting.

'Lovely,' he said.

His cock was pulsating. She was sure she was going to come in seconds rather than minutes. She dropped her bound arms over his head and hugged his body. 'It's wonderful, Master,' she said, because it was true.

He twisted his body from side to side to screw himself deeper into her, but he did not try to withdraw.

At her side she saw Angela picking up the smaller of the two dildoes he had got out earlier. She raised her head and watched as the girl sucked the dildo into her mouth, wetting it with her own saliva, then directed it down between his buttocks. Suddenly Malcolm's whole body arched up off her, as Angela pushed the dildo into his anus. A second thrust produced the same reaction.

Sandra heard a humming noise. Less than a second later

she felt a deep, powerful vibration seize his cock. Angela had turned on the motor inside the phallus.

'Oh, God,' he moaned. He lifted himself up on straight arms, staring down into her eyes. She could see the ecstasy on his face. But he wasn't the only one who was affected by the constant vibration. With his cock as the conduit, it was spreading through Sandra too. The longer it went on, the stronger it seemed to get. Her clitoris, stretched out tautly between her labia, was quivering in sympathy and producing sharp needles of pleasure. The whole of her vagina was trembling too, clenched convulsively around his phallus.

He cried out loudly, a noise that was not a word. His buttocks went rigid and Sandra felt his cock jerk against the confines of her cunt. She was sure she could feel his ejaculation, but the hot spunk that spattered out of him tipped her over the edge too. Her orgasm exploded. She used all her strength to wriggle herself down on him, then allowed the pleasure to wash over her.

'Master,' she whispered, the word heightening everything she felt.

Chapter Eight

It hadn't been easy; the estate was vast. The brick walls must have run for at least a thousand yards on either side of the gates, then gave way to high fencing topped with barbed wire. All tabloid journalists were used to identifying security measures, often aimed precisely at them, and Cherry recognised the tell-tale responders set in each fencing post, indicating that the perimeter fence was protected by electronic security as well. There was no way in without being discovered.

It was difficult to stake-out the entrance too. The closely-planted forest offered no hiding places for a car anywhere along the lane that led to the gates. The best she could do was to park back on the main road, pulling her car up on to a grass verge partly hidden by some thick shrubs, and hope that there was no other way for the Rolls to come out.

After two days she was beginning to wonder. She'd seen no one use the lane down to the gates, either coming out or going in. Either the house was well-provisioned or deliveries were made through another entrance. Or late at night. Cherry hadn't been able to watch for forty-eight hours continuously. She'd had to eat and sleep and take a shower. She'd gone into the local village and, though there was no hotel, she'd found a small pub where they did bed and breakfast and the food was reasonable. She'd stayed parked in the road during daylight hours and early evenings, but gone back to the pub after nine when she reckoned that the Rolls was unlikely to come out again.

She'd sent the reels of film to her office and received them back the next day by courier. The eight-by-ten prints were in colour, some of them quite good enough to sell to a pornographic magazine. Though their genitals featured in the close-ups, there were full-length shots that made it perfectly clear who the genitals belonged to, which is exactly what Cherry had intended. She was dozing off on the early evening of the second day when she heard the screech of tyres. She snapped awake. The sun had already set and the twilight was gloomy, but there was no mistaking the big boot of the Rolls and its rectangular arrangement of rear lights.

Cherry fired up the Ford and sped off down the road after it. The car was heading into the village about four miles away. There was no other traffic so Cherry hung back not wanting the blond chauffeur, who she could see was driving the car, to be able to catch sight of her.

The village was small and hilly, its main street leading down to a cove where crab boats were moored, the stone houses and small shopfronts a picture-postcard idyll of Cornwall. The Rolls found it difficult to manoeuvre in the narrow streets, but headed straight for the centre of the town. To Cherry's astonishment it pulled into the small car park at the back of The Old Red Lion, the pub where she was staying.

It appeared the driver was playing right into her hands, she thought, grinning. She turned the Escort into the car park right behind the Rolls. As the big car rolled into a parking place, she drove up beside it and got out.

'Hey, what a great car,' she said. 'It's huge.'

The blond man got out and locked the car. Its central locking system made a loud clunk. He examined Cherry critically. She was wearing a tight, clinging white top and a short red skirt. Her slender legs were sheathed in champagne-coloured tights and she wore spiky-heeled red shoes.

'I'm just the chauffeur,' he said.

'What, is this your night off?' she asked. It was obvious

that it was. His uniform had been replaced by corduroy trousers and a check shirt.

'Yes.'

'Then how about you buy me a drink. I'm new in town.'

He looked at her suspiciously. 'All right,' he said, though he didn't look very happy at the thought.

'Cherry Austin,' she extended her hand.

'Curtis Canfield.' He shook hands briefly as if he suspected she had a contagious disease.

'Don't worry, I won't bite,' she said, grinning. Ignoring his reticence, Cherry shouldered her capacious handbag and took his arm.

They walked through into the saloon bar. The pub was decorated with mementoes of the fishing industry, the ceiling hung with nets and lobster baskets, and the walls with stuffed fish and ancient photographs of men and women fishing by various long forgotten means. Though it was not cold outside, the early summer temperature well above average, there was a small coal fire in a grate around which several customers were huddled.

'What do you want to drink?' Curtis said, with little enthusiasm.

'Gin and tonic,' Cherry said. She spotted a table in the corner where they would not be overlooked. That was likely to be important, after all.

She watched as the pretty barmaid served Curtis his drinks. He was obviously a regular as he was greeted with a warm smile and a great deal of banter. From her body language, the way she angled herself at him, Cherry was sure the barmaid would have liked to get to know him a great deal better. She caught her throwing envious glances in her direction, and if looks could kill Cherry would undoubtedly already have begun to feel ill.

'Here,' he said, putting her glass down. He had brought himself a pint.

'Is this your regular routine?' Cherry asked.

'Yes. Thursday night off.'

'Where do you work?'

'Big castle just up the road.'

'Must be a very rich man.'

'He is. Very private too.' That was clearly intended as a rebuff. He didn't want to talk about Manville.

'Manville Mason, right?'

He looked at her askance. 'How did you know that?'

'Do you know, you're a very attractive man?'

'How did you know who I worked for?'

'A lot of women would kill for that colour hair.'

'What the hell is this?'

'And you're obviously very fit.' She squeezed his bicep. It felt like steel.

'I asked you a question. What do you want?'

'Aside from your body? Do you know the barmaid's really got the hots for you?'

'I'm leaving.' He got to his feet.

'I think you should look at these first.' Cherry pulled the brown manilla envelope from her bag. It was covered with stickers from the courier company that had delivered it to the pub first thing this morning.

Curtis looked confused. 'What are they?'

'See for yourself. I think you'll be impressed. Actually some of them are quite artistic. The rays of the sunlight filtering though the trees. It *was* a beautiful sunset.'

He sat down again and took the envelope. Flipping it open he took out the photographs.

'Christ, where did you get these?' His mouth fell open. He flicked from one to another, examining each with equal astonishment.

'I'd have thought that was obvious. I followed you down from London. She's pretty, isn't she? I can see why you were so keen. Are you always so forceful?'

Curtis put the photographs back in the envelope quickly, looking around to make sure no one else had seen them.

The Master's Diary

'What do you want?'

'Is Manville Mason a jealous man?'

'What do you mean?'

'I imagine that beautiful brunette was not your date, Curtis. You were taking her to Manville. I imagine he might be very annoyed if he found out his chauffeur had taken advantage of her on the way down.'

'On the other hand, he might not,' Curtis said.

'Fine. So you won't mind if I send these photographs to him?'

Curtis's face showed his alarm. His ability to bluff would not have made him a good poker player. 'You can't do that,' he said.

'Oh, I can. And I will. Unless you help me.'

'Help you do what?'

'I'm a journalist, Curtis. I want to do a story on Manville. I just want a little information.'

'What sort of information?'

'Like, for instance, who was the brunette?' She tapped the envelope.

'I don't know. One of his women. I just drive the car.'

'Oh you do a great deal more than that, Curtis. I've seen it for myself.'

'Have you read Manville's books?'

'One of them.'

'Then you know.'

'Sorry? You'll have to spell it out for me.'

'The book, the women . . . I mean, it's all for real.'

'What's for real?'

'The women come to the castle to be . . .' He looked around to make sure no one could overhear him, '. . . slaves. Manville's slaves. They live at the castle. All the stuff he writes about is true.'

Cherry felt herself flush. That was not what she'd expected. She wasn't at all sure how she had imagined the brunette fitted into the picture with Angela Blake but she hadn't imagined anything as bizarre as this.

'You mean he does all that stuff in the book?'

'All of it.'

'How many women are there?'

'There's four at the moment.'

'Including the brunette?'

'Yes. But there's Marion too.'

'Marion?'

'She sort of runs it all for Manville.'

'Like the character in the book, can't remember her name?' She wished she'd read the book more carefully.

'Right.'

'And the brunette was the latest edition?'

'They all have to go through a test. If they pass . . .' He opened his hands in a shrug.

Cherry rooted in her bag. She found the photograph of Angela Blake and showed it to Curtis. 'Is she one of them?'

'Yes,' he said. 'She's been there for a month at least.'

Cherry smiled. This was going to be the scoop of the decade. 'You see, that wasn't so difficult, was it?' she said. She was thinking about what she had to do next. She needed proof. Curtis's word was no good. She had to get photographs and try to see inside the castle for herself. And she had to get an interview with Angela Blake.

'I could lose my job,' Curtis said, his face wreathed in worry lines.

'Don't worry, your secret's safe with me. As long as you co-operate.'

'I've told you the truth.'

'And I appreciate it. Now I want you to do one other thing for me.'

He looked apprehensive. 'What?'

'Smuggle me in.'

'What! I can't do that.'

'Yes you can. And you will,' Cherry said firmly. 'And what's

The Master's Diary

more, you'll do it tonight. What time are you expected back?'

'No later than ten.'

'You see – the perfect opportunity.'

'What if Manville finds you?'

'Don't worry. I'll say I came in with the groceries. I won't mention you. Promise.'

'Once I get you inside, you're on your own.'

'Agreed.'

Curtis picked up his beer and drunk half of it.

'What do you usually do on your night off?'

'Have dinner here. They do good food.'

Cherry felt a growing excitement in the pit of her stomach. Seeing the photographs again and all this talk of the castle and its slaves, the fact that such a place actually existed, had created a knot of arousal she found hard to ignore. It came as something of a shock to her to realise that she didn't have to ignore it. She had the means to that particular end right here in the manilla envelope.

'You're a big boy, aren't you, Curtis?' After all, she had Curtis completely under her thumb and could see no reason at all why she shouldn't exercise her power.

Curtis blushed. 'Not particularly.'

'Oh, but you are. I've seen it for myself, after all. A sight like that makes a girl . . .' she squirmed on her seat, '. . . hungry. Did you know I happen to be staying here?'

'No.'

'I've got a nice room at the back with a nice comfortable bed. Wouldn't you like to see it?'

'Not particularly.'

Cherry laughed. 'Curtis I don't think I'm making myself clear. Perhaps I should spell it out for you. We've got a couple of hours to kill. I want you to take me up to my room. Now. I'll tell you what I want you to do with me when we get there, if you can't come up with your own ideas. Have you got that?'

'You're a real bitch, aren't you?' he said.

'You were a greedy little boy. You made a mistake. Now you've got to pay for it,' she said, standing up. 'Come on. I'm not that unattractive, am I?'

Curtis got to his feet. Cherry took his hand and marched him across the bar, the barmaid's eyes following them both. She knew Cherry was staying in the hotel and would probably have guessed where they were going. She smiled at Curtis and scowled at Cherry in quick succession.

The bedroom was on the first floor. It overlooked the car park.

'That's better,' Cherry said, closing the bedroom door and leaning against it. Her heart was thumping.

'What do you want?' Curtis said, staring at her with an expression of distaste.

'I'd have thought that was obvious,' she said. 'Come here.' She beckoned him with her index finger.

Grudgingly he stepped forward. She reached up and kissed him on the mouth, licking her tongue against his lips. He did not react, keeping his mouth firmly closed.

'You'll have to do better than that,' she said, pressing herself into his body, her belly worming against his.

And he did. He threw one arm around her neck and the other behind her knees and scooped her into his arms effortlessly. He strode over to the bed and dropped her down on it, then fell on top of her. His hand thrust up under her skirt as his mouth screwed against hers. As his tongue plunged between her lips he wrestled her tights down at the front, pushed his hands underneath them and into the crotch of her panties. He pulled it aside and drove his fingers up into her vagina without the slightest hesitation, reaming into her until they could go no further, his knuckles hard against her labia.

'Is that what you wanted?' he hissed, breaking the kiss for a second, then resuming, chewing on her lips hungrily and not letting her answer.

Her vagina had not had time to react and was dry. But

The Master's Diary

this sudden intrusion produced an instant liquidity that slicked his fingers as they stroked back and forth. His other hand groped her chest, moving down inside the neckline of the tight, white top to find her breasts. His hand squeezed the soft flesh, then pinched her right nipple so hard it made her gasp. It also made her sex contract around him sharply.

'You little bitch,' he said. He pulled himself up to his knees, his fingers still buried in her sex, and used his other hand to unbutton and unzip his trousers. He pulled them down with his cotton briefs, then took his cock in his hand. His burgeoning erection hardened rapidly in his fist.

'Lovely,' Cherry said, raising her head to look at him. She wriggled her body down on his fingers and felt an enormous wave of pleasure.

'I'll show you,' he said angrily.

He pulled his hand out from between her legs, extracting it from her tights with difficulty, then caught her by the hips and spun her on to her stomach. He flipped her skirt up over her hips and grabbed the waistband of the tights, pulling them down over her pert, round arse. He got them to her knees, then went back for the small white panties that had folded themselves into the cleft of her buttocks. These were pulled to her knees too.

Cherry levered her bottom up towards him, so he could see the lips of her sex. This sudden assault had created a pulsing core of arousal centred in her vagina where his fingers had been. But it was spreading out rapidly, her clit and her nipples already involved, the rest of her body catching up as her nerves were set on edge.

Curtis tore off his shirt, then grasped Cherry by the hips, pulling her into a kneeling position. He pushed his hands between her legs, caught the crotch of the tights and panties in his hand and wriggled them down over her knees and down to her ankles. Stripping off her shoes he pulled the two garments over her feet.

'Open your legs,' he said, his voice thick with passion.

Cherry obeyed, squirming her knees apart. She felt his hand travel over her buttocks and down between her legs, momentarily parting her labia. Then he gripped her firmly on the flanks again and pulled her back towards him, just as he pushed forward. His cock jabbed into her wet and silky sex. He thrust up as far as he could go, the crown of his cock butting against the neck of her womb.

He did not pull back. His fingers dug into the flesh of her hips, pulling her back on him as he pressed forward, seemingly determined to bury himself in her, his cock rocking slightly from side to side as it nosed millimetres deeper.

Cherry felt her sex clinging to him. Right at the very top of her quim she could feel his glans twitching. Her sex was stretched in every direction by the size of him, her labia and her clitoris pulled taut. Now she knew exactly what the girl in the little copse had felt. Instantly, she felt herself coming, the sensation of being so completely filled, of having his sword of flesh so deep inside her, making an orgasm inevitable. As the flood of feeling coursed through her, it was accompanied by a marvellous sensation, as her sex seemed to be opening for him, letting his cock in deeper, into some secret place. Whether this caused a second orgasm or just a second phase of the first she could not tell. All that mattered was the squirming pleasure that raked through every nerve.

Curtis paid no attention to her ecstatic distress. He began pounding into her, pulling his cock almost all the way out of her, then lunging back in, using all his considerable strength to thrust into her as powerfully as he could. Each stroke seemed to take him deeper, opening her up further, his glans penetrating into new depths, where her nerves were raw and untried.

She gasped at each impact but he was moving so fast, his hips sawing back and forth with such speed, that the noise became almost continuous, an increasing crescendo of sound.

And that egged him on. The more she wailed the more he

wanted to make her wail, his anger still consuming him. His whole body was concentrated on driving his cock into her, stabbing her with it.

Cherry was barely aware of her voice. She was not aware of anything but her sex. Everything had narrowed down to the tight tube of flesh that was being battered so relentlessly. It was totally out of control. He seemed to have breached some secret barrier in her cunt and was buried in a place no man had been before, a place where every nerve was capable of feelings so acute they were creating yet another orgasm. Her sex gripped him tightly, trying to hold him in place, every muscle locked rigid, her voice producing a noise like some dying animal. The whole pub could probably hear her, but there was not a single thing she could do about it.

This time he stopped the hammering thrusts. He felt her body gripping him and waited until the rigor had dissipated.

Cherry felt him slowly withdrawing. 'No,' she cried.

She wanted to feel him spunk. She wanted that as much as she'd wanted anything.

'I thought you'd got what you wanted,' he said.

'It's your turn . . . don't you want to come?'

'What, did you think I'd finished with you?' he mocked. He grasped her hips tightly again and directed his cock upward into the little corona of her anus.

'No,' she repeated for a different reason.

'Yes,' he said.

She twisted her head around to look at him. He was staring down at the cleft of her buttocks and grinning broadly.

'You're too big.' She had been buggered before but not by a man as big as Curtis.

'You can take it.'

He thrust forward. The ring of muscles resisted. He thrust again. The muscles relaxed and his glans slid into her rear, the juices from her own sex providing the necessary lubrication.

Cherry felt an explosion of pain. She cried out. He had

only penetrated an inch of so but it felt like her anus was on fire. He was readying himself to push again.

'No,' she begged.

He ignored her. His cock pressed forward. The searing pain got worse. Then, suddenly, she felt something else. It wasn't like the pleasure she had as he fucked her so aggressively, but it was pleasure nevertheless, a pleasure on the same frequency as pain and just as intense. She moaned as it rolled over her in big waves, the crests lifting her nearer to ecstasy, the troughs dropping her closer to pain.

He thrust forward again. She could feel his balls banging against her labia. Another set of waves rolled out, but though the pleasure was even more acute there was no accompanying pain this time. She began to wallow in the intensity of the feelings, abandoning her fear. It was quite different. In her quim she had been aware of him as part of her, getting as much feeling from his cock as from the throbbing nerves of her vagina and clitoris. But in her rear she seemed only to be able to feel him, every vein and ridge of his erection, every pulse of blood somehow magnified so they took her over completely.

His left hand was sliding around the top of her thigh. She felt it brush against her downy pubic hair, then descend into her labia. It parted the rubbery folds of flesh and found her clitoris, not a difficult feat considering it had swollen to the size of a lozenge. Trapping it between his thumb and finger he pinched the little bud of flesh, then pulled it up towards her belly. Cherry moaned. The sharp pang of pleasure this produced shot through her body, making her rear passage contract around his cock. This, in turn, set off another volley of sensation from the tortured nerves there, the pain now almost totally banished by the extremes of pleasure.

She was coming again. But he wasn't finished with her yet. The fingers deserted her clitoris and pushed up the long slit of her sex to her vagina. Before she realised what he was going to do, he had done it, plunging two fingers – or was it three? – deep inside her, then sliding alongside his erection, the two only separated by the inner surfaces of Cherry's body.

Pain momentarily gained prominence again. The fingers stretched her rear almost as much as they stretched her vagina, and shards of pain lanced through her sex. But, as before, they were followed by a pleasure so extreme it felt like something she had never experienced before.

Her orgasm was overtaking her rapidly. What's more, she knew he was coming too. It was difficult to keep track of what was happening. The huge waves rolled over her. She felt herself lifted by them, carried along like something that didn't have a body any more and was floating. That didn't mean she didn't feel every twitch and spasm of his cock, or that each movement didn't provoke a new flood of sensation. His fingers were pounding in and out of her, imitating what his cock had done minutes before. She realised he was using them to finger his erection, almost as if he was wanking himself inside her. For some reason that idea aroused her even further. Suddenly her body turned to jelly, the tightness of her anus disappearing. He penetrated deeper, taking her over completely, no resistance left.

That's when she felt his cock jerk reflexively, his fingertips moving against it, pressing the flesh of her vagina backward into it. Immediately, his spunk spattered out into her. She could feel every jet. Each produced a spate of feelings so strong that if she had not already been coming, she would have come over and over again. It felt as though that's what she did anyway, one peak of pleasure giving way to another.

In time, though how long she did not know, his cock softened. His fingers were pulled from her body. His soaking wet cock dropped out too. She rolled over and looked at him. He was still angry, the expression on his face set.

'Am I off the hook now?' he said.

She smiled. 'That wasn't so bad, was it?' She felt a trickle of wetness escaping from her anus. It made her shudder.

'Am I off the hook?'

'Just smuggle me into the house and you have my word those photographs will never see the light on day. Unless you'd like to keep them, for old times' sake?'

'No thank you.'

She picked up the phone.

'What are you doing?'

'Ordering something to eat. I'm starving. Will you join me?'

The boot of the Rolls was carpeted and spacious. There was a rug in there and it was quite easy to get comfortable. Cherry had climbed inside as soon as they'd got to the turn-off to the lane.

She heard the gates clanging as they opened and heard the noise of the tyres change as the tarmac surface gave way to the gravel of the driveway. The car rolled as it took several bends, then turned left sharply. After a minute or two it turned left again then came to a halt. Cherry heard an electric motor whirring and a loud metal clunk. The car started forward, then stopped. The engine was turned off. The electric motor whirred again and again there was a metal clunk.

Cherry heard footsteps. The boot lid opened.

'Hi,' she said in a whisper.

'We're here,' he said grudgingly.

'So I gather.' She scrambled out of the boot. They were in a large garage. Standing next to the Rolls was a bright red Ferrari Testarossa, and next to that, a metallic silver Aston Martin DB5. More prosaically, at the far end was a Jeep and a light blue Ford Transit. 'I see Manville likes his cars.'

'He can afford them.'

'How do we get into the house?'

'*You*. I'm not allowed in the house. I live in the stable block over here.' He pointed in the direction of the garage door.

'All right, so how do *I* get in?'

'Follow me.'

He led the way to the back of the garage. A small door

The Master's Diary

opened out on to a courtyard. Cherry gazed up at the back of the imposing Victorian 'folly'. She had dressed for stealth, a black Lycra body over opaque black Lycra leggings and black calf-length boots.

'Which way?' she whispered.

He took her hand and pulled her towards the back of the castle. There were several doors. Curtis headed towards one of them. He tried the handle. It was locked.

'Locked,' he said.

'So I see.'

'Come on. I don't think they lock up very securely. Not with all the perimeter security.'

There were no lights at the windows. They edged their way along the back wall, trying every door and window, but they were all locked. They turned the corner and were greeted by a flood of light coming from the downstairs windows at the front. There was the sound of music too, the lyrical strains of a Mozart opera.

'The curtains are open,' Curtis said, stopping dead in his tracks.

'Let's try the other side,' she said, pulling him back the way they had come. They walked the length of the castle and were just about to turn the corner on the other side when Cherry spotted a small, half-open window set at shoulder height. 'There,' she said.

'Too small,' Curtis, whispered.

'No it's not. I can get in there. Just lift me up.'

'You'll get stuck.'

'Don't be ridiculous. Come on, Curtis. Lift me up and you're off the hook. And don't worry. If I get caught I promise I won't mention you.'

'Right. Face the wall. Open your legs.'

Cherry did as she was told. She felt Curtis bending over and suddenly his head was projecting through her thighs. With her crotch firmly settled on his neck he straightened up.

Trying to ignore the rush of feelings this unusual manoeuvre had created, her whole nether region distinctly sore from the hammering he had given it, she reached up to the window and pulled it open. Using his shoulder as a stepping stone she squirrelled her way in, until her waist was resting on the windowsill.

Inside she could see a small larder. Fortunately, there were sturdy shelves on all the walls which she could use as a ladder to make her way down to the floor.

Outside she heard Curtis's footsteps receding into the distance. She was on her own.

The larder door opened with a creak that she thought would attract the attention of the whole house. She waited in the corridor outside expectantly but heard nothing move. The distant tinkle of Mozart echoed through the halls.

Carefully she tip-toed towards the front of the house. She hadn't really planned what she was going to do. She supposed the best thing to do was to find Angela Blake and ask her to explain her fascination with Manville Mason. Then she would demand to see Manville, face him with her evidence and ask him to confirm or deny her story. She had parked her car on the main road at the end of the lane. A quick walk to it and she could drive overnight to London, ready to see her editor first thing in the morning. It would make his day. It would make his week and possibly his whole month. They would put on at least 100,000 copies. What's more the story had legs. Once it was public knowledge, Cherry was sure she could trace more of the women who had spent time at the castle. With any luck some of them might be famous too. The story would run and run.

Finding Angela Blake was another matter. She had asked Curtis, but he had no idea about the layout of the house let alone where the slaves were quartered. She wished she'd read the book more carefully. She seemed to remember the slaves had been kept in cells at the top of the house. Or was it in the dungeons? She decided to try upstairs first.

She worked her way into a vast vestibule. Light spilled from

The Master's Diary

what was clearly the living room. She could smell the smoke of a log fire and hear the strains of Don Giovanni quite clearly now – '*Madamina, il catalogo è questo delle belle che amò il padron mio.*' She reached the foot of the stone staircase and crept up to the first floor. The corridor was lit brightly and she had no trouble seeing a smaller staircase at the far end. She walked along the carpeted hallway.

'*Qu'est ce que vous faites?*'

The voice stopped her in her tracks.

'*Pas ici.*' The tone was annoyed. She turned around to see a small, stout man with short legs and a shiny, bald head approaching her rapidly. 'What are you doing here?' he snapped.

'I . . . I . . .' She couldn't think of a single thing to say.

'I wasn't expecting you until the morning. No one told me you were coming early. What are you doing wandering about here?'

'I just thought—'

'Did no one tell you to wait?'

'No, I just—'

'*Tant pis.*' He grabbed her arm, his fingers fat but powerful. '*Vous êtes ici, maintenant.*' He pulled her in the direction she had been heading, towards the narrow stone staircase. 'Up,' he said releasing her at the bottom.

Cherry climbed the stairs, not at all sure what she should do. He had undoubtedly mistaken her for someone else, but if she told him the truth now he would throw her out, and any chance of getting to see Angela Blake would be gone. What's more, security would be increased and she was unlikely to get another chance. The opportunity for an exclusive would be gone. If she wanted the story she had no choice but to go along with him.

The staircase ended in a short corridor with two doors on either side and a large door at the far end. To one side of the stairs was the shaft of an ancient lift, caged in with elaborate gilt.

'*Allez, allez* . . .' he said, indicating the door at the far end.

He waddled ahead of it and opened the door, then stood aside for her to enter. The room beyond was large and plain. There was a rectangular table, a large antique walnut cupboard, a matching chest of drawers and a Windsor chair. The walls were stone and the floor polished wood.

'This is most inconvenient. Does the Master know you're here?'

'No,' she said truthfully.

'I haven't even got anything ready for you to wear. Most inconvenient. Most inconvenient.'

'I'm sorry,' she said.

'The room's not ready. The other girl doesn't leave until the morning. Oh well, it seems I have no choice. Get your clothes off. We will just have to improvise.'

'My clothes?'

'My dear girl, what on earth do you think you are here for? The parade's at eleven. Since you're here you'll have to line up too. If the Master found out you'd arrived early and weren't displayed, he'd be furious. Especially since it's for his cousin. Come on, *vite*.'

Cherry hesitated.

'*Vite. Vite*. Don't start your time here with a punishment.'

Cherry realised she had no choice. As the little Frenchman turned to the cupboard, she reached down and unclasped the three poppers that held the crotch of the leotard in place. It sprung free. She pulled it over her head. She unzipped her boots and skimmed down her leggings. She wasn't wearing panties or a bra.

Was it her imagination or did the fact of standing naked in this oddly anonymous room with a total stranger provoke a sharp pang of arousal? Perhaps it was just a reaction to the extremes of passion she had experienced with Curtis earlier. Surely what she should feel was embarrassment, not this breathless excitement?

The little man turned around. He had draped a complicated

leather harness over his arm. He appeared not to be the least interested in her naked body.

'Kneel,' he said, with absolute authority.

Chapter Nine

Henri had taken Sandra and Angela up together, dealing with Angela first, making Sandra wait in the doorway while the blonde stripped, then locking her in. Two doors in the corridor were already locked, so Sandra guessed the other slaves had been returned before them.

The single, opaque white light-fitting on the ceiling of the cell was controlled by a switch in the hall outside. Last night, after Henri had deposited her in her cell and locked the door, the light had gone off some ten minutes later. Tonight the procedure was the same. He waited while she stripped off the black lingerie and shoes, then locked the door after her. She just had time to shower and clean off her make-up before the light went off.

Sandra lay on the bed in the dark. The corridor light was left on all night, so some light spilled under the door, but it was only a faint line in the otherwise total gloom. The experience with Malcolm had left her exhausted. He had shown remarkable powers of recovery. Unlocking the cuffs he had insisted on taking Angela while she knelt on all fours on the bed, with Sandra behind him using the vibrator on his scrotum. But, despite her tiredness, it proved impossible to sleep. Her mind was whirling. She had too many things to think about. The thought that she had come so close to rebelling made her turn cold. She remembered what Manville had said about every slave reaching a breaking point and hoped that this had been hers. She didn't want to have to go through that again.

She thought about Angela too. She knew, of course, that her own desire to be submissive was shared by other women, indeed even by other men. That was the fountainhead of Manville's book. But knowing it rationally and actually seeing it were two different things. The fact that Angela's excitement was such a mirror image of her own had been a revelation. The fact that the girl obviously luxuriated in everything that was done to her validated Sandra's own feelings. And being with her, seeing her reaction to Malcolm, had made it easier to sort out precisely what she felt, and helped her to avoid the mistake that would have ended her adventure almost before it had begun.

There was another factor too. Angela was only the second woman she had been intimate with. The idea that she might be receptive to sexual advances from another woman had grown from merely thinking about Angelica and the role that character had played in the book. Marion Chandler, the role model for that character, had proved that the lust Sandra had harboured towards the fictional lesbian was capable of being developed into something real and very tangible. But what had happened with Marion had occurred in a context of absolute domination, with Marion a surrogate for the Master.

Sandra had hoped that a more equal pairing would provoke feelings that were just as strong. And it had. She had no doubts on that score now. In fact, though what Angela had done to her and what she had done to Angela had been at Malcolm's behest, she began to wonder if the passion she had felt with the girl could be explained purely as result of her obedient submission. Or had the process that had put her in touch with the deepest streams of her sexuality found another tributary?

She thought about the Master too. She wondered when he might call for her. His seeming lack of interest was deliberate, she was sure. He wanted her to understand that his attention was not something she could take for granted. The image of his hand running along the dark blue stocking of the long-

The Master's Diary

haired blonde stuck with her. How much she wished it had been her, how much she longed for him to treat her to even that meagre contact!

She wondered what he had meant about other members when he'd been talking to Malcolm in the dining room. She could make no sense of the remark. Members suggested some sort of organisation and it was clear from what Manville had said it was a secret one. The thought that the reality of what went on here was not confined to Manville or his castle was almost too much to take in.

It was difficult to know how long she had lain awake. She supposed she must finally have drifted off to sleep eventually because the noise of the key in the lock startled her awake. Breakfast was pushed through the door.

Following the same pattern as yesterday, the day was eventless. She ate breakfast and lunch without seeing a soul. She expected the door to open at any moment and Henri or Marion to enter, ready to take her to her Master but, though she heard footsteps outside on two or three occasions, they did not come for her. She tortured herself with the thought that Manville had asked for one of the other girls, in preference to her. She began to wonder if he wanted her at all, whether he had just brought her here to serve his guests and never had any intention of using her himself. In the car, after all, he had barely touched her. Even when she had been bound and exposed on the metal frame in the Hampstead house he had made no attempt to do anything but watch, so quietly that she hadn't realised he'd been there.

The awful truth might be that he would never give her his time, consigning her to limbo. When the five days were up, he would send her away without a second glance.

As the day progressed, as the footsteps came and went outside in the corridor but never approached her door, Sandra became more and more depressed. At one stage, in a mood of defiance, she sat on the bed and began to play with her sex, trying to energise her clitoris by prodding it to and fro while her other hand squeezed one of her tenderised nipples. But her body stubbornly refused to be cajoled into any sort of sexual feeling. Her clitoris was totally unresponsive and as a result of the total absence of sexual passion, the pain from her nipple was not transmogrified into any semblance of pleasure. Even her vagina refused to liquefy, despite her efforts to conjure up the events of last night. She gave up in disgust, annoyed at her own body's unresponsiveness. Defying her Master was not that easy it seemed. His control was pervasive.

She had no idea what time it was when, finally, the footsteps clacked on the stone floor and the noise of the key in the lock set her heart beating ten to the dozen. At last, she said to herself. At long last.

The door opened.

'Up.' It was Marion.

'What is it?'

'Aren't you forgetting something?' Marion's voice was cold and hard. She was wearing a black silk robe belted tightly at the waist, and high-heeled black satin slippers.

'Mistress.'

'Just come over here.'

Sandra scrambled to her feet. As her breasts swung against her arms her sore nipples reacted with a stinging pain, a thousand little needles lancing into them. She winced.

'Are they sore?' Marion asked with no real concern in her voice.

'Yes, Mistress.'

'I bet they are.'

'What's going to happen, Mistress?' Sandra knew she wasn't supposed to ask such a question, but after a day of neglect she was anxious to know her fate.

'Don't you know better than to ask questions? Put these on.'

Marion was holding white leather pants. She handed them to Sandra, who stepped into them and drew them up her legs. They were like a pair of hot-pants, the leather tight. It

The Master's Diary

covered the whole of her belly at the front, but the back was a different matter. The leather had been cut away to completely expose the two fleshy ovals of her buttocks, with only a narrow thong running up between the cleft of her bottom to the waist. This central divide was very tight and had the effect of separating her buttocks as well has emphasising their nakedness.

'And this,' Marion said. This time she was holding out a white leather bra, but as Sandra discovered, it had no cups, only a web of leather straps that surrounded her breasts, in the centre of which was a shiny metal ring that circled each nipple.

'All right, now follow me,' Marion said, as Sandra clipped the leather around her body. The cold metal surrounding her nipples made them pucker instantly. Perhaps that was the intention.

Marion marched down to the narrow staircase. Sandra followed. They got to the first floor and when Marion turned towards the Master's bedroom, Sandra felt her heart thumping like a drum in her chest. It looked as though her worst nightmare was about to be dispelled.

The redhead opened the door without knocking and shepherded Sandra through. She took her by the arm and led her all the way across the room to a small door on the other side. The door was already ajar. She pushed Sandra inside.

The room beyond was long and narrow and lined, on one side, with racks of clothes and, on the other, with custom-made drawers with glass fronts. Most of the clothes were men's and obviously belonged to Manville, but there was a small section of women's dresses, mostly made from silk and satin and lace. At the far end was a large, full-length mirror. Marion marched Sandra to the mirror, then opened one of the glass-fronted drawers, taking out a small cosmetics case. Quickly and expertly she dusted Sandra's cheeks with blusher and made up her eyes. She painted on a line of lipstick and brushed on mascara. Putting the case back she took out a hairbrush and a tortoiseshell hair slide.

It was a different experience from the last time Sandra had been made-up. Then, she had not been able to see what was being done to her. This time she could see her face change in front of her eyes. That didn't mean it was any less odd a feeling, or any less thrilling. The fact that she was not even allowed to make herself up underlined her lack of choice in every other area. Her needs and desires were simply irrelevant.

'Turn around,' Marion said, then brushed Sandra's hair and folded it into the slide at the nap of her neck. 'That's better.' There was a long rack of shoes under the clothes rails and again, though most of them were for men, at one end there was a section of women's high-heels. Marion rooted among them, turning up a pair of white shoes with a gold-coloured, spiky heel. They were not as high as the ones Sandra had worn last night.

'Put these on,' Marion said, dropping them on the floor.

'Am I here to see the Master?' Sandra asked, unable to contain her curiosity. She climbed into the shoes.

'You're here to do what I tell you to do.' Marion took her arm and piloted her back into the bedroom. She positioned her at the foot of the bed. 'Stand there,' she ordered, sitting down on the armchair with the matching footstool. She pushed the stool away and crossed her long legs. Ultra sheer white nylon sheathed her legs. She tossed her foot up and down impatiently, the black satin slipper balanced on her toes.

Sandra stood perfectly still. She thought she could hear a noise coming from the bathroom. Her pulse was still racing. She was certain now that the Master had asked specifically for her. If that was the case she was determined to show him she could be as perfect a slave as Angela, a 'natural' like her. Even if he planned to torment and disappoint her as he had the first time she had been brought to his bedroom she wouldn't mind. After the despair she had felt this afternoon, even that would be better than his neglect.

The bathroom door opened. Manville had obviously been

taking a shower. His hair was wet and apart from a small towel wrapped around his waist he was naked. He was using another towel to dry his hair.

'How charming,' he said, staring at Sandra. 'She looks quite obscene dressed like that, doesn't she?'

'She has a very good figure,' Marion said.

'Yes, she does.' He walked up to Sandra, his eyes roaming her body. He raised his hand and touched her cheek. It was the sort of gesture of tenderness she had craved. His touch was electric. She shivered. His hand descended to her nipples surrounded by the metal rings. He stroked each one with the tip of his finger as gently as if he were brushing the wing of a butterfly.

'Are they sore?'

'Yes, Master.' Her mouth was so dry her voice croaked, hardly able to pronounce the words.

He raised his dark brown eyes to look into hers. Their impact on her was transfixing. 'I'm not supposed to have favourites. You know that, don't you?'

'Yes, Master.'

'I have to treat all the slaves equally. But there is something about you. What shall I call it? An acceptance. A willingness. It runs deep.' He looked as though he was about to say something else, then changed his mind. His tone of voice became more businesslike. 'My cousin is visiting tonight. He will be able to choose from all the slaves. You will be paraded for him later. But first I thought . . .'

He nodded to Marion. The redhead got to her feet and stripped off the silk robe. She was completely naked underneath it apart from white stockings with deep, white lace welts that clung to her long, sensuous thighs of their own accord. Her big, very round breasts rode high on her chest, apparently needing no support, their nipples already erect. Her pubic hair was thick and curly. It had been trimmed into a neat triangle.

'Do you want her bound?' she asked.

'No, I don't think she needs it.' The Master stretched himself out on the bed, propping his head against the pillows and crossing his ankles. 'But a blindfold, I think.'

Sandra saw Marion smile. The redhead walked to the bedside chest of drawers and slid open the bottom drawer. She extracted a long, thick strip of black silk. Quickly, she wrapped it around Sandra's eyes, knotting it so tightly the silk pressed against her eyeballs.

Darkness descended. The sound of her own breathing seemed suddenly to intensify. It was short and irregular. She heard Marion moving but could not identify in which direction. Then she felt the heat of her body at her side again.

'I want you to bend over, spread your legs wide apart and grasp your ankles.' Marion's voice was emotionless.

Sandra did as she was told. She had been facing away from the bed so knew this position would provide Manville with a perfect view of the whole plane of her sex, tightly covered by white leather. Her long hair trailed on the carpet. She started as Marion's hand touched her hip. It glided over Sandra's bottom, following the strip of tight white leather down to her sex, then caressing each naked buttock in turn.

'Which one?' Sandra heard the redhead ask.

'The crop,' the Master replied.

It didn't take much imagination to guess what they had planned for her. The leather pants exposed her buttocks and the position she had been made to adopt tilted them upward at the perfect angle, but if Sandra still needed confirmation Manville had just given it to her. She was to be whipped. She tightened her grip on her ankles, determined not to protest.

Marion's hand rested on the small of her back. Sandra heard a swish of air and a line of pain burnt its way horizontally across her bottom. She gasped. Immediately she heard a second swish and another cut of the whip sliced across the ample curves of her flesh, making them quiver. It was followed by a third. Two of the strokes had intersected and the pain was most intense at that point, but the whole of her bottom seemed to have turned to fire. She could feel the heat radiating out. But it was radiating inward too, and that was what was affecting her most. As with the pain she had felt from the silver nipple-clips, her body had found a way to convert pain into overwhelming pleasure. She felt her pussy respond with an extraordinary flood of sensation.

'Three more?' It was Marion's voice again.

'Oh, yes, I think so.'

Thwack. There was no pause between the Master's voice and the cut of the whip. This stroke was the lowest so far and the most painful, the flesh trapped against the bone. Even though the sharper the initial pain, the sweeter the rush of pleasure that followed it, Sandra was not sure how much of this she could take. In the blackness behind the blindfold she tried desperately to keep control, her fingers locked around her ankles like claws of steel.

Thwack. The noise echoed around the room. Sandra could no longer distinguish exactly where the whip fell. Her whole bottom was seething. But the pain was gradually giving way to pleasure, the cut of the whip on flesh creating a sexual sensation that vibrated every nerve in her body.

Thwack. Sandra moaned. It was quite obviously not a moan of pain. The heat radiating from her buttocks was matched by the fire in her sex. She actually thought she could feel her juices running out of her quim. Her clitoris was so swollen it had forced its way out from between her labia and was rubbing against the tight leather crotch of the pants. As for her nipples the soreness they had felt earlier only increased their sensitivity. They were pulsating, creating waves of pleasure on the same frequency as the pleasure from her pussy.

'You can see she loves it,' the Master said.

'And this?'

Marion's hand touched Sandra's back. It descended to her buttocks where it had been moments before. But its effect now was dramatic. Sandra almost lost balance as the cool fingers and palm of Marion's hand caressed the tortured, burning flesh, circling each buttock in turn. For a moment Sandra thought she was actually going to come. It was as though every inch of her buttocks had been turned into an erogenous zone, quite as sensitive and responsive as her clitoris, the fingers creating a trail of pleasure.

'Stand up,' Marion said, pulling her hand away.

With relief, Sandra straightened up. The movement created a whole new panoply of sensations in her bottom which she tried desperately to ignore.

She felt Marion's fingers working at what passed for a bra. The leather slackened and was pulled away. Marion was standing behind her. Sandra felt the heat from her buttocks bouncing back off Marion's belly.

'She's shaking like a leaf,' Marion said.

'I like to see that.'

Marion wrapped her arms around Sandra's body, crossing them over the front of her chest, then cupping her breasts in her hands and squeezing none too gently. As the feeling lanced through her tender nipples, Marion stepped forward, her silky soft belly rubbing against Sandra's red-wealed buttocks. The wave of feeling this double assault produced made Sandra throw her head back and cry out, the noise rattling in her throat. For the second time in so many minutes she was on the point of orgasm. In the darkness behind the blindfold she saw fluorescent scarlet light. She found herself rubbing her buttocks from side to side almost unconsciously, her body hungry for the sensation this produced.

Marion's hands dropped to the waistband of the pants. She unbuttoned them and unzipped them. 'Take them off now,' she said quietly, moving away.

Sandra eased the pants down her legs, not without creating a tingle of pain as the leather slid down her bottom. She allowed them to drop to her feet then stepped out of them.

'Do you think we should have her shaved?' the Master said. Previously his voice had seemed detached, but Sandra hoped she was not imagining that it had become slightly higher pitched.

'Yes, I think we should.' Marion said. Sandra felt the woman's hand brushing against her curly pubic hair. 'We should have her pierced too.'

'She may not get that far,' the Master says.

'But if she does?'

'I'll think about it. Take the blindfold off now.'

Marion's fingers loosened the black silk. She let it fall to Sandra's neck, then unknotted it, sliding it down over her breasts. She covered both of them with it and sawed it across both nipples.

The Master, Sandra saw, had pulled the towel away. His mushroom-shaped cock was erect and he had circled it with his fist.

'I want you to kneel on the bed, on all fours,' Marion said, finally letting the silk fall to the floor. 'With your legs spread apart.' She patted Sandra's rump to indicate that she should do it right away.

Sandra did as she was told.

'Higher up,' Marion ordered.

Sandra crawled up towards the Master, until her hands were level with his waist. She could have dipped her head forward and sucked his cock into her mouth with the greatest of ease. It was a temptation that had to be resisted. She could see it was slicked with his own secretions.

Looking over her shoulder Sandra saw Marion laying on her back on the bed behind her. Then she wriggled forward until her face was immediately under Sandra's sex.

'Now straighten up and lower yourself on to my mouth,' Marion said, her voice as calm as if she had been ordering Sandra to make a bed.

Sandra straightened her back. She could see Marion's head lying between her thighs. Slowly, she lowered herself down on to her mouth, her sex already spasming at the prospect of what was to come. She looked at Manville, whose eyes were locked on the apex of her thighs.

Sandra felt as if her pussy were melting over Marion's mouth, hot and liquid, the hard bud of her swollen clitoris the only geographical feature in a sea of pliability. But it was soon joined by the rigidity of Marion's tongue which plunged into the morass and found its target, pushing the hard little bud from side to side. At the same time, she worked one arm under Sandra's thigh and prodded her fingers upwards to Sandra's vagina. In a second, two fingers were playing at its mouth, not penetrating but scissoring apart, stretching the opening this way and that.

The heat from her bottom and the incessant throbbing had not slackened but as Marion's fingers and tongue probed her pussy the two sets of feeling seemed to connect, feeding off each other, the one amplifying the other. The feeling in her rump was changing too. Whereas before the whole area was alight, every inch burning with the same intensity, now each of the six weals was distinct and separate, each forming a line of sensitivity.

In seconds, Sandra was coming. The physical sensations were coalescing with the mental, the fact of what Manville had said to her and the way he was looking at her now, his erection clearly showing he was taking pleasure in her, making her mind run quite as wild as her body. The fears of the afternoon had proved to be totally unfounded and her relief was as palpable as Marion's well-practised tongue.

That was not to say that of all the feelings that coursed through her, it was not Marion's tongue that was the most provocating. The redhead had found the epicentre of Sandra's sexual being and was exploiting it ruthlessly. The tiniest of movements, the slightest flick of the tip of her tongue, produced an earthquake of response. Sandra was coming. In fact she was sure her orgasm had started the moment she'd lowered herself on to Marion's mouth but this orgasm was not short and sharp, but long and luxuriant, whirling and eddying through her body, constantly re-defining itself, affecting different areas with different intensities, unwilling to release its grip.

Eventually it died, though not without a whole series of tremors and aftershocks. She fell forward, supporting herself on all fours again.

Marion squirmed away. She 'walked' up the bed on her knees until she was directly in front of Sandra.

'You know what I want you to do now?' she said.

Before Sandra could reply, the answer became obvious. Marion scissored her long legs apart on either side of Sandra's body and lay back on the bed, arching her sex up off the sheet, her labia opening, the hair that surrounded them already plastered back by her wetness.

Sandra did not hesitate. Her orgasm had not sated her lust. She wanted to feel the softness of a woman's sex again. She dropped her head down and brought her mouth to within an inch of Marion's quim. Sandra could smell the flowery aroma of her perfume mixed with the much more basic scent of sex. It was an intoxicating combination. She inhaled deeply. She could see the whole of the redhead's plump labia and the little puckered hole of her anus. She stuck her tongue out and began by licking the whole furrow of it, from anus to fourchette, spreading it apart with the whole breadth of her tongue. Then, experimentally, she pressed the tip of her tongue against her anus. She felt the little ring of muscles relax and her tongue sink inward. Marion moaned. She screwed her tongue deeper.

The redhead was undulating her hips. Sandra saw that she had grabbed both of her breasts in her hands and was squeezing them, her fingers almost buried in the spongy flesh. She eased one up towards her mouth, baring her lips so Sandra could see her teeth pinching the dark brown bud.

Sandra moved her tongue up to the redhead's clit. It was not difficult to find. She pushed it back, then tapped it, making her tongue into a tiny hammer. She felt Marion's body vibrate with each blow. With the fingers of her right hand she played the same game Marion had played on her, easing her fingers into the mouth of her vagina, then spreading them apart, stretching the flesh like an elastic band. Then she pushed two fingers as deep as they would go. The sensation of touching a woman as intimately as this was still new enough to thrill her completely. She felt her own sex throb just as if it had been penetrated, a startling empathy between the two. Her clit, too, appeared to share the same reciprocity. As Sandra began to drag Marion's clitoris from side to side, hers responded exactly as if the same thing were happening to it.

She could feel Marion was coming. The silky wet walls of her vagina were expanding and contracting rhythmically and her clitoris was pulsing wildly. The muscles in her thighs were becoming increasingly stretched too, the taut, lacy welts of the stockings cutting a groove in her flesh. Then she too trembled. Sandra saw her stretch her arms out above her head, her fingers stretched out too, as though trying to clutch at something. She cried out loud, one long, continuous keening sound.

Sandra suddenly realised the Master was no longer at her side. She could not see him. Her view was restricted by Marion's thighs. But then she felt his weight moving behind her.

The shock of his touch was as electric as it had been before. His hands gripped her hips, almost at the same time as she felt his cock, hot and rock hard, nudging between the soft wetness of her labia. The mental shock was as great as the physical. She had wanted this from the first day she had met him. Longer than that, in fact, since she had wanted the Master he had written about since the first day she'd read the book, fantasising that she was in Clara's place.

The sword of flesh did not waver. It thrust forward right into her vagina, riding up on the flood of her juices until it was so deep inside her she could feel the glans against the neck of her womb and his pubic bone grinding into her buttocks. She felt a hundred sensations at the same time. Her tortured bottom responded with a stab of pain as his belly slapped into it. Her vagina contracted around him reflexively. Her clitoris pulsed at the same speed as her heart and her nipples puckered even more tightly, stretching the rest of the flesh of her breasts tight like tenterhooks. She pressed her mouth down on Marion's sex, sucking on her labia, wanting that sensation too, the delicious softness of a woman and the thrusting hardness of a man. She came so quickly that there seemed to be no gap between feeling the first signs of the onset of orgasm and the orgasm itself, the explosion of feeling dwarfing what she had felt before.

Manville began pounding into her, his balls swinging against her labia on the inward stroke. Sandra could feel every inch of him, every pulse of blood, every ridge and vein. Her orgasm only made her more aware, concentrating her whole being on the phallus that lanced into her.

She felt him driving himself faster, his powerful muscles plunging his cock deep inside her. Then, at the moment when she was sure he must lose all control, his hands, like talons, clutching at her hips, he pulled right out of her, jammed his cock into the cleft of her bottom and came, a parabolic arc of spunk jetting out of him and spattering down on Sandra's back and buttocks. A second gush exploded with almost as much vigour. And still more oozed out of him, running down over her buttocks, hot, wet and sticky.

'Has Andrew arrived?' the Master asked.

'Yes,' Marion replied. 'He's in the sitting room listening to Mozart.'

'Is everything ready for him?'

'Yes. Henri's going to take the others to the library.'

'You'd better take her back then.'

Marion had got up off the bed and was wrapping herself in the black silk robe. 'Are you coming down?' She stooped to pick up the discarded leather pants and bra.

'No. Let him get on with it. He doesn't need me. I'm going to do some work.'

'Up,' Marion said to Sandra, pulling her by the arm.

Sandra was completely dazed, as if not really in contact with the world. She glanced back at Manville as Marion guided her towards the door. He had taken a big, leather-bound notebook out of the bedside chest and had rested it on his knees and was now writing in it rapidly.

'One day, I'll have you to myself,' Marion said as they walked up the narrow staircase. 'I'm looking forward to that.'

There was a hint of menace in Marion's tone, but Sandra didn't care. She was incapable of feeling anything but the pleasure that vented from the hard core of satisfaction her Master had created.

In the short corridor at the top of the stairs Sandra was not surprised to see that all the doors of the other cells were open and their occupants gone. Henri was standing in her cell, looking impatient.

'There you are,' he said.

Sandra saw a leather harness lying on the bed. There were shoes and clothes too.

'She's all yours,' Marion said.

'I see you have given her a little colour.' Henri was looking at Sandra's bottom.

'I went easy on her,' Marion said with a cruel smile. 'She won't be so lucky next time.'

Henri picked up one of the garments on the bed. 'Put this on,' he said to Sandra. He was holding up a black body. It was made from exactly the same sort of dernier of nylon used for stockings and was therefore almost transparent.

'The other girl has arrived.'

'What other girl?'

'The replacement. I thought she was not due until tomorrow.'

'She wasn't.'

'Well, she's come tonight. I've put her in there.' He nodded towards the end of the corridor. 'I thought I'd take her to the library too.'

'I don't understand. I didn't hear a car.'

Henri shrugged.

Sandra had climbed into the body. The nylon was tight and flattened her breasts back against her chest slightly. The legs were cut high on the hip, revealing the crease of her pelvis, the gusset so narrow it disappeared between the folds of her sex, cutting up between her buttocks and leaving them completely exposed, the six distinct pink stripes across the white flesh making it quite obvious what had been done to her.

'Now those,' he said, indicating the stockings on the bed. They were black too with the same self-supporting lacy welts that Marion was wearing. Sandra sat on the bed. She had forgotten the weals on her buttocks and winced as they reminded her of their presence. She drew the stockings up her legs. Marion watched as the sheer, shiny nylon encased her legs, the tight band of elastic under the wide black lace dimpling the flesh of her thigh. The stockings were long, their tops almost brushing her sex.

'Help me, will you?' Henri said, picking up the leather harness. It comprised of two arm-length leather straps, attached to which were three leather cuffs. He handed Marion one of the straps and she immediately pulled Sandra to her feet and spun her around. She wrapped the first cuff around the top of Sandra's left arm and buckled it tight. The second was secured just above the elbow and the third at the wrist.

Henri had performed the same function on Sandra's right arm. Then he began threading a single leather lace through the D-rings on the inner side of each cuff, criss-crossing them over Sandra's back, each pass drawing her arms together more tightly, forcing her shoulders back and her chest out. He tied the lace off at the wrist.

'*Bon*,' he said.

'Good enough to eat,' Marion said. Her hand trailed down the front of the nylon body. She touched both of Sandra's nipples. They were still puckered and stuck out from the nylon like buttons.

'It is time,' Henri said. He picked up a leather collar from the bed and buckled it around Sandra's neck. A metal leash was already clipped to it. He took the leash and led her out through the cell door.

'What's the new one like?' Marion asked.

'Don't you know? I thought you tested all *les femmes*.'

'Not all. Sometimes Manville decides for himself.'

'Well, I think she will be very much . . . what do you say . . . up the road.'

'Up my street?'

'*Exactement*. If Maurice does not choose her you can have yourself a little treat, *mais non*?' The little Frenchman handed Sandra's leash to Marion. 'Wait here, I'll go and get her.'

He walked to the end of the corridor, opened the larger door and disappeared inside.

Chapter Ten

Cherry hadn't the slightest idea what she was going to do. There was nothing she could do. Before the odd little Frenchman had started to draw the leather straps around her body she had at least had the chance to tell him the truth, even if it meant that any chance of getting to see Angela Blake and writing her story would disappear. Now, however, with the complex bondage harness securely in place, she had no choice. She was trapped and powerless, having no option but to stand exactly where he had left her.

The leather the little Frenchman had used to encase her body while she knelt in front of him was tight and unyielding. It consisted of a type of corset that was more like a cuirass, made from stiffened white leather, shaped to cinch the waist so tightly it created an hour-glass figure, the effect further emphasised as he tightened the lacing at the back, making it difficult to breathe. The corset did not cover her breasts, two crescents at the top tucking neatly under them, but a thick leather strap extended up between them to a collar that had been buckled around her neck. Another much longer strap descended from the collar at the back and attached to this were two stiff leather cuffs, one on top of the other, just below the level of her shoulder-blades. Cherry's wrists had been strapped into these, forcing her arms back and upward, and making her elbows stick out. Henri had then pulled the long rear strap up between her legs and buckled it to the front of the corset at the bottom, the wide leather burrowing its way uncomfortably into her buttocks and digging into the soft flesh at the top of her thighs.

A large ball of black rubber had been crammed into her mouth and secured by a white leather strap that the Frenchman had buckled at the back of her head. Ordering her to stand, he'd then completed the outfit by cramming her feet into high-heeled, calf-length leather boots. Cherry had never worn heels of this height. They forced her feet into an almost vertical position. As what appeared to be an afterthought, the man had wound a small white strap around her ankles and cinched it tight, making it impossible for her to take even a single step. Why he had done this she was not sure as he had locked the door of the room before he bustled away. Perhaps it was just a way of increasing her discomfort.

That, as far as she could tell, had been half an hour ago. She had stood, unable to do anything to ease the ache from her cramped shoulders, or the pain in her calf muscles and feet that the high-heels caused. She could shuffle forward slightly, a millimetre taking a huge amount of effort, working her feet against the ankle strap, to try to bring some relief by using her leg muscles. She could bend her knees to ease the bite of the leather between her thighs, but that only caused her legs to cramp and couldn't be sustained for long.

Her imagination ran riot. She was completely helpless. She tried desperately to remember Manville Mason's books. She had only read *The Master's Diary* quickly, for the purposes of research, and although she remembered the setting was a carbon copy of the castle she found herself in now, she couldn't recall much of what had happened. There were slaves and a tall, beautiful redhead who had used the girls for her own purposes, and a Master, of course, but what he had done and what else had gone on in the castle she just could not remember.

She looked down at her body. Her small, round breasts jutted out over the white leather. Her nipples were hard. She could see the leather strap emerging from her thighs and snaking up over her flat stomach. She realised, with something of a shock, that she had been unconsciously wriggling her hips from side to side, sawing her pubis against the strap, and that this was resulting in little ripples of pleasure emanating from her clit. Despite the cramp in her muscles and the overall discomfort, her body was asserting another agenda.

Oddly, perhaps, it wasn't until that moment that she thought about Peter Simmons, and what he had done to her. The memory produced a shudder of feeling that also caught her by surprise. Before watching the video with him, then improvising on its contents, Cherry had never had the faintest interest in what her sub-editor would have described as 'kinky' sex. Now, standing alone in this room, bound in an elaborate and specially designed bondage harness, in the middle of what was clearly a circle of people who shared the same proclivities, the apprehension she had felt began to change to a knot of excitement. If she was honest with herself, what Peter had done to her had aroused her deeply. It didn't take much of an effort to feel the same about the gag and the tight leather straps that held her now.

If she rubbed her thighs together she could angle the leather straps between her legs right up against her clitoris and produce a sharp stab of pleasure. She wished she could have remembered the book. Was there some sort of initiation ceremony for the newcomers? The Frenchman had mentioned a parade. What on earth would that involve, and who were the others he'd mentioned? Would one of them be Angela Blake?

Footsteps echoed outside the door. She listened intently. She thought she could hear voices but they were indistinct. After a while there were more footsteps but this time they were coming closer. She heard the key being inserted in the lock. Her heart started to pound.

The little Frenchman marched in. He dropped to his knees in front of Cherry and released the white strap that held her ankles together. Jumping to his feet again he took a shiny chain from his pocket and clipped it into a D-ring in front of the white collar around her neck. He took the leash in his right hand.

'Follow.'

Cherry tottered forward with small, diminutive steps, fearing that she might fall over. She was not prepared for the sight that greeted her in the corridor outside.

A tall, elegant redhead was holding another leash attached to a collar around the neck of a stunning, long-haired brunette. She recognised the brunette at once. It was the girl she had followed down from London, the one she had photographed with Curtis. Cherry couldn't decide which of the women was the most beautiful. The redhead was dressed in a black silk robe and satin slippers while the brunette was wearing a tight nylon body which was so transparent Cherry could see the big orbs of her breasts and the thick, but neatly trimmed, thatch of her pubic hair. Like her, the brunette's arms were tightly bound.

The redhead examined her critically.

'She's pretty, Henri,' she pronounced.

'I have no interest in such things,' the Frenchman said, airily.

'Well, I do,' the redhead said. She took a step towards Cherry and looked into her eyes. 'Look at her, she's so excited. Does she need the gag?'

The Frenchman shrugged.

The redhead walked up to Cherry. 'You're not going to scream, are you?' she asked.

Cherry shook her head.

The redhead unbuckled the white leather and pulled the rubber out of Cherry's mouth.

It was her chance to tell the truth, to escape from this nightmare. But Cherry said nothing.

'Bondage turns you on, doesn't it, girl?' the redhead said.

'Yes.' The truth was she didn't want to escape. Not now. Not with the way her body felt. It was obvious she was not the only one who could sense her arousal.

The Master's Diary

'Don't you know better than that?' the redhead admonished, slapping the strap of the gag against Cherry's thigh. The thwack of leather on flesh reverberated along the stone corridor. 'Say it.'

Cherry wasn't sure what she had done wrong.

'You need to be taught a lesson,' the redhead said, bringing the strap down again, a cut that left a red mark on Cherry's thigh. She traced her hand over Cherry's breast and down over her stomach. She seized the strap that rose from between her legs and pulled it up, making it dig deeper into her sex. Cherry gasped. 'Don't worry. I will be available to teach you everything you need to know.' The redhead was smiling a crooked smile, one side of her mouth higher than the other.

'*Allez*, Marion. We've got to take them down.'

Handing the gag to Henri, who stuffed it into his already bulging pocket, the redhead turned and led the brunette down to the lift. The four crammed into the small cage and descended to the ground floor. The music Cherry had heard earlier was still playing, the opera drawing to a close. Cherry had always loved the opera and knew Don Giovanni well. The fact that she was hearing it in such extraordinary circumstances only served to make her situation seem even more bizarre.

Marion opened the grille and pulled the brunette out by the leash. They walked in tandem behind the staircase. The redhead opened a large oak door set in a lancet arch.

Beyond the door was a large room with a high, vaulted ceiling and a massive Gothic fireplace. Logs burnt brightly in its grate, occasionally showering sparks up the chimney as one log fell from the pile. Every wall of the room was lined with shelves and every shelf was filled with books. There were whole sections of antique books bound in leather, with titles hand-tooled in gold. There were rows of paperbacks and a column of large art books. In one corner Cherry saw Manville's books, identical copies of all the editions of all his works in various languages. There were several in Japanese.

Standing in front of the fire were three other women. Each

was dressed in the same sort of *outré* costumes that she had been forced into, though each was different. There was a blonde, with long, very silky hair hanging down her back. She was wearing a red patent leather basque and red, thigh-high leather boots in the same material. Her arms had been pulled into long, red leather gloves that reached up to her armpits. The gloves had a series of eyelets all the way down one side, which had been laced together behind her back, so her arms were held tightly against each other. Standing beside her the second woman was bigger. She had wavy chestnut-coloured hair and had been dressed in a loose, peach-coloured camisole made from a semi-transparent silk. Cherry could see her big, pendulous breasts underneath it. A pair of tiny G-string panties in the same material covered her mons, its straps so tight they were buried in her ample flesh and barely visible. Two wide, white leather straps had been buckled tightly around the top of the woman's thighs, again biting into her soft flesh, and attached to each of these was a smaller cuff, into which her wrists were secured, effectively binding her arms to her sides.

And then she saw her. The third girl was also blonde and though her hair was cut into a neat bob and looked entirely different from the last picture Cherry had seen of her, there was no doubt that the girl was Angela Blake. She was dressed in an incredibly tight and very shiny yellow catsuit. It clung to every curve of her figure, but holes had been cut into the material to expose her breasts and the whole slit of her sex. The exposed flesh seemed white and vulnerable in contrast to the tight material that surrounded it.

The two new arrivals were led up to the other women and made to stand at their side.

'I'll go and get him,' Marion said.

'Is the Master coming?'

'No.'

Marion walked out of the room. The Frenchman followed her, closing the door behind him.

The Master's Diary

Cherry wondered what to do. She was just about to blurt out who she was and tell Angela she'd come to help her but soon thought better of it. It was more sensible to wait until they were alone. There was no telling how the other women would react. She thought she saw a faint smile of acknowledgement pass between the brunette and Angela that might have indicated friendship, but the other women were an unknown quantity. For the moment she decided she should do absolutely nothing to reveal herself. She was surprised at how passive the girl was, but obviously, if she had been here for some time, she had become inured to her imprisonment and the complicated bondage. Besides, she probably realised that there was no means of escape at the moment. The library door was almost certainly locked and even if it was not, where could they go? They couldn't drive, bound like this. And they could hardly run through the grounds and get over the fencing. The only thing to do was to wait until they were not so tightly bound.

As she had walked ahead of her down the corridor, she had noticed the pink marks that crossed the brunette's buttocks and was sure there was only one explanation for them. That thought tempered the excitement the tight bondage had created. She was prepared to go so far for a story, and no further. The pain of the bondage had been endurable because of her own recently discovered proclivities, but she didn't think she wanted to be whipped. Whatever happened, her first priority now was to look for a means of escape for herself and Angela.

Of course, this was a much bigger story than she'd ever imagined. She had expected to find Angela in some sort of lovelorn state, infatuated with Manville Mason and perhaps involved in some of his avowed and perverse sexual practices. She had not dreamt that she would be held in bondage with three other women. Once she escaped she would bring the police back and free them all and be the first reporter to break the story, able to write all the sordid details from first-hand experience. Her editor would be delighted.

'Well, now . . .'

The door had swung open. A tall, handsome man with a mop of thick black, curly hair walked into the room. He was in his early thirties, with a rugged face, hollow cheekbones and a square chin. His dark brown eyes had a family resemblance to Manville's.

'There's one extra than usual. She arrived early,' Marion said. She had stripped off the robe and was wearing a black satin basque, its long suspenders clipped into glossy back stockings, and matching panties. Her hands were gloved in black satin too and she held a riding crop in one of them.

'So I see,' the man said. He was dressed in a crisp white shirt and a blue tie which had been pulled down from his collar, the top button of the shirt undone. His trousers were a navy-blue and he wore black loafers. He walked up to the girls. 'This one's new,' he said, indicating the brunette.

'And this one,' Marion said, coming up to Cherry. She pressed the tip of the crop under Cherry's chin, forcing her to raise her head.

'You know my preference,' he said. He was looking Marion in the eyes. 'It's a shame about you. All the times I have been coming here. I've always wondered if you might change your mind. Do all the guests feel that way about you?'

'I don't know.'

'I fantasise about it sometimes. Imagining you . . . You're a gorgeous woman, Marion.'

'I'm never going to change my mind, Maurice. No man interests me. I don't mind them watching, but the idea of a man touching me . . .' Cherry saw her shudder.

'If there weren't so many other delights I'd be heartbroken,' he said, smiling broadly. He came up behind the brunette. 'I bet you've had some fun with this one already. Did you do this?' He was looking at her buttocks.

'Yes.'

Maurice pressed himself into the girl's back. He wrapped

a hand around her body and circled his palm against one of her breasts. 'Lovely. I'll take her.' He walked around to the bigger woman. 'Very Rodinesque,' he said. Then he came up behind Cherry. 'I'm feeling greedy,' he said. 'Her too, I think.'

Cherry saw a hint of excitement flare in his eyes as he strode back towards the door.'

'Where do you want them?'

'Down here, I think. Don Giovanni has made me feel distinctly playful.'

'It's supposed to have the reverse effect.'

'If I'm going to hell, I need to practise,' he said grinning.

As he disappeared through the door Marion came up to Cherry. She picked up the metal leash that hung down between her breasts, then pulled her over to the brunette. Picking up her leash too she led both girls out of the door and down the corridor.

'In here,' she said.

She had opened another door in another lancet-arched doorway. She released the chains and signalled that they should go inside, but she did not follow them, merely closing the door behind them. Cherry noticed that she did not lock it, however.

The room filled Cherry with horror. It was small and dimly lit, its walls and ceiling were painted black. Positioned in the middle of the floor was the sort of table doctors use for examinations, except that it was lower and had a padded suede top. Attached to the top of each of its sturdy wooden legs were leather straps. There were other straps hanging from the underside of the frame all the way down its length. Above it, crossing the ceiling, was a solid wooden beam, suspended from which were a series of metal rings and pulleys. Chains and leather cuffs hung from some, white nylon rope from others. But that was not what had caused Cherry's alarm. On one wall was a wooden rack, two parallel pieces of pine into which notches had been cut at regular intervals. Sitting neatly in the notches were a selection of different whips, some long and thin like the riding crop Marion had carried, others thick and short. There were hooks at the bottom of the rack too, and from these hung more instruments obviously designed for the same purpose as the whips. There were tawses, wooden paddles, a thick leather strap with its end split and a multi-lashed whip, each lash made from a leather thong, and each thong knotted at the end.

'Christ we've got to get out of here,' Cherry said. 'Can you get at these straps if I come up behind you?'

'Don't be ridiculous.'

'Can't you see what he's going to do to us? Do you want to be whipped again? Look at that lot. Come on. She didn't lock the door.'

'What are you talking about?' The brunette was looking at her as if she were mad.

'Don't you see, it's a chance.' Cherry wasn't thinking about Angela Blake now. The only thing that concerned her was to avoid being trussed up on the table while the man got his pleasure from applying the wicked-looking whip of his choice. 'Look, I'm a reporter. If we can escape we can bring the police back and rescue all the girls.'

'What sort of reporter?'

'I'm doing a story on Angela Blake. The blonde. The short-haired one in the library.'

'I thought I recognised her.'

'Right, let's move. I was hoping to get out of here with her. But it doesn't matter. I can interview her when we get back with the police.' That was true. It wasn't going to make any difference to the story as long as they could get out now. 'For Christ's sake, get me out of this thing.'

'Angela doesn't want to escape.'

'What do you mean?'

'None of us do.'

'Don't worry, Manville will be arrested. He won't be able to find you.'

'It's not that. We're here because we want to be. If we wanted

The Master's Diary

to leave we only have to refuse an order. We'd be sent away immediately.'

'I don't understand.'

'I think you do. I saw it in your eyes when you came into the library. You were excited. Don't tell me you weren't.'

Cherry found herself blushing. 'That was . . . I just . . . I . . . I experimented, once . . .' She couldn't think of how to explain it. But there was no denying what the brunette had seen. 'But I don't want to be whipped.'

'If you refuse, you will be sent away. It's that simple.'

'And if I don't?'

Suddenly the door opened and Maurice walked in. He was wearing a white cotton robe. His legs and feet were bare.

'Well, isn't this cosy?' he said.

Cherry expected the brunette to say something, but she remained silent. The man stood in front of her, took her cheeks in his hand and kissed her full on the mouth. Cherry could see their tongues vying for position, their lips mashed together hungrily, and felt her sex pulse. When he stepped away from her, a large bulge tented the front of the robe. He pulled the robe aside and Cherry found herself staring at his big, circumcised erection. A second pulse inside her pussy made her quiver.

'One blonde and one brunette, the perfect combination,' he said. He stood in front of Cherry and dipped his head to kiss her on the mouth. She felt his hot tongue plunge between her lips and his arms encircling her waist, crushing her body into his, his erection hard against the strap that bisected her stomach. A surge of pleasure coursed through her. Instinctively she tried to wrap her arms around him but the tug of the leather cuffs reminded her that this was not an option. That sensation of restraint, however, caused another hard, throbbing pulse of desire. It made her body tremble.

'My, you are needy,' Maurice said, obviously quite aware of her excitement. 'We'd better deal with you first.'

He broke away and went back to the brunette. Cherry saw

him unbuckling the leather harness that held her arms behind her back. The girl moaned as the leather fell away and she brought her arms around in front of her body.

'Now unstrap her arms,' he ordered as he slipped out of the robe. His body was athletic and muscular, as if he took a lot of exercise, his arms and legs thick, his stomach flat and his chest broad.

The brunette came up behind Cherry and unbuckled the first cuff. As her arm dropped out of it she felt a sharp stab of pain, the nerves pinched for so long in the same position now given their chance to protest. The other arm reacted in exactly the same way. She rubbed them in turn and rotated her shoulders to get rid of the cramp.

'Now this,' the man said, tugging on the strap that ran down Cherry's back. The brunette unbuckled it from the collar then moved around her body and released it from the front of the hardened leather corset. There were red marks where it had cut into the top of Cherry's thigh. It dropped to the floor.

'Much better,' Maurice said. 'Does that feel more comfortable?'

'Yes,' Cherry said.

'Yes, what?'

Cherry looked puzzled. She didn't understand what he meant. She looked at the brunette who was standing behind the man. She mouthed a word at her.

'Yes, Master,' Cherry said, lip-reading.

'I think you should show your gratitude, don't you? Get on your knees.' He pressed her shoulder to emphasis the point.

Cherry dropped to her knees. It was quite obvious what he expected. This whole situation was so extraordinary she hadn't the slightest idea what she should do. If what the brunette had told her was true, she only had to refuse to take the man's cock in her mouth and she would immediately be released. But that would mean she would lose the story. If they sent her away she'd never get to interview Angela Blake. Even if she was not a prisoner in the castle it was still a good

The Master's Diary

story. She told herself that was her rationale for keeping quiet. Nothing to do with the growing excitement that was making her cunt throb. She opened her lips and leant forward, gobbling his big cock into her mouth and sucking it hard.

She had always been good at this. Several of her boyfriends had told her she was the best they had ever had in this department and she was determined to show Maurice what she could do. She sucked on his glans, then ran her tongue around the ridge underneath it, all the way around it two or three times. Then she forced his whole erection as deep as it would go, until his glans was pressed against the ribbing of her throat and she had to resist the impulse to gag.

'Mmm . . .' He put his hands on her head. 'I've obviously made a good choice. Now you,' he said, indicating that the brunette should kneel at Cherry's side.

The girl did as she was told. He pulled his cock from Cherry's mouth and directed it towards the brunette, who sucked it in quite as eagerly as Cherry had done. After a minute or so of her attentions he pulled it out again, swinging back to Cherry. She slipped the solid rod of flesh between her lips and felt a huge surge of passion as he forced it deep. Her sex pulsed and her clitoris twitched against her labia.

'It's tempting girls, it really is. But . . .' he pulled away, '. . . the night is young. Up, both of you.'

They both got to their feet. Cherry thought the brunette was looking at her strangely as if trying to work out what she was thinking.

'You first,' he said pointing at Cherry. 'At least to begin with.' He went to the table and patted the end of it. 'Let's get you a little more uncomfortable, shall we? Sit up here.'

'No, Master,' Cherry said, suddenly seeing the whips again. She couldn't decide whether fear or excitement was dominating her emotions.

'No?' He raised a thick black eyebrow. 'I hope that you don't mean that.'

'I . . . please, Master.' She realised her excitement had the upper hand. That hard, hot cock had felt so good in her mouth, and she couldn't stop thinking about how it would feel slipping into her quim. She didn't want to stop now.

'Please?' he queried. 'What does that mean?'

Cherry took a deep breath. Trying to control her conflicting emotions she walked to the table and hoisted herself up to sit on the end where he had indicated.

'Good,' he said, approvingly. He stroked her thigh and leant forward to kiss her on the mouth. It was a long, lingering kiss that melted her from the inside. Her heart was thumping so loud she was surprised he couldn't hear it. 'Now lean back,' he said as his lips moved away. He was smiling, a thin, knowing smile. He put his arm around her neck and eased her back on to the suede. Her body rested on the table top with her legs dangling over the end of it.

Maurice reached under the surface. He pulled a wide leather strap up over Cherry's shoulders.

'Raise your arms above your head,' he said.

As she did as she was told he buckled the leather just above her breasts. Then he pulled another strap up and secured it around her waist, tying her down to the table and making it impossible for her to sit up. He stretched out her hands to the top corners and secured her wrists with the leather straps. Now only her legs were free.

Cherry's body trembled again. Bondage seemed to thrill her in a way she simply did not understand. She thought of the explosive orgasm she had experienced with Peter. These bonds were a great deal tighter and more effective that the improvised variety he had employed and her excitement seemed proportionately more extreme.

'Help me,' he said to the brunette, who had knelt impassively, waiting to be told what to do.

She got to her feet. The man took hold of two nylon ropes threaded through pulleys hanging from the wooden beam directly over Cherry's head. A leather cuff was secured to the end of each. He pulled the ropes down the length of the table then handed one to the brunette. He picked up Cherry's ankle and stretched her leg out horizontally, buckling the leather cuff around the white leather boot and signalling to the brunette to do the same.

Lying staring upward, as she was, Cherry could see the white ropes from the pulleys were fed through a gearing mechanism of some sort. A single rope emerged from this which stretched diagonally over to the wall behind her head, where it was attached to a winding block and a handle. Satisfied that the cuffs were secure, Maurice walked to this block and began turning the hand. The ratchet in the block made a loud clicking noise. Slowly but inexorably, Cherry felt her feet being pulled up back towards her body. The pulleys were spaced well apart and by the time Maurice stopped reeling the rope in, her legs were not only doubled up over her body, her ankles over her shoulders, but spread out in a wide V-shape.

Cherry raised her head to look down her body. The tight leather corset still held her in a grip of steel. Below it she could see her sex, open and exposed, her short pubic hair not hiding her labia. For some reason the view and the feeling of total vulnerability it portrayed aroused her more deeply than anything she could remember. Her whole body was throbbing, each pulse producing a hot thrill of pleasure. She was sure juices were leaking out of her sex and running down between her buttocks. She did not understand the reason she felt this way but there was no time to analyse it now.

Maurice stood at her side. His hand caressed her shoulder. His fingers moved to her breast. He flicked one against her nipple. The surge of feeling this tiny movement produced made Cherry moan.

'Very sensitive,' Maurice said. 'I like that.'

She saw him turning towards the rack of whips.

'No!' she cried, fear making her body turn cold.

'Sh . . .' he said. He took down a short, thin whip with a leather tassel at the end.

'Please, don't whip me,' she begged.

'Don't make me gag you,' he said, standing at the foot of the table.

Cherry used all her strength to struggle against her bonds. The leather straps held her secure, not giving an inch, but the feeling of total helplessness provoked an enormous wave of passion that coursed through her body, making her face flush a bright red. At that exact second Maurice cracked the whip down on her upturned buttocks.

A stripe of pain seared across her soft flesh. She opened her mouth to scream but before she could a second stroke fell, lower on her buttocks this time, and then a third, so high it was almost on the top of her thigh. The scream was stifled because the pain was turning to a sensation she had never felt before. Just as the bondage had created a new fund of pleasure, so the three lashes that burnt across her buttocks caused the most extraordinary feelings. Needles of pain lanced into her but they were routed directly to her sex and in the milliseconds they took to reach it had turned, miraculously, into stinging, sharp pleasure that set every single nerve alight. She could feel heat radiating out from her bottom, but it radiated inward too. Her clitoris felt as though it were on fire. Instinctively, wanting to touch herself as badly as she'd ever wanted anything, she struggled against the leather that held her so tightly. The unyielding bondage laid another layer of sensation on her overwrought body. And that's when she realised that this was not just academic. Her body had gathered it all up into a tight, hard ball centred on her clit and she was beginning to come.

It was shaming, but there was nothing she could do about it. She saw him raise the whip again. Her body clenched in anticipation, and this itself produced a new thrill. Then the whip whistled down, again delivering three strokes in rapid succession. Three stripes burnt into flesh that had never been treated in this way, their nerves raw and untried. Three sharp pulses of pain flooded through Cherry's body. Three intense waves of pleasure reached her sex. Her body went rigid, every muscle and sinew stretched against the bondage, making the leather creak. She made a noise that was a mixture of a scream and a moan of pure delight. Her orgasm rushed through her, making her body quiver.

'Did you see that?' Maurice asked the brunette.

'Yes, Master.'

His hand stroked Cherry's buttocks. It created another wave of feeling almost as pronounced as her orgasm. She moaned loudly. She couldn't believe she was capable of responding in the way she had. It embarrassed her and excited her equally. Her face was still flushed.

'It's in your blood, isn't it?' he said.

What did that mean? 'I don't know, Master,' she muttered.

'Oh, take it from me. I've seen a lot of Manville's little slaves. You're very responsive.'

She looked at his hard, naked body. His cock was sticking out from his body like the lever of some strange machine. It was so hard she could see each individual vein, like cords of string wrapped around the shaft. A tear of fluid was dripping from the slit of the urethra. But what she was feeling now was not a new sensation. It was exactly what she had felt with Peter. The fact of her bondage, of being unable to move her body at all, made her throbbing sex, by contrast, the only part of her that felt free. It was clenching convulsively as if to underline the point, each movement producing new shards of pleasure. She wanted to feel that big phallus reaming up into her more than she'd ever wanted anything in her life.

Fortunately that was exactly what Maurice had in mind.

'Come here,' he said to the brunette. He pointed to a spot at the side of the table.

Cherry raised her head to look at her as the brunette moved forward. It was not difficult to read her expression. What the man had done had affected her almost as much as it had affected Cherry. Her big brown eyes were slightly gazed, and she was breathing in short pants through her mouth. Her nipples were knotted into tight, dark brown buds.

'Let me see you play with her tits,' he said.

The brunette raised her hands and stretched them across Cherry's chest. To Cherry it seemed they were moving in slow motion. She had never been touched intimately by a woman before. She followed the girl's hands as they moved towards her breasts. They squeezed her flesh back against her chest and she felt a wave of pleasure mixed with a sweet, sickly sensation. The girl's hands were warm. Her fingers found both Cherry's nipples and pinched them lightly.

'Oh . . .' Cherry gasped. What was happening to her? Shouldn't she be revolted and desperate to escape this treatment? Shouldn't she tell the man enough was enough? Her nipples tingled. They had never felt this sensitive.

Maurice had positioned himself at the end of the table. He stepped forward so his cock nestled against her buttocks. Cherry gasped again, the heat of his phallus almost as extreme as the throbbing heat her buttocks continued to produce.

'Oh, yes,' she moaned.

'Yes, what?' he said sternly.

'Please, Master.'

All thoughts of escape, of her story, of Angela Blake, had disappeared. Minutes before, all she had wanted to do was run. Now the reverse was true. What she wanted to do now was wallow in the luscious sensations that emanated from every erogenous zone.

Maurice slid his cock up and down the deep furrow of her labia. She could feel her own juices coating it, making its journey slippery.

'Please . . .' she said again. This was the most delicious torture. As he pushed upward, his glans rapped against her clitoris, producing a huge surge of pleasure. She felt his fingers moving under his cock and suddenly one of them was pressing into her anus. The little crater was so wet from her spending that it offered little resistance and he slipped his finger deep inside, screwing it around.

'Please . . .' She was not sure whether slaves were meant to beg. That is what she was now, of course. Wholly and totally. A slave. His slave. She didn't care what he did to her as long as he put that big, pulsing phallus inside her. She raised her head to look down at him. She could see the pink glans appearing from the top of her labia as he sawed it back and forth. The only movement she could make was to wriggle her buttocks from side to side and she did that, trying to show him how desperate she was.

In one smooth movement he withdrew his finger, pulled his cock back and plunged into the furnace of her cunt. She was so wet, and her buttocks tilted up so high, that he reamed right up into her, deeper than she thought any man had been, his glans not only touching the neck of her womb but pressing it back forcibly.

There was not a second's hesitation in her body's response. A surge of sensation renewed everything she had felt moments before, except this time the process was accelerated, her orgasm seizing her so quickly it took her breath away. She felt her sex grasp the steel-hard rod inside it as tightly as a fist, not letting go again until the waves of exquisite pleasure had finally ebbed away.

But it was not over. Her eyes had been closed by the force of her orgasm but as she opened them again a new sensation was overtaking her. She looked up and saw the brunette's hand snaking down over the hard leather corset to the soft hairs on her mons. Her labia had been spread apart by the breadth of the man's cock and, tipped up as she was, she could actually see the little pink nub of her own clitoris. The girl's finger was heading towards it.

'No . . .' she moaned. But it was the sort of no that very definitely meant the opposite. She watched with absolute fascination as the girl's middle finger tapped against her clit, then dragged it from side to side. Her sex convulsed, gripping the shaft buried inside it again. The two sensations combined. She could feel every inch of the man's phallus. It was throbbing so much she knew he was going to come. And she wanted that. She also wanted the wonderful, delicate caresses the brunette was giving her clit. If she was revolted by the thought of being touched by a woman, her body did not register it. All that she could feel was yet another burgeoning orgasm.

She wanted to feel his spunk. She wanted to feel the tight bonds that held her so completely and the six lashes that had suddenly begun to throb again. She wanted to feel the woman's finger.

'Christ . . .' the man hissed between his teeth. His hand wrapped around her upturned legs for support and he shuddered. Cherry felt his cock kick wildly inside her and a hot wetness jetted into her sex. The brunette's hand reached forward and grabbed the base of his cock, squeezing it tightly as if trying to milk it. As a result the heel of her hand ground against Cherry's exposed clit. It was all too much. Once again Cherry's body tumbled into orgasm, her body once again stretched rigid against the leather straps that held it so tightly.

Chapter Eleven

'In here.' Maurice pulled them inside his bedroom door and closed it behind them.

The bedroom was large. There was a double bed covered by a dark green counterpane that matched the thick wool carpet. The man turned on the lights, then dimmed them to a pleasant glow.

'Over here,' he said.

Sandra's body was aching. She looked across at the small blonde. The marks of the girl's bondage hadn't faded yet, and there were pink lines around her wrists and the top of her breasts. The tight leather corset and the boots had protected her waist and ankles. She had watched the girl's obvious excitement with envy, her whole body desperate for the same sort of release. Her desire had turned into a real physical pain in the pit of her stomach.

'Get her stripped,' Maurice said.

He sat on the edge of the bed.

Sandra began to unlace the corset at the back. She could feel the heat the girl's buttocks were generating and remembered how hers had reacted in the same way. The feeling only served to fuel her own need. She dropped to her knees at the girl's feet and pulled off her white boots one by one.

The girl had been unstrapped from the table downstairs. Without explaining his intentions Maurice had slipped back into his robe, then shepherded both girls up here to his bedroom, his taste for bondage and discipline clearly satiated.

She hoped the same did not apply to all his sexual appetites and clung to the idea that he would hardly have bothered to bring them up here if that were the case.

'All right, over here,' he ordered, looking at the blonde, then pointed at a spot on the carpet in front of him. She walked over to him immediately. 'Kneel,' he said.

Sandra watched the girl kneel. She wasn't sure whether to be relieved or disappointed when the man opened the robe to reveal a growing erection. On the one hand it was proof that he wanted more but, on the other, he was concentrating all his intentions on the blonde. Sandra saw him guide his phallus between her lips. The girl's cheeks dimpled as she sucked on him.

'Take that off,' Maurice said, glancing up at Sandra. 'Leave the stockings,' he said as an afterthought.

Sandra pulled the clinging nylon body off her shoulders and skimmed it down her body. Its narrow gusset had buried itself so deeply between her labia that she had to tug it sharply before it could be pulled clear.

'Mmm . . .' the man said, looking at her, naked now apart from the lace-topped stockings. He could see that her black pubic hair was plastered back by the wetness from her sex. 'Now come here and lie on the bed.'

Sandra obeyed. Her sex was throbbing. As she moved, her big breasts jiggled up and down, provoking all sorts of feelings in her hard nipples. She watched the girl's mouth bobbing up and down on his cock, which was now as large as it had been earlier. She lay on the bed behind him.

He twisted around to look at her. 'Open your legs,' he said.

Sandra did as she was told, spreading them apart and bending them at the knee.

'Touch yourself for me,' he said.

Sandra slid her hand over her flat stomach. Her fingers explored the slit of her sex until they found her clit. It was swollen and felt hot to the touch. She pressed it back. Her body reacted with a flood of feeling so strong it made her

The Master's Diary

snap her head over to one side. She could not see the girl now but heard the slurping noises she was making as she plunged her mouth on to the man's cock.

'Come on,' the man encouraged.

Sandra did not want this. She wanted him. She wanted to feel what the blonde had felt. As she'd caressed her bound body in the room downstairs, she'd felt the huge tremors of orgasm that had crashed through it, as well as seen them, the girl stretched out against her bondage. Every spasm in the girl's body had produced an equal response in her own. No wonder she was feeling strung out and incredibly needy. She would not be able to stop herself coming if he made her go on, but reluctantly she did as she was told. She moved her finger up and down, dragging her clitoris with it.

Maurice pulled the blonde's head away from his cock and got up.

'I want to see you together,' he said, pulling the naked girl to her feet.

Sandra saw the girl looking down at her body, examining her exposed sex. She arched it up towards her and saw an expression of what she could only interpret as fear flash over the blonde's face.

'Come on,' the man said.

The blonde knelt on the bed at Sandra's side. She looked deep into her eyes as if trying to tell her something. The message got through. Sandra was sure she had never done this before. If what the girl had told her was true, if she was a reporter who had somehow smuggled herself into the castle, she supposed that was not surprising. If she was not a slave, not part of the Master's collection, she would not have realised what was involved. She had been quite obviously turned on by bondage and by the strokes of the whip. And she had responded to Sandra's touch. But there she had no choice. This was entirely different.

'She's new, Master. She's never done this before,' Sandra said, hoping to get the girl off the hook. It was not entirely altruistic. If Maurice took pity on her he was more likely to move on to Sandra herself.

'How very interesting,' he said. His eyes sparkled with excitement. 'Let's see what happens.'

'It's all right,' the blonde said. The look in her eyes had changed. The fear had gone. She reached forward, tentatively and touched one of Sandra's big, fleshy breasts, cupping its weight in her hand. Her fingers tweaked at the nipple as if testing to see exactly how hard it was. The sensation caused Sandra to raise her hips reflexively.

'Come on, then,' the man said impatiently. He had got to his feet and was staring down at them.

The girl leant forward. Sandra felt her mouth kissing the side of her waist. It worked its way down over her navel until she felt it hesitate as it got to the thick hair of her pubis. Then with a determined effort, she wrapped her arms under Sandra's thighs and plunged her mouth on to her sex. Her mouth was wonderfully soft and hot, her tongue exploring between her labia until it butted hard against Sandra's clit. Enthusiastically, like a puppy that had just discovered an exciting new game, it began to circle the little bud of nerves while her fingers worked under Sandra's buttocks and began probing the mouth of her vagina. The girl was growing in confidence every second. Sandra felt her fingers working their way up into her vagina. She was rubbing them against each other rapidly as she pushed them right up to the knuckle.

Sandra couldn't think about the girl any more. She had her own feelings to cope with. However inexpertly, the blonde was creating great waves of pleasure in her over-wrought body. But she tried to hold herself back, wanting more. She tugged at the girl's thigh, trying to let her know that she wanted to return the compliment. The girl must have realised what was required of her and swung her thigh over Sandra's shoulders.

The blonde's sex was poised above Sandra's head. She could see every detail, its outer labia and the smoother inner lips pursed around the scarlet mouth of her vagina. The whole plane of her sex glistened. The blonde held it there, four or five inches above Sandra's mouth, as if wrestling with herself as to what she should do. It was the final commitment, Sandra knew. When she had been in the same predicament with Marion she had had no choice and that fact, and her devotion to everything the Master represented, had seen her though. But as far as she knew the girl had none of those feelings. She had got herself into this situation for entirely other reasons.

Suddenly she felt a distinct tension leave the girl's body. She had made her decision. As her tongue circled her clit Sandra saw her body descending. She welcomed the soft, spongy labia with a kiss, kissing it like a mouth, darting her tongue out to penetrate her vagina.

Though not as new to this as the blonde, Sandra was still inexperienced enough at lesbian sex to be shocked at just how easily she could respond to the pleasures of another woman's body. What she had felt with Angela was repeated again. Their bodies were joined. Eagerly, Sandra sent her tongue to search for the girl's clit. She was not surprised to find it hard and distended, the hammering the man had given her still affecting it. She circled it carefully and rhythmically, while she worked two fingers into her vagina to complete the circle. The girl learnt quickly. What Sandra did to her, she did to Sandra instantly. As Sandra circled her clit and plunged her fingers into her sticky sex, the girl did the same, adopting exactly the same rhythm. As her own body began to throb, unable to bottle up all the pent-up feelings to which she had been prone for the last hour, she felt the girl's body pulsing too.

Having decided she was going to allow herself to indulge in this way, the girl was obviously not regretting her decision. Sandra knew the blonde was coming just as certainly as she knew she was coming herself. Their bodies melted together, clinging to each other for support, the wetness at the centre of both of them somehow melded together. Sandra was sure she came first, the explosion of feeling rocking her body from side to side, but the girl came soon after. They were so close and so in tune that her orgasm renewed and refreshed Sandra's, making her feel as if she were coming again.

They were locked together, rocking their bodies against each other, responding to the same impulse, wanting to husband the exquisite feelings for as long as possible.

'Very pretty.' The sound of the man's voice came as a shock to Sandra. As much as she wanted him minutes before, she had become so involved with the blonde she had forgotten all about him. 'Well, that obviously wasn't too difficult,' he said. He had stripped off the robe and was standing at the foot of his bed. If anything his erection was even larger than it had been downstairs. It was throbbing visibly, little pulses of blood coursing through the prominent veins.

He took the blonde's shoulder and rolled her over to one side.

Sandra's passion was instantly revived. To her astonishment a surge of lust raced through her, as urgent as the one she had felt as she'd entered the room. She arched her buttocks off the bed, presenting her sex and her long, stocking-sheathed legs to him, the lacy welts emphasising the creaminess of her thighs. She clutched at her own breasts, lifting them up towards him too.

He knelt on the bed. For a terrible moment Sandra saw him looking at the blonde and thought he was going to take her. But he didn't. His eyes swivelled back to her and he moved between her legs. He lunged forward. His cock didn't touch her labia. It centred on her vagina and drove right up it. There was no subtlety and no finesse. He was just pounding into her, his buttocks rising and falling like a steam-hammer, every ounce of his considerable strength concentrated on that single action.

He drove up into her, higher and higher. Sandra saw the blonde get to her knees. Over his shoulder she watched as the girl pushed her finger down between his heaving buttocks. She found his anus and pushed into it. The effect on the man was immediate. Sandra felt his cock kick and jerk against the tight confines of her vagina. The movement was so so strong it set her off too, a rush of pleasure making her sex clench around him. This, in turn, caused him to kick even more strongly, creating a vicious circle from which neither of them could escape. She saw the blonde screw her finger around in his anus and then felt his cock recoil. But that was all. After that her orgasm overwhelmed her. Somewhere in the middle of the huge waves of passion she thought she felt a hot wetness spreading at the centre of her sex, but it was only a vague awareness compared to the pulsating pleasure at the forefront of her mind, her body clutching the rock-hard phallus that was buried so deeply inside it.

Eventually he rolled off her. He got up and went into the bathroom.

'Are you all right?' Sandra asked the girl in a whisper.

'What's happened to me?' she said.

'Don't you know?'

'I came here to get a story. Look at me. My whole body's still trembling.'

'He was right about you. It's in your blood. You're like all of us.'

'I don't know what that means.'

'Don't you?'

'No. But, my God, after that I'm certainly going to find out!'

Sandra woke early. After her windowless cell she was unaccustomed to the dawn filtering in from the little gaps in the curtaining that covered the large window of Maurice's bedroom. Maurice had not summoned Henri to take them back to the cells and they had spent the night in the large bed, with Maurice on one side and the two girls side by side on the other, all three exhausted by their efforts.

Once awake, Sandra found it hard to get back to sleep. She had too much on her mind. She tried to remember exactly what the girl had told her. If the Master discovered her presence, which she was sure he was bound to do, she was afraid he might blame her for not immediately telling Maurice that she was an imposter. The truth was, it had never occurred to her for a moment to do so. It had looked, at the beginning, as if the girl was going to confess herself, and by the time it became apparent she was just as turned on by what was going on as a real slave, Sandra had been too wrapped up in her sexual feelings to intervene.

She had no idea how the girl had managed to infiltrate the house, or how Henri or Marion had not been suspicious. They had obviously accepted her as one of the slaves and dressed her accordingly. But if the girl told the Master the truth and mentioned her confession in the punishment room, Sandra was going to be in serious trouble, ironically at the moment when her relationship with Manville was at its most rewarding. She could not forget the things he had said to her or the considerable privileges he had granted her. If this girl's arrival destroyed all that she wasn't sure she would be able to stand his anger and what would certainly be a subsequent rejection. She could cope with endless hours in her cell if she knew at the end of it she would be called to her Master again. But after this she was sure he would punish her for her complicity and the rest of her time at the castle would be spent in isolation.

There was one way out, she realised suddenly. She must try and help the girl escape, now before anyone was up.

Quickly she nudged the girl awake, ready to put her hand over her mouth if she made any sound.

'Mmmm . . .' the girl moaned, opening her eyes.

'Sh . . .' Sandra warned. 'He's still asleep.'

'Me too,' the girl said, rolling over.

'You've got to wake up,' Sandra hissed.

'Leave me alone.'

'You've got to escape,' Sandra said.

The word registered on the girl's consciousness. She shook her head and sat up. 'What?' she said.

'Escape. How did you get in here?'

'The chauffeur smuggled me in.'

'And what about Henri?'

'The Frenchman? They must be expecting a new arrival. He mistook me for her.'

'How?'

'I don't know. I think she's due this morning and he thought she'd come early.'

'Right. So you've got to get out before he discovers his mistake. As soon as the real girl arrives they'll be looking for you.'

'I'm not sure I want to go.'

'You've got to. I'll get into big trouble.'

'Hey, what's going on?' The man rolled on to his back and opened his eyes. 'Well, look at you two. Don't you look pretty.' Sandra could see the outline of the man's cock under the single sheet that covered them. It was as erect as it had been last night.

'We didn't mean to wake you, Master,' Sandra said.

'Bet you did, and in more ways than one,' he grinned, glancing down at his erection. He sat up, wrapped his arm around Sandra's neck and kissed her full on the mouth, twisting his body into hers. Despite her anxiety she felt a surge of pleasure as his hand slid under the sheet and squeezed her breasts.

Sandra tried to control her feelings, still looking for a way to get the blonde out of there. But the girl had other ideas.

'Lovely,' the blonde said. She got up on her knees and pulled the sheet down. Grasping his erection in her hand she wanked it hard, then dipped her head and slipped it into her mouth. Sandra felt the man's body start. He kissed her more violently, crushing their lips together as his tongue forced its way deep into her mouth. His hand left her breast and dived into her lap. It wriggled between her thighs and then turned inward, his finger plunging into her vagina.

As the blonde sucked his cock, Maurice dropped his head

to Sandra's breast and closed his mouth over her right nipple. The flesh went from soft and flat to hard and protuberant in less than a second. He pinched the hard flesh then transferred his mouth to the left. Before she realised what he was doing he had pushed her back on to the bed, pulling the blonde's mouth from his cock and moving down between her legs, his tongue replacing his finger in her vagina.

Sandra's body shuddered. She writhed around on the bed while he moved his tongue from her vagina up to her clit and caught hold of the blonde's ankle. The blonde realised what she wanted immediately. She crawled up the bed and positioned her sex above Sandra's face. Sandra wrapped her arms around the girl's thighs and pulled her down on to her mouth. She probed with her tongue until it was butting up against her clitoris, then dragged it from side to side exactly as Maurice's tongue was doing the same to hers. It was too late now, Sandra realised, to do anything about escape.

And she was right.

'*Voila! Ca y est. Elle est ici.*' Henri's voice was breathless and excited.

Sandra struggled to sit up, extricating herself from between the blonde's thighs.

'*Vite. Vite.*'

The little Frenchman had flung the door open and barged into the room. He was standing at the foot of the bed, gesticulating wildly, pointing at the blonde with one hand and waving towards the door with the other.

Manville Mason walked in. He raised a single eyebrow as he surveyed the tableau. Marion Chandler came up behind him.

'*Elle. Elle.*' Henri said pointing at the blonde.

'What is all this?' Maurice said, sitting up. He wiped his mouth with the back of his hand and covered himself with the sheet. 'Is anything wrong?'

'It appears that there is,' the Master said sternly, looking at the blonde. 'Who are you?'

The Master's Diary

'Cherry Austin,' the girl said at once.

'And what are you doing here?' Marion said. She was wearing a tight white top and a pair of jeans and looked as though she'd just got out of bed.

'I'd have thought that was pretty obvious,' Cherry said. She sat up but did not bother to cover herself.

'How did you get in here?' the Master asked.

'Through a window at the back. I'm a reporter if you want the truth. I came here to do a story about Angela Blake.'

Sandra felt a hand tighten around her heart. She saw Manville's eyes glance at her with disapproval and feared the worst. Marion's eyes were cold too.

'What sort of story?'

'Oh you know the sort of thing, surely? She ran out on quite a famous pop star. We wanted to know why. And now I do.'

'I see. Who helped you? You didn't get in here by yourself.'

'I did. I'm very resourceful. I waited by the gate and sneaked in behind your Rolls last night.'

'I found her wandering about downstairs,' Henri said. '*Naturallement*, I thought she was the new girl. When she said nothing. When she allowed herself to be bound and taken to the parade . . . well . . . who would have known?'

'The new girl has just arrived,' the Master said calmly. 'That's when Henri realised his mistake. Did you know?' He had directed the last question to Sandra.

'Of course she didn't,' Cherry said quickly. 'Nor did he. What would have been the point in my telling either of them?'

'So what are you going to do now?' the Master asked.

'I am going to write my story. I am going to describe in loving detail everything that goes on here. The way I was dressed up and bound. The boots I was made to wear and that leather corset. What all the other girls looked like. All the details of that little room downstairs with all that complicated apparatus. What shall I call it? The bondage room? Whatever. Of course I'll have to describe what this gentleman did to me and how this beautiful brunette helped him out. Then there was everything that went on after that when we came up here. Quite a story, don't you think? Not forgetting her role in all this,' she nodded at Marion. 'And that's just my experience. Naturally, I shall write about Angela Blake. How you had her trussed up and ready to serve your guests. I wonder what her father will make of that. Or her ex-boyfriend for that matter? Quite a story.'

'All the women are volunteers,' the Master said weakly. Sandra could see he was trying to calculate the consequences of the girl's revelations.

'I know that. In a way, that only makes it worse.'

'You'd better get out now. Where are your clothes?'

'Ask him,' she said, nodding at Henri.

'Go and get them, would you?' Manville said to the Frenchman.

'Don't you think that would be rather a waste?'

'What do you mean, a waste?'

'I mean exactly what I say.' Cherry got to her feet. 'Thanks to this gentleman, I am very aroused. I was hoping you'd like to take me to that bondage room again. With this gorgeous redhead.' She walked over to Marion and ran her hand across her breasts. 'You could watch while she amused herself with me. You wouldn't find that too arduous, would you? You see, I'm certainly going to write my story but whether I send it to my newspaper is rather up to you. I'm a reasonable woman. I've always believed in fair exchange being no robbery. If you are prepared to let me come to the castle on a regular basis, then obviously I won't want to publish all the gory details of what goes on here, would I?'

The Master allowed himself the faintest of smiles. 'I suppose not.'

'Good.'

'All the women here have to be tested to determine their suitability,' he said. 'You might find that you will not enjoy yourself as much as you think.'

'If you ask me, she's a natural,' Maurice said. 'I told her that.'

'That remains to be seen.'

'Then test me,' she said, adding coquettishly, 'Master.'

Manville walked to a chest of drawers on the side of the room. He opened the top drawer and took out two long strips of black silk. Coming back to stand behind the blonde he wrapped one carefully around her eyes. He took her hands, crossed them in the small of her back and tied them together with the second strip.

'Take her, Marion,' he said.

Cherry bowed her head as she was guided across the room. She was smiling broadly.

They were nearing the end of the journey.

'So good,' he said quietly.

They were siting in the back of the Rolls. Sandra was kneeling in front of the Master. She had tried to swallow all his spunk but some had escaped and trickled down her chin. He wiped it away with the tail of the black silk scarf that banded her eyes.

'Thank you, Master.'

He leant forward and unknotted the scarf. It fell to the floor. 'Sit up here now. We're nearly there.' He pushed his softening cock back into his trousers and zipped up his fly.

She sat next to him, wondering if Curtis had been able to see what she had done to the Master.

'You have to make a serious decision, Sandra,' he said. 'I want to explain something to you. Most of the women who come to me regard it as a sort of holiday. An escape from their normal, possibly drab lives. But there is another dimension. There are other . . . shall we call them members?'

'Other men?' She remembered the conversation he'd had with Malcolm.

'Not only men. Other men and women who like myself

have the facilities for total privacy and the inclination towards . . . dominance. Some of the women who come to me find that they want to take it one step further, to explore deeper. Do you understand?'

'I think so.'

'They send specially selected women to me. I send suitable candidates to them. They are, if you will, *in loco parentis*. You would have to serve them as totally and absolutely as you serve me. There can be no exceptions to that rule. Some have very big establishments. All are implacable. You could expect no favours.'

Sandra thought about that, looking at Manville's face. She glanced behind her for a moment and saw Cherry driving her Escort. She had followed the Rolls all the way from the castle, though this time Curtis was aware of her presence.

'Have you given Cherry this choice?'

'No. I think I may do after her next visit. She has all the right qualities.'

'Do you want me to do this?' she asked.

'Yes,' he said simply.

'May I ask why, Master?'

'If you think about it, you will realise the answer to that question yourself. If you do not come up with the answer then you should not go.'

Sandra was dressed in the same type of cotton lingerie and dress she had travelled down in. She was surprised when the Master had told her he wanted to accompany her. Now she guessed this was the reason.

'When you come back to the castle next month you can give me your answer,' he said.

'And if I say no, will it mean I can't come to the castle again after that?'

'Certainly not.'

In the last three days Sandra had gained confidence. The more she accepted the role of a slave the more pleasure she gained from it. It appeared that Cherry had passed the tests and was invited to stay at the castle, having been installed in one of the cells. They had been picked by one of the guests last night, and taken to the same punishment room they had shared with Maurice, extending and developing the pleasure they had taken from him and from each other.

Marion, too, had been much in evidence. Sandra had greatly enjoyed her experiences with Angela Blake and Cherry Austin but Marion's sexuality was as complex as the Master's. What she wanted from the slaves, singular and in pairs, was demanding. But Sandra was eager to learn and determined that she would please her, whatever the cost.

In fact she wondered if the other 'members' Manville had talked of would resemble the redhead. She could imagine a female Master like her, cold, cruel and not easily satisfied. Could she face such a taskmaster?

The Rolls pulled up outside her building. She saw Cherry park immediately behind it.

'I'll send Curtis for you in two weeks,' the Master said. He handed her the house keys she had given to Curtis on the outward journey.

'Thank you, Master,' she said.

'And be ready with your answer.'

'Yes, Master. I will.'

He smiled thinly but did not get out of the car. She stood on the pavement and watched the Rolls pull away, staring at her own reflection in the opaque black windows. He had given her lots to think about.

'Hey, come on,' Cherry said as she locked her car. 'He'll be here in thirty minutes. We've got to get ready.'

'Right.'

Sandra led the way into her house. In the kitchen they opened a bottle of wine. They took it into the bedroom.

Exactly thirty minutes later the doorbell rang. Sandra pressed the button on the entryphone to let Michael in. She had phoned him from the castle and told him she was anxious to see him.

'Hi,' she said, opening her flat door before he could ring the bell.

He stared at her. She was wearing her scarlet satin basque, sheer black stockings and high-heel shoes. She had flattened the bra cups of the basque under her breasts so they were lifted up and out. She was not wearing panties.

'You look great.'

'Thank you.'

He gathered her in his arms and kissed her on the mouth, his tongue hot and wet between her lips.

'God, I want you,' he said. It was evidently true. She could feel his erection bulging against her belly.

'Good, because I want you too. And I've got a little surprise for you.'

She slammed the front door and led him towards the bedroom.

'I want you to wear this,' she said. There was a little hall stand by the bedroom door. She had put the sleeping mask on it in preparation.

'Is this another one of your games?'

'Of course.'

'Fine by me,' he said.

She slipped the mask over his eyes and made sure it fitted securely. Then she opened the bedroom door.

'This way,' she said, taking his hand and leading him to the bed. She unbuttoned his shirt and tore it off, then attacked his trousers. He raised one foot after the other while she pulled off his shoes and socks, then his trousers and pants. His erection stuck out from his belly. It was already wet.

'So responsive, Michael, that's what I like about you.'

She dropped to her knees in front of him and sucked it into her mouth. She forced it as far down her throat as it would go, then pulled right back and circled the ridge of his glans with her tongue.

'Kneel on the bed,' she directed, getting to her feet again.

She pushed him forward so he kneeled in just the right place. 'Perfect.' She jumped on to the bed. 'Now see what you can find.'

Michael edged forward, his cock throbbing. She could see how desperate he was. His knee butted against a nylon-covered thigh and he crawled along it until he felt the nylon give way to naked flesh, soft and very warm. He could feel the heat of her labia radiating out towards him.

'This is very sexy,' he said. It was true. He imagined her lying there in front of him with her legs spread wide open, her sex exposed. He pushed his cock out and felt it nosing into the heat and wetness of her sex.

'Oh, that's so good,' she moaned. 'Come on fuck me, now, Mike. I know you want to.'

He did. He dived forward on to her and rammed his cock deep into her body. And that was when he realised something was wrong. Despite the shock of pleasure he got as he penetrated the silky wet folds of her sex, right up into her, something was not right. First, as he had fallen on her, there had been no pneumatic chest to squash against. Second there was no thick hair where he ground the base of his cock into her body.

'What's going on?' he said, rearing up on straight arms.

'This,' Sandra said, tearing off the blindfold.

He stared down at the short but slender blonde who he was already impaled inside. She was spreadeagled across the bed naked, her ankles and wrists tied to the corners of the brass bedstead by leather straps. He felt her sex clench around him in a vice-like grip. She smiled, arching her head back with pleasure.

'And this,' Sandra said. She leant forward and kissed Cherry full on the mouth, while her hand squeezed one of the girl's round, pert breasts. Then she pulled away grinning. She ran her hand over Michael's back and down between his buttocks, cupping his balls. 'Does she feel good?'

'Yes,' he said breathily, not sure he could control himself

as Sandra's hands squeezed his scrotum rhythmically as if she was milking it.

'Come on then, you know what to do.'

'God, Sandra, this is so exciting.'

'I know. And it's only the beginning, Michael.'

And, of course it was.

Headline Delta Erotic Survey

In order to provide the kind of books you like to read – and to qualify for a free erotic novel of the Editor's choice – we would appreciate it if you would complete the following survey and send your answers, together with any further comments, to:

> Headline Book Publishing
> FREEPOST (WD 4984)
> London
> NW1 0YR

1. Are you male or female?
2. Age? Under 20 / 20 to 30 / 30 to 40 / 40 to 50 / 50 to 60 / 60 to 70 / over
3. At what age did you leave full-time education?
4. Where do you live? (Main geographical area)
5. Are you a regular erotic book buyer / a regular book buyer in general / both?
6. How much approximately do you spend a year on erotic books / on books in general?
7. How did you come by this book?
7a. If you bought it, did you purchase from: a national bookchain / a high street store / a newsagent / a motorway station / an airport / a railway station / other . . .
8. Do you find erotic books easy / hard to come by?
8a. Do you find Headline Delta erotic books easy / hard to come by?
9. Which are the best / worst erotic books you have ever read?
9a. Which are the best / worst Headline Delta erotic books you have ever read?
10. Within the erotic genre there are many periods, subjects and literary styles. Which of the following do you prefer:
10a. (period) historical / Victorian / C20th / contemporary / future?
10b. (subject) nuns / whores & whorehouses / Continental frolics / s&m / vampires / modern realism / escapist fantasy / science fiction?

10c. (styles) hardboiled / humorous / hardcore / ironic / romantic / realistic?
10d. Are there any other ingredients that particularly appeal to you?
11. We try to create a cover appearance that is suitable for each title. Do you consider them to be successful?
12. Would you prefer them to be less explicit / more explicit?
13. We would be interested to hear of your other reading habits. What other types of books do you read?
14. Who are your favourite authors?
15. Which newspapers do you read?
16. Which magazines?
17 Do you have any other comments or suggestions to make?

If you would like to receive a free erotic novel of the Editor's choice (available only to UK residents), together with an up-to-date listing of Headline Delta titles, please supply your name and address. Please allow 28 days for delivery.

Name ....

Address ....

....

....

If you enjoyed this book here is a selection of other bestselling Erotica titles from Headline

FAIR LADIES OF PEACHAM PLACE	Beryl Ambridge	£5.99 ☐
EROTICON HEAT	Anonymous	£5.99 ☐
SCANDALOUS LIAISONS	Anonymous	£5.99 ☐
FOUR PLAY	Felice Ash	£5.99 ☐
THE TRIAL	Samantha Austen	£5.99 ☐
NAKED INTENT	Becky Bell	£5.99 ☐
VIXENS OF NIGHT	Valentina Cilescu	£5.99 ☐
NEW TERM AT LECHLADE COLLEGE	Lucy Cunningham-Brown	£5.99 ☐
THE PLEASURE RING	Kit Gerrard	£5.99 ☐
SPORTING GIRLS	Faye Rossignol	£5.99 ☐

Headline books are available at your local bookshop or newsagent. Alternatively, books can be ordered direct from the publisher. Just tick the titles you want and fill in the form below. Prices and availability subject to change without notice.

Buy four books from the selection above and get free postage and packaging and delivery within 48 hours. Just send a cheque or postal order made payable to Bookpoint Ltd to the value of the total cover price of the four books. Alternatively, if you wish to buy fewer than four books the following postage and packaging applies:

UK and BFPO £4.30 for one book; £6.30 for two books; £8.30 for three books.

Overseas and Eire: £4.80 for one book; £7.10 for 2 or 3 books (surface mail)

Please enclose a cheque or postal order made payable to *Bookpoint Limited*, and send to: Headline Publishing Ltd, 39 Milton Park, Abingdon, OXON OX14 4TD, UK.
Email Address: orders@bookpoint.co.uk

If you would prefer to pay by credit card, our call team would be delighted to take your order by telephone. Our direct line 01235 400 414 (lines open 9.00 am–6.00 pm Monday to Saturday 24 hour message answering service). Alternatively you can send a fax on 01235 400 454.

Name ....
Address ....
....
....

If you would prefer to pay by credit card, please complete:
Please debit my Visa/Access/Diner's Card/American Express (delete as applicable) card number:

Signature .... Expiry Date ....